The Sinister Sitcom Caper

A Sandy Fairfax Teen Idol Mystery
(Book 2)

by

Sally Carpenter

COZY CAT
PRESS

ISBN: 978-1-939816-23-8
Printed in the United States of America

Cover design by Ginny Glass
http://www.wordsugardesigns.com/

1 2 3 4 5 6 7 8 9 10

Dedicated to

DAVY JONES
(1945 to 2012)
Teen idol and daydream believer extraordinaire

Acknowledgments
In 2000 I moved from the Midwest, where I had grown up, to Los Angeles. My first job in La-La Land was working as a tour guide/page at Paramount Pictures, the hardest work and most fun I ever had. In the daytime the pages conducted the studio tours for the tourists. In the evenings they ushered the audiences for the sitcom shoots. Oftentimes the shoots took place at the other studios in the area. Many times the backstage production was more entertaining than the show itself. Those experiences and my imagination led to this book.

Mammoth Picture Studio is fiction, a blend of the various studios I had the privilege to visit. Many of the elements are factual, such as the sitcom rehearsal and shooting schedule, the back lot and ghost legends. The story omits a number of crewpersons in an effort to streamline the cast and focus on the key characters. All of the characters are fictitious and are not intended to resemble any living or dead person. No animals were harmed in the writing of this book.

My thanks to the following:
    Patricia Rockwell, for giving my series character a home
    The supervisors and pages of the Paramount Guest Relations team
    Dr. D.P. Lyle for information regarding the murder weapon
    Sharon Goldstein for details about classical music
    Carl Adler of the Valley Mustang Club for the description of Sandy's car
    Chris Lynch for information about Sandy's motorcycle
    Karen McCullough for my blog design and setup (http://sandyfairfaxauthor.com.)
    My colleagues of Sisters in Crime

MONDAY: TABLE READ
Chapter 1: Getting Together

My first day back on the studio lot in fourteen years and I stepped on a dwarf.

"Watch it, mac!" he said.

I put the black gym bag holding my script and dance shoes on the floor and removed my motorcycle helmet so I could see the person I almost squashed. I pushed that stubborn lock of blond hair out of my baby blue eyes.

"I'm sorry; I didn't see you down there," I said.

"I guess not." He spoke in a high-pitched voice. "Next time I'll send up a flare."

Can't blame me for overlooking him. I stand six-foot-two, a bit more in my riding boots, which I had on, and this guy couldn't have been more than four feet tall on tiptoe. With only a couple of work lights turned on in the soundstage, I couldn't see him in the shadows. But I had to work with the man for the next five days so I tried to make amends.

"Did I hurt you?"

"Naw, I'm tough. Gotta be in this business."

Although his torso was a normal size, his head was too large in proportion and his legs and arms, too short. His stubby fingers held a script—about forty hole-punched pages held together with metal brads. He was close to my age of 38.

I unzipped my black leather jacket, tucked the helmet under my left arm, and held out my right hand so he could reach it. "I'm Sandy Fairfax. I'm the guest star on the show this week."

He shook my hand with a surprisingly strong grip. "Yeah, I know who you are. The substitute. The second-stringer. The fallback guy. The producer tried to get some of the other over-the-hill teen idols for the part, but they all said no. Smart guys. They knew that a spot on this turkey would wreck their careers. I assume you're here only out of desperation."

When my agent said I'd landed a guest spot on a sitcom, I assumed he meant a respectable show like *Rosanne* or *Frasier* and not *Off-Kelter*, the lowest-rated dud of the 1993 fall season. This wasn't the way I planned my comeback. But how dare this pipsqueak say I'm second best. My ten gold records sold more copies, and my mug beautified more covers of *Tiger Beat* magazine, than all those other pop stars of the 1970s.

"A job's a job. And you play the next-door neighbor. You're Little Joe Graves."

His face scrunched up in a frown. "Jo*seph*." He emphasized the last syllable. "Jo*seph* Graves."

"But in your movies you're listed in the credits as–"

"Yeah, yeah, I know. That was back in the days when the little people in the business all had kiddie names. Now I want a grownup image so I can get better jobs."

"You already have a job."

"Not for much longer."

Joseph wandered into the center of the room and onto the master set, the living room/kitchen/basement workshop setup of the Kelter home used in every episode. He gazed at the three flimsy canvas walls—the front of the set was left open for the cameras—that seemed so real on TV but looked rather cheap up close.

"Nobody's expecting a renewal after this episode. The studio thought a big name guest star this week might pull in the viewers. Nothing personal, Sandy, I don't think even *you* can help our ratings."

I understood his concern. A new series only received six episodes to find an audience before the network signed on for a full season. Six weeks is hardly enough time for people discover a show in the multi-channel world of cable TV. My own hit series ran a glorious four years, but that was back in the day when viewers had the pick of only three networks.

A new voice called out. "Sandy Fairfax! Glad you could make it!"

A 20-something man all in black—black hair, black plastic-rim glasses, black T-shirt, black shorts, black shoes—hurried in from behind the set; his footsteps echoed in the hangar-sized building. He carried a pasteboard clipboard with a script nestled under the clip, and he wore a headset. He shook my hand firmly.

"I'm Carl McIntire, the assistant director. Welcome to *Off-Kelter*. The guard at the front gate called and said you'd arrived. Did you find a parking spot?"

"Yes, I left my Harley in Lot Five."

"Great. Did you get a script?"

"Right here."

I picked up my gym bag with my left hand (I'm a southpaw) and fumbled with it until Carl relieved me of my helmet. With my hands freed I unzipped the bag and removed the pages that the messenger had brought to my house last week. After my first reading of the script I was tempted to use the pages as kindling in the fireplace. A second reading made me want to set fire to the writers' office.

"Good, good." Carl turned his attention to the little person. "Hello, Joseph. You're here early."

As the dwarf approached us, he pulled the world's fattest cigar from the pocket of his jacket and rolled it between his fingers. "I wanted to look over my lines before the battle-axe showed up. Whoever cast her on the show apparently had a lobotomy."

"The final casting decisions went through the producer."

"Like I said. Excuse me, gentlemen. I need a smoke."

Smoking is not allowed on the sets, so he headed for the meat-locker-style stage door. Joseph pushed the door's panic bar with both hands and stepped outside.

I asked, "Who's the battle-axe?"

Carl's chuckle sounded forced. "Don't mind Joseph. That's his nickname for Elsie Bloom. She plays the housekeeper on the show. Did you have any trouble finding the stage?"

"No, not at all. This is where I filmed my show."

"No kidding!" His eyes grew wide. "I didn't know that. You shot *Buddy Brave, Boy Sleuth* in here?"

I smiled. "Yeah, and also next door on Stage 15."

"Then you must feel right at home."

"We had the standing sets in here. Buddy's underground laboratory was in that corner." I pointed. "And the Spy Central office was over there along with the interiors of Buddy's house. Stage 15 had the swing sets. But otherwise the place looks the same."

"We've made a few changes. Let me show you."

He turned on the overhead lights that bathed the stage in a warm glow. When I say "stage," I don't mean like a raised theater platform. The Kelter family rooms stood in the center of the vast concrete floor, surrounded by empty space for the swing sets, the temporary interiors that changed weekly according to each new script. Thick, quilted padding covered the outer walls to block out the street noise. A bank of raised bleacher seats, something that never existed on my show, faced the set. The first row stood about seven feet from the floor and narrow steps on both sides of the bleachers led to the seats. The first two rows consisted of the chairs reserved for the studio hotshots and special guests; tourists sat on the back benches where they could watch and (hopefully) laugh during the shooting. TV monitors hung from the ceiling so those in the back rows could see the action on the floor. The sound engineer and other technical personnel sat behind a glass window behind the back row.

Carl flipped a switch to start the air blowers that cooled the stage. "We can seat an audience of 220. Have you done a sitcom before, Sandy?"

"No, only single camera shows," which included my guest spots on *Charlie's Angels*, *Fantasy Island* and *The Love Boat*.

"Not much difference, except that we shoot the scenes in order and, of course, we have the audience."

"What if I make a mistake?"

"We stop for retakes. Will the audience bother you?"

I bluffed. "No, of course not."

I tried to picture the bleacher seats filled with enthusiastic fans, but failed. If this episode of *Off-Kelter* turned out as dreadful as the ones I'd watched at home, the guests might turn ugly and attack the cast. I haven't appeared on camera for a number of years and I didn't need a hostile audience to watch me struggling to get back in the game. But for Carl, I put on a brave front because I couldn't afford to lose this job. The industry isn't kind to teen idols once they outgrow their cute pin-up phase.

The AD slapped me on the back. "You'll be great, Sandy. You'll love working with this cast. They're good people."

A noise by the wall drew my attention. A man from craft services was setting out food and beverages on a wooden table. Everybody loved the craft services people. During long shooting days, a well-stocked table provided an oasis of refreshment for the cast and crew.

Carl followed my look. "Get yourself something to eat, Sandy. But first, let me put your things in your trailer."

"Trailer? Don't I get my old dressing room?"

"I'm afraid not. Harv's using it."

Of course the largest dressing room in the soundstage went to the star of *Off-Kelter;* whereas, I, as the one-time guest, was exiled to less desirable quarters. I'd lost my ranking as the former top dog at Mammoth Picture Studio. I handed my gym bag and helmet to Carl but I kept my script as well as my jacket on because the air conditioning was working its magic all too well. The AC's great when you're on the set working under the hot lights, but otherwise a person could freeze. Carl excused himself as I headed for the craft services table. I tucked my script beneath my armpit, and filled a Styrofoam cup with coffee from a metal urn.

"Good morning, Sandy. I have a Mountain Dew for you." The craft services guy reached into a cooler on the floor and removed a chilled can. "I was told to stock some for this week."

My agent, Marshall Ellis, was on the ball; he must have told the producer about my preferences. Nothing gets a good performance out of actors like pampering the actors like gods.

"Thanks. I'll have one later. In the morning I need coffee."

"It'll be here in the cooler whenever you want it." He returned the can to the ice-filled container.

I scanned the table for something to eat. "No brownies?"

"I put out the desserts after the lunch break."

"On my show they always stocked brownies." Because I pitched a fit if my favorite snack wasn't available when I craved one. Chocolate gave me a nice sugar boost right before shooting stunts and action scenes. "Didn't my agent say I like brownies? The soft, gooey kind?"

"I was told that you were watching your weight and I should have some low-fat options available."

I'm gonna fire my agent. "Right now I need something to get me going. Got any high-fat options?"

"I have doughnuts. Will that do?"

The guy opened a cardboard box full of oversized, still-warm doughnuts. I salivated as I reached into the box—and stopped. As much as I hated Marshall for fussing about my weight, my recent years of heavy drinking had left me in dreadful shape. If I didn't slim down, the cameraman would need a panoramic lens to keep me in the shot. So I look a plastic knife and cut one of the doughnuts in half. I put one half on a paper plate and then helped myself to a foil pan full of cooked bacon.

Before I took a bite, a newcomer interrupted me. "You don't want to eat that."

The blouse on this young, stunning blonde was unbuttoned far enough to reveal considerable cleavage. Her tight miniskirt showed off some great curves and long, smooth legs unencumbered with pantyhose. Ten toes tipped with red polish peeked through her high heel sandals. One thing I liked about showbiz was the number of attractive women I'd had the pleasure to work with over the years. If you're going to spend long hours on the set in close contact with someone, it helps if she's easy on the eyes. But I didn't need a co-worker criticizing my food choices.

"And why not?" I replied.

"You're filling your body with a disgusting glob of fat, chemicals and sodium. Ingesting animal products will cause aggression, premature aging and clogged arteries."

"Elsie, let the man have what he wants." Joseph had returned from his smoke-out. The heavy odor of premium tobacco clung to his clothes. I'd quit my own smoking habit years ago, but I still appreciated a quality leaf blend. To the craft services guy he said, "The usual, please."

The guy placed several slices of the bacon and a hard-boiled egg onto a plate. He handed the plate, along with a Styrofoam cup of orange juice, to Joseph.

"See what I mean?" she said. "Red meat stunts your growth. Right, Little Joe?" She burst into a chorus of "We Are The Lollypop Kids."

"Shut up, Elsie!"

"Oh, lighten up, Joe. Aren't you a *big* enough to take a *little* teasing?"

He lowered his voice. "Don't embarrass me in front of the guest star."

She smiled and fluttered her long, fake eyelashes at me. "He's so *small* minded, don't you think?"

Her attempt to flirt with me might have worked if she wasn't acting like a jerk. I tried to diffuse her teasing with humor. "I thought short jokes went out of style with *The Terror of Tiny Town*," the 1938 all-midget musical western filmed long before the days of political correctness.

Those lashes stopped batting and her eyes darkened. "I guess shorty needs a big, tall man to stand up for him."

Joseph said to me, "C'mon, let's go before she spreads her rabies."

With food in hand, he trundled away as quickly as his legs could go. I followed. I'd wait until Elsie cooled down before making further conversation. Starting the work week by fighting a cast member was never a good strategy. She stayed behind at the table, filling a plastic bowl with cottage cheese and banana slices. On the show, Elsie Bloom played the Kelter family's housekeeper, Miss Tucker, although none of my real-life maids ever looked this good. One of the show's lame ongoing jokes was that Miss Tucker had the hots for her diminutive neighbor, played by Joseph. Apparently Ivan Constantine, the show's producer, thought a five-foot-ten-inch woman standing next to a dwarf looked hilarious. Maybe the actor guy was correct about Ivan having received a lobotomy.

Joseph sat down at a long, rectangular table set up in front of the set and started eating his food. Folding chairs surrounded the table on all sides. I set my food on the table beside him.

"Look on the bright side, Joseph. If the show's cancelled, you won't have to work with Elsie anymore."

"She needs to retire so *nobody* has to put up with her."

A middle-aged man dressed in jeans and a denim jacket ran up and embraced me in an unexpected bear hug. "Sandy Fairfax! How the heck are you?" After releasing me he grabbed my hand and pumped it as if he was priming a pump. "Welcome to the show! Wonderful to have you here! I've been looking forward to working with you."

Anyone who watched TV in the 1980s would have recognized Harv Brandon, the star of the hugely popular family sitcom *Anyone Home?* and the man who *TV Guide* dubbed as "America's Most Loveable Dad." Like many actors who achieved astounding success on one show (including yours truly), Harv failed to generate a post-series career. After his show folded Harv was absent from show biz except for a handful of flop movies and the game show circuit. He still had that friendly, open face—the "neighbor next door" look—but he'd grown thin and gaunt.

I pulled my hand from his grip. "Glad to meet you, Harv. I loved your work in *Anyone Home?*"

"Thanks, Sandy, and you were fantastic on your show. Wow, you still look great." How nice of Harv not to mention my extra poundage. "You're hiding the fountain of youth in your back yard, aren't you?"

"I'm just blessed with good genes, I guess."

Joseph gestured toward the craft services table. "Looks like the battle-axe is getting her morning jollies."

Elsie stood nose-to-nose with a young, muscular guy who sported perfect teeth and a photogenic face. If he weren't an actor, I'd eat my boots. The man rubbed Elsie's bare arms and whispered sweet nothings at her. In seconds they were smooching and groping with wild abandon. If the action heated up any more, they'd have to continue in Elsie's dressing room.

"Who's the guy?" I asked. "I haven't seen him on the show."

With one hand Harv lifted his purple-and-gold Lakers cap and scratched his bald spot. "Don't you recognize him? He's in all the tabloids. That's her boyfriend, Troy Rawlins."

Troy and Elsie gave each other one last smoldering look of affection before he left through the back exit door. Meanwhile, Carl had returned and informed me that my things were in the trailer; he'd show me the location after the table read.

Then a familiar but unwelcome voice cut through the chatter. "All right, people, we're running late. Let's get started."

At the far end of the table stood a man in a red polo shirt; he was pushing forty-five years as hard as he could. He set a briefcase atop the table, opened it and removed a script and a set of store-bought reading glasses. He put the glasses on his face and flipped through the pages. His hairline had receded from when I'd last seen him. His face had the leathery, wrinkled look of someone who had spent too many days in the SoCal sun with too little sunscreen. If he ever tried to smile—little chance of that happening—he'd crack his face.

I almost fainted from disbelief. "Carl, is that who I think it is?"

"That's Royce Jobbe, the director. He told me that the two of you had work together on your show."

More like we'd fought together. Back in the day, Royce was a young buck who had arrived in L.A. with dreams of directing gritty, award-winning movies. Instead he was stuck on *Buddy Brave*, babysitting an out-of-control teen star. I complained to Royce about the bad scripts, his ham-fisted approach and the lack of safety procedures for the stunts. He, in turn, yelled about the way I strayed from the script (can I help it my improvised lines were better?) and my lack of acting talent. Royce also groped the female guest stars and threw his ego around so much he could have tried out for the Olympic shot put team.

Our shouting matches were legendary. When we started fighting, the crewmembers had a good ten-to twenty-minute break before we wound down. During our last show together, Royce was so obnoxious I punched him. He cancelled the rest of the day's shooting while he went home with a bloody nose. Next day he showed up with a bandaged beak and a lawyer who tried to sue me for battery. I called in *my* lawyer and the legal eagles duked it out while we finished shooting. After we wrapped, I told Royce I never wanted to work with him again.

So here we were.

Royce glared at me over the half-moon lenses of his glasses as if challenging me to step over the line first.

As much as I dreaded the task, I might as well say hello and get it over with. I walked over like a man approaching a firing squad and extended my hand.

"Good morning, Royce."

"Fairfax. How nice to see you again." He spoke these lines with all the enthusiasm of a patient about to undergo a colonoscopy. Then he gave my hand such a limp handshake I was ready to check him for vital signs. "I want you to know you were not my first choice for a guest star. Or even my second or third choice."

I gave him a sly smile. "Royce, I'm likewise excited about working with you again and have full confidence in your ability to turn out a spectacular show."

"Cut the crap, Fairfax." He nodded toward the table. "Take a seat anywhere." He turned his attention to the script. He wasn't reading, just ignoring me so I'd go away.

Before I had a chance to sit, Elsie screamed. "What are you doing? Are you trying to kill me?"

Chapter 2: A Must To Avoid

Elsie dumped the contents of her coffee cup into a trashcan beside the table and spat out a mouthful of brown liquid as well. "How dare you put milk on the table!"

The AD rushed to the table. "What's the problem?"

She said, "Craft services knows full well that I only take non-dairy creamer. I don't eat or drink anything from animals."

"Sorry, Miss Bloom," said the attendant. "I have a new person working for me and she must have forgotten about the creamer."

"What's her name? I want her fired."

"Elsie, it's all right," Carl said. "Let it go. No harm done." The unfortunate employee was shaking in his sneakers. "It won't happen again, Elsie. From now on I'll personally bring in your creamer."

Joseph spoke loud enough for those around him to hear. "Too bad someone didn't put poison in her coffee."

The cast of any show is like a family, and this one was truly dysfunctional.

Dottie Hendricks, a grande dame of stage and screen, paraded into the building with a flourish. Only a talented character actress like Dottie could make a production out of unbuttoning her jacket and removing her headscarf. She wore leather knee boots, a load of gaudy costume jewelry, a moleskin skirt with a wide leather belt and a colorful blouse. On the show she played Harv's mother, although with her face lifts and dyed hair she looked more like his sister. Dottie's character was a crazy scientist whose basement inventions launched the fantasy sequences in each episode. She set her purse on the craft services table and fetched a doughnut. Apparently at her age she didn't need to worry about her weight.

Elsie sipped her coffee (sans creamer). "How's the queen bee today?"

Dottie glared from behind her eye tucks. "When I was your age, we respected our elders."

"When you were my age, movies didn't have sound."

The metal bracelets on Dottie's arm jangled as she loaded her coffee with cream and sugar. "But when the microphones were turned on, my dear, we had something intelligent to say. And we didn't slobber all over our boyfriends in front of God and the world."

"At least *I* have a boyfriend."

"How nice for you, Elsie. I've buried three husbands. I can't imagine you'd ever stay faithful to one man."

Elsie balled up her fists and took a step towards Dottie. Carl stepped between the women and gave a nervous smile.

"All right, ladies, why don't we all sit down and get started?"

I parked myself in an empty chair beside Joseph. Harv started to take the seat on the other side of me, but Elsie bumped him with her hip and slipped in. She slapped her purse—a monstrous thing covered in neon-pink fake fur, beads and silver glitter, all attached to a silver shoulder strap—on the table. My ex had a closet full of purses, but if she had owned anything this hideous, I'd have buried it in the yard. Royce took the command position at the end of the table and Carl sat beside him. Dottie sank into the chair across from me, which left Harv facing Elsie across the table. The writers entered and sat in folding chairs several feet from the table. Considering the script they'd cobbled together for this week, they were wise to keep their distance from the actors.

Elsie said to Dottie, "What kind of nail polish is that?"

The diva flaunted her long red nails, sharpened a point. Although Dottie's face was smooth, the wrinkled skin hanging from her boney fingers belied her age.

"It's called jungle red, my dear. Thanks for noticing, but I don't think this shade would suit you."

"Yeah, it's the sort of color an *old* woman would wear."

Before another volcano exploded, Harv interjected, "So, Dottie, how was your weekend?"

Before she could answer, Royce yelled, "Where are those blasted twins?"

"Maybe they're running late," said Carl. "Should I call the house and see if they've left?"

"If they don't show up in two minutes, I'll have them written out of the script."

Apparently the kids heard the threat, because two teenage girls, mirror images of each other, ran in and headed straight for the craft services table. Missy and Molly Jones loaded up paper plates with doughnuts. A man trailed close behind the girls. No, wait; on second glance, the person was actually a woman built like a guy, short and stocky with close-cropped hair. Her muscular arms and thick legs bulged out from the short-sleeved blouse and capris. If she'd stop scowling, one might even say she was pretty.

"Don't eat that garbage! You'll ruin your diets!" The woman snatched the plates from the girls and tossed the food in the trash bin. "You girls will get fat and ugly and nobody will cast you in another show."

"Mom, I'm hungry." I couldn't tell the twins apart, so I don't know which one spoke.

"I don't see why. You had a big bowl of granola for breakfast."

One girl stuck her finger in her throat and made gagging noises. The other one said, "Granola tastes like poop."

"Mrs. Jones, we need the girls over here right away," Royce said.

The girls grabbed sodas from the cooler but mama made them return the cans and take bottles of water instead. She hustled the young actresses to the table. Mrs. Jones dropped her suitcase-sized handbag into the empty chair at the opposite end of the table from Royce. The girls sat, one on each side of mama's chair. They opened their scripts and bent their heads over the pages, but instead of reading, they whispered among themselves. Harv gave the girls a cheery good morning greeting but they only mumbled something in reply.

"Mrs. Jones, please take a seat, we need to start," said Royce.

Instead, the woman pulled a rolled-up magazine from her bag, marched over to Elsie, and whacked the actress on the head with it.

Elsie jumped to her feet. "You witch!"

Royce snapped, "Mrs. Jones, that was uncalled for. Sit down."

The mother fixed the director with a look that could have set a wildfire. "You tell this harpy to stop spreading lies about my daughters!"

She threw the magazine onto the table. The glossy unfolded to reveal Elsie's perky face smiling from the cover of *Buzzword Now*, a disreputable monthly rag that covered the L.A. entertainment and nightclub scene, or rather, uncovered the featured person of the month in a scandalous photo spread. Formerly known as *Buzzword*, the slimy magazine had gone out of business years ago but recently a tasteless entrepreneur had resurrected it, not that anyone was clamoring for more copies. If Elsie wanted to advance her career, she'd make better progress by investing in acting lessons than in posing for nude photos.

Mrs. Jones jabbed a forefinger on the magazine. "In this interview, that piece of scum says my girls sleep around and smoke pot and want to act in dirty movies!" The finger then started poking Elsie's voluptuous chest. "That's a bald-faced lie and you know it!"

Elsie slapped the hand away. "You think your precious little darlings are so squeaky-clean? Ha! They got you fooled!"

"You call this magazine and retract what you said or you'll be sorry!"

"Yeah, like I'm scared of you, big mama."

Exasperated, Royce said, "Ladies, we don't have time for this. We're behind schedule. Mrs. Jones, if you have something to discuss with Elsie, wait until the lunch break." As Mrs. Jones stomped to her chair and sat, the director spoke in a low voice, "Elsie, I need to speak to you later, okay?"

"Sure, Royce." She smiled, batted her lashes at him and almost purred out loud. Did those two have something going on?

"It's regarding a memo I received."

As Elsie sat, her smile turned upside down.

One more person—actually, a person with an animal—arrived to complete the *Off-Kelter* cast. The woman in an unpretentious dress wasn't an actor but the dog on her leash played the Kelters' pet, Scruffy. According to the credits at the end of the show, her name was Frances Fontenay. She moved a folding chair within a few feet from the table, close enough to hear the actors, and sat. She ordered the dog to lie down, and the terrier mix obediently relaxed at her feet as she dug a script from her satchel.

Between the twins, the dwarf, the dog and the fantasy sequences, this show had more gimmicks than Batman's utility belt.

Royce said to the assembled clan, "I'm sure most of you already know our guest star this week, Sandy Fairfax." He managed to say that without a trace of resentment.

"Samuel, how nice to meet you," Dottie said.

"Sandy. My name is Sandy."

"Of course it is. How silly of me. Sandy, a pleasure to meet you."

Harv told the twins that I had starred on *Buddy Brave, Boy Sleuth*. From the boredom on their faces, they had obviously never heard of my show. Some people really know how to deflate one's ego.

"All right, I hope everyone had a pleasant weekend," Royce said. "Let's begin, top of the show, page one." He put on his reading glasses and opened his script.

Elsie reached inside her purse and rummaged around. "Wait, we can't start yet."

"Why not?" Royce peered at her over his lenses.

"My wetting drops. I need to put in my eye drops."

"Elsie, everyone's ready to go."

She removed a small white plastic bottle from her handbag. "This desert air dries out my contacts and my eyes get itchy."

"Take out your contacts and squint."

"Won't take a second." She opened the bottle, threw back her head, squeezed a drop into each eye, and then blinked. The other actors reacted with annoyance by staring into space, glancing through their scripts or brushing lint off their clothes. Finished, Elsie capped the bottle and returned it to her bag, which she dropped to the floor with a thud. Royce glared at her and ordered the cast to start. Since my character didn't show up until scene four, I sat back and listened. The show opened, as usual, early morning in the Kelters' kitchen. The twins engaged in typical sibling squabbling while Miss Tucker set out breakfast for them.

After a few minutes, Elise slapped her script shut and shouted at the writers. "When are you guys going to write me some good jokes?"

"We don't need to change the words," said Joseph, "just the actress."

She set her thick, red-lipsticked lips in a tight line. "Who made you a drama critic?"

"The best acting you ever did was convincing your boyfriend that you liked him."

"Okay, everyone calm down, please," Harv said. "No need to start the week on a bad note, right, gang?"

Royce turned to the writers and asked if they could punch up Elsie's jokes. From the looks on their face, they'd rather punch her in the kisser, but they dutifully nodded.

But Elsie wasn't finished grumbling. "And I'm only in a couple of scenes this week. I'm not getting enough exposure!"

Joseph eyed her cleavage. "I wouldn't say that."

"They're trying to write me out of the show!"

"Elsie, I counted the lines," Royce said. "You, Dottie and Joseph have about the same amount of screen time."

"Harv has way more lines than I do."

"That's because he's the star of the show."

And not you, I wanted to add.

"Calm down, Elsie." Harv reached across the table and patted her hand, his voice flowing like liquid salve. "I'm sure it's just an oversight. The writers are doing the best they can."

She whispered something to Harv. I'm hard of

hearing in one ear (a casualty of the decibel-busting audience screams during my concert days) and I couldn't hear what she said. But his eyes grew wide, his jaw dropped and his face turned into a mask of fear.

Harv coughed nervously. "You'll have more lines next week, Elsie, I'll personally see to it." He flipped through his script, pretending to study his lines in an effort to hide his reddening face.

The drama between the cast members was far more interesting that the muddled script. The plot involved the theft of athletic trophies from the display case at the school where Clarence Kelter worked as a career counselor. Clarence had to recover the awards before the big homecoming dance or the visiting alumni would not make any donations (seems to me that Clarence should ask the alums to pay for a security system). Mr. Kelter refused to call the police because of the bad publicity for the school, which provided a flimsy excuse for this week's fantasy sequence: Momma (Dottie) had invented a time machine that transported the clan back to the 1940s where Clarence hired a Sam Spade-type detective named Sammy Shovel (get it?) to find the missing trophies. The real mystery in the story was why the producer cast a blue-eyed, cherub-faced former teen idol with a blonde ponytail as a tough guy private eye. And for some unexplained reason not only did Mr. Shovel find the purloined prizes but he also performed a parody of the "Singin' in the Rain" dance sequence. I think the writers had a few drug-induced fantasies of their own when they scribbled this script.

My first scene came up and I read my lines as a hard-nosed, streetwise shamus, a mix of all my favorite tough guy actors from those wonderful classic films like *Little Caesar* and *The Maltese Falcon*. I wanted to play against my usual wholesome persona and expand my acting range in an effort to impress future casting directors.

Royce stopped me. "Sandy, what are you doing?"

"I'm reading the lines."

"No, I mean, what's that voice you're using?"

"It's how I picture the character. You know, a world weary, man-of-the-streets P.I."

"Sandy, this is a comedy. We're not doing *The Godfather*. You're going too dark. We want light and funny."

"All right, Royce. What would you suggest I do?"

"Why don't you do the character like Buddy Brave?"

My blood pressure shot up to the high ceiling. "Royce! I am not playing this character like a teenage pipsqueak who isn't old enough to shave!"

"Just give it a shot, will you?"

When I was the star on my own show I could push the directors for what I wanted, but as a guest I didn't have that luxury. He knew he had me.

I spoke through gritted teeth. "I'll see what I can do, Royce."

I was cruising through my lines when, right in the middle of a long speech, a hand squeezed my knee. This surprised me so much, my voice squeaked, but I recovered, hopefully before anyone noticed. I glanced at Elsie and she fluttered those alluring eyelashes at me. Her fingers walked up my leg and I panicked. Don't get me wrong; I love a woman's touch. If we were sitting at a bar, I'd pursue her invitation. But when I'm at work I save the cootchy-coo for later. Elsie blew me a kiss and I shot her an angry look. I turned away from her, hoping she'd get the hint. Joseph watched us, his lips curled in a bemused smile.

Carl prompted me on missing a line and I apologized. Elsie had me so distracted I'd lost my place. I jumped back in the scene and soon Elsie's daring digits were once more making their way along my inseam. Her fingers hovered dangerously close to my crotch. I crossed my legs and kicked her.

She screamed. "You broke my ankle!" Elsie rubbed her shin and moaned in mock pain, giving her best performance of the morning.

I put on my most contrite face. "I'm terribly sorry. Did I accidentally kick you? I was just stretching my legs."

Royce glared at us. "Can we please finish this scene before midnight?"

Elsie scowled at me, but I didn't care. The read through continued without further incident. Harv, Dottie and Joseph were far better actors than this show deserved. They tried hard to breathe some life into the limp lines. With the twins, I wasn't sure if they were simply acting like real disinterested teenagers or if they wanted to spend the day at the beach. At one point we stopped so Frances could tell me about some business I'd have with Scruffy—he'd jump on the P.I.'s desk and lick my face. Sounded simple enough (little did I know . . .).

At long last we reached the final scene, the tag, where the family once more gathered in the living room to generate some parting jokes and a cozy feeling. The cast argued with the writers about their lines for several minutes until the AD called for a lunch break at about one-thirty. Elsie was the first on her feet. Before rushing out the stage door she handed her fuzz ball handbag to a production assistant and told (not asked) him to put it in her dressing room. Harv left to record a radio spot for the America Family Foundation, a nonprofit charity he endorsed. Mrs. Jones, thankfully, took her girls somewhere else.

Joseph turned to me and chuckled. "Hey, Sandy, nice job of giving the battle-axe the brush off. I saw that tramp making googly eyes at you."

"Maybe she's a fan."

"Don't flatter yourself. She pulls that same routine with all the men guest stars."

Joseph excused himself for a luncheon appointment. I stood, stretched, and realized that after that coffee I needed to make a pit stop. If I remembered correctly, the soundstage had a small restroom for use by the crew, extras and the PAs (production assistants, the young gofers trying to break into the business by doing grunt work for minimum wage). Behind the set I found the hallway that led to the various dressing rooms, offices, and storage areas. I gratefully occupied the single stall, unisex restroom. As I was washing my hands afterwards I heard voices just outside the door. I finished wiping my hands, tossed the paper towel in the metal wastebasket, and pressed my good ear against the door.

"She's such a witch." Sounded like one of the twins.

"Let's think up something really nasty to get back at her."

"Yeah! I got an idea."

The footsteps faded away and then a door slammed. The girls must have gone inside a dressing room. I left the restroom and met Carl in the hallway.

"Sandy, there you are. I was looking for you. If you don't have plans, I'd like you to join me for lunch. I can bring you up to speed about the Friday night taping and answer any questions you have about the show."

Having a luncheon companion sounded great so I readily agreed. I waited for Carl to deposit his clipboard and headset in the production office, a small room with little more than file cabinets, old desks and chairs, and a couple of PAs to answer the mostly-quiet phones. We left the comfort of the air-conditioned cocoon for the bright sunshine of a warm SoCal day. I removed my leather jacket and flung it over my shoulder, holding it in place with one finger hooked under the collar. My baby blues took a second to adjust to the sunlight and another moment to comprehend what I saw walking down the street.

A space alien with a ridge of razor sharp fins running down its back and horns on its elongated, grasshopper-like head approached us. The creature held a laser rifle in its claws.

Chapter 3: Get It Right Next Time

The monster seemed to stare at us with its two huge black eyes. The thing wore brown leather pants and a shiny metal breastplate over its green scaly skin. The creature had no shoes, only two huge feet with thick pads on the soles and curled claws.

Carl waved with nonchalance. "Hi, Troy."

The alien returned the gesture with its webbed fingers, grunted something in what I assumed was a language from another planet, and walked by.

"Troy?" I asked. "That was Troy as in Elsie's Troy?"

"Yes, he plays Commander Ump'teck on that sci-fi show, *Space Posse.* They film next door to *Off-Kelter.*" Carl gestured at Soundstage 12 (movie lots don't have a Stage 13 because that's unlucky). "Troy comes over to see Elsie during his breaks."

"I don't see how Troy can get romantic in that makeup."

At the end of the street Carl showed me the trailer I'd be using. Who needed to go to the gym for a workout when one had to walk a distance for a costume change? We climbed the trailer's steps. The interior only held the bare necessities: a chair, short couch, wall mirror, small shelf and drawer for makeup and a minuscule bathroom with shower, sink and toilet. My old dressing room could have accommodated three of these shoeboxes. The AD showed me the closet where he had stashed my helmet and gym bag. We left the cramped quarters and saw a small group of people coming toward us. Based on the way they snapped photos and craned their necks to gawk at the buildings, these folks were obviously tourists. I admit the studio looked impressive on a first-time visit. I too was star-struck when my then-manager, Jarvis Lycowitz, brought me here at the tender age of 18 for my screen test. The college-aged woman leading the group wore what looked like a uniform: maroon pants, vest and beret with a long-sleeved gold shirt. The vest's left breast sported a Mammoth Picture Studio logo.

"Here comes another tour group," Carl said. "Let's go this way."

He steered me away from the tourists and through a narrow passageway between two soundstages that deposited us on yet another street.

"Back in the '70s we never had tourists on the lot," I said. "When did that change?"

"Ivan Constantine hired the pages and set up the tour groups about eight years ago as another money maker for the studio."

"When did Ivan start working for Mammoth? He used to be in real estate."

"I'll bring you up to date on the studio politics over lunch."

The commissary, a gray, nondescript one-story building, provided a cafeteria for the below-the-line employees and extras as well as a more exclusive dining area with wait staff for the suits. When I worked on my show, I rarely stepped foot inside the commissary, but not by choice. My so-called lunch breaks were crammed with interviews, photo shoots for the teen magazines, discussions over the next record or concert, or quality time with a young lassie in my dressing room. Small wonder I was skinny back then; I never had time for a decent meal.

The long serving line in the cafeteria moved quickly.

We picked up our plastic trays and metal silverware and made our selections. Some of the servers and cashiers looked familiar, only older and grayer. Nobody made a fuss over me because the studio employees were used to seeing celebrities. Carl found a small round table near the wall. I draped my jacket over the chair back. We sat and placed our paper napkins on our laps. At another table, a green *Space Posse* creature carried on an animated conversation with a blue-skinned woman dressed in a skimpy bikini outfit covered in rhinestones. On her head sat an enormous headpiece with pink and white feathers.

"Now that's something you don't see everyday," Carl said.

"What's that?"

He pointed his spoon at the aliens. "A Gorgandian having lunch with Princess Alea of the Kamorra tribe. Those species are sworn enemies."

Only in Hollywood.

I tore open my mustard packet and doused my all-beef hot dog with condiment. "So give me the scoop on Ivan the Terrible."

Ivan was the only son of the current Mammoth studio head, Leo Constantine, and his first wife. When I worked on my show I'd met the kid (everyone called him that, even now) at some obligatory social functions, but I never had any business dealings with him. He'd earned the nickname from his surly attitude toward anyone he deemed beneath him, which was just about everyone on the planet.

Carl talked in between bites of his soup and salad combo. "The younger Constantine wasn't interested in the studio until recently. He begged his father to let him produce some shows."

"I heard rumors that Ivan didn't do well in real estate. Some of his more expensive retail developments failed."

Carl shrugged. "You know how rumors go. You'll probably see Ivan at the Thursday run-through, if not before."

"How nice." I hoped Carl didn't pick up the sarcasm in my voice.

The AD named some of the other programs Ivan had produced, mostly sitcoms, and all of them flops that lasted less than a season.

"Sounds like the kid doesn't have the knack of developing anything." I opened my ketchup packets and drowned my fries in the red sauce. "If Ivan's such a dud, why does daddy keep him on the payroll? Outside of the fact that he's family?"

"It may not be Ivan's fault. It's the nature of the business. Most new shows don't take off. One of these days he'll come up with a winner. It's just a matter of time."

"From what I've heard, Mammoth doesn't have much time." When I decided to get back into the business I started reading the Hollywood trade papers again. "Last year the studio released more bombs than the army in World War II."

"It's a dry spell. I'm sure things will be picking up soon. Ivan has a number of shows in development that sound promising."

"At the risk of sounding presumptuous, is the kid thinking of taking over pop's position?" I skewered some ketchup-laden fries with a fork and crammed them into my mouth.

"It's possible."

"Isn't Leo afraid that the kid will turn Mammoth into another Roach Studios?"

I was referring to a Hollywood story without a happy ending. In the early 1900s, producer Hal Roach Sr. created his famous studio, dubbed the "laugh factory to the world," that created hundreds of comedy films with the likes of Our Gang, Harold Lloyd, and Laurel and Hardy. But when his son lost the Culver City studio to creditors, the chuckles were silenced forever. The buildings were torn down in 1963 and replaced with stores and an auto dealership. Now only a small plaque embedded in the ground gives any indication of the site's former greatness. I couldn't bear the thought that the home of *Buddy Brave* might suffer the same fate.

"Things change, Sandy. By the time Leo steps down, a whole new regime might be in place and Ivan might have moved on to something else." He glanced at the wall clock. "We better get back."

I picked up my jacket and we placed our trays and dirty dishes on the conveyor belt leading into the washing area. During our walk back to Stage 14, Carl asked me how many seats I wanted reserved for the Friday night taping.

"Seats?" I asked.

"Cast members can bring in guests to watch the taping. I'll make sure some chairs are set aside for your family and friends."

Friends? I was avoiding old drinking buddies so they wouldn't push me off the wagon. Family? A rift wider than the Grand Canyon existed between me and my parents and siblings. Girlfriends? I'd recently broken up with my latest in a long line of neurotic women. My kids? I'd have to plead with Becka to let them visit me. Undergoing open-heart surgery without an anesthetic sounded far less painful than asking my ex for a favor.

"Can I get back to you on that?"

"Why don't I put you down for two and you can let me know if you need more."

"Fine, thanks."

Back at Stage 14, one of the PAs handed me the script that I'd left behind; maybe I should tether the pages to my wrist. I wasn't on for a couple of scenes, so I put on my leather jacket and sat in the bleacher seats for a bird's eye view of the action. The actors gathered on the master set, scripts in hand, and worked through the cold opening, the first scene before the opening credits. Royce and the AD sat in canvas chairs facing the scene. Mrs. Jones stood just off to the side of the set where she could keep a sharp eye on her two charges seated at the Kelter kitchen table (California's strict laws regarding child actors mandated that a parent or guardian must be on the set with their youngster at all times). As the scene progressed, the mother grew increasingly angry and no wonder: Elsie constantly complained about the twins. The actress griped when Molly stepped on her line and when Missy bumped into her as she moved upstage. When Elsie dropped her script and bent over to pick it up, her miniskirt hiked up just a little too much. Molly made a crude remark about the situation and Missy giggled. Elsie stood and threw a lewd comment back at the girls.

Mrs. Jones shouted, "Don't talk to my girls like that and don't show off your nasty butt like a hooker!"

The actress threw her script onto the kitchen table and stomped over to Royce. "Can you get that old bag off the set? I can't work with her here!"

"Take it easy, sugar." Sugar? Did these two have more than a professional relationship going on? "Don't let her get to you."

"Look at the way she's staring at me. She's trying to put a hex on me."

Royce whispered something to the AD, who then set up a metal folding chair beside the director.

"Mrs. Jones, would you please sit over here?" Royce said, indicating the chair.

The mom made a brief protest but at Royce's insistence, she obeyed. Elsie picked up her script and the actors finished the scene without further ado. Mrs. Jones hustled her darlings out of the building and the action then moved to the living room set. Royce gave the actors their blocking: Elsie and Joseph standing side-by-side stage left, Harv sitting on the sofa and Dottie upstage right (toward the back of the set). Royce called for action and the actors started the scene—but they didn't get far. After a few minutes, Elsie slapped Joseph on the head with her script.

Royce stood. "What's going on?"

Elsie yelled, "Joe's looking up my skirt!"

"You wish," the dwarf replied.

She yanked on the hem of her miniskirt, as if that would cover anything. "And this isn't the first time he's done it, the little pervert!"

"Why would I do that?" he retorted. "There's nothing up there worth seeing."

"That's it!" She took a step towards Royce. "I'm reporting Joe for sexual harassment!"

Royce approached Elsie and placed his hands on her shoulders. "There's no need for that, Elsie, darling." His voice was soft and soothing. "We don't need that kind of trouble. A legal issue would only upset you. Why don't you stand over there by the bookcase?" Royce eased the gal over to the bookcase standing at the foot of the stairs. "That's it. Perfect. We can still get you in the shot."

"Thank you," Joseph said. "Now I can breath again. Elsie's perfume is worse than the smog layer."

The actress screamed, "You nasty, little—"

"Please, please." The director held up his hands. "Everyone, calm down. Let's keep it civil. Elsie, pick it up from your line, 'What if they find out?'" He returned to his canvas chair. "And action."

She recited the line with the same flat delivery as her table read. This didn't bode well. During my scenes,

Elsie's lack of focus might suck the energy right out of me.

Time for Dottie's line. She said, "I might have what's needed downstairs."

Carl corrected her. "Dottie, the line is 'I've got just the thing for you in the basement.'"

The actress held her script as far away from her face as she could and glanced at the page. "Really? That can't be right."

"That's what my script says," Harv interjected.

Royce said, "Dottie, why don't you use your glasses?"

"Royce, dear, those dreadful spectacles pinch my nose."

"Just wear your glasses for rehearsal, Dottie. You won't need them once you've memorized your lines."

"I *have* memorized my lines! I learned my role thoroughly. I'm a professional."

"You can't remember anything," Elsie scoffed. "Last week's taping took forever because you kept blowing your lines."

Dottie shot back, "At least I *act* when I say my lines."

"If airhead Elsie can learn lines," Joseph quipped, "then they're pretty easy to remember."

Elsie stomped over to the dwarf and I could swear she was ready to pick him up and toss him off the set. Harv intercepted Elsie and tried to console her. Meanwhile, Dottie stepped over to the edge of the set (the "edge" being a line of tape on the floor) to talk to the director.

"Royce, be a sweetheart and let me improvise. As long as I get the gist of the line, where's the harm?"

"Because, Dottie, the other actors need to hear the cues so they can say *their* lines."

She gave a big sigh. "So much fuss over such a silly

little line."

"Dottie, please put on your glasses so we can move on."

All this time, the eyeglasses in question were hanging around Dottie's neck on a gold chain. Maybe she thought the eyewear worked better as a necklace than as a reading aid. With a good deal of theatrics, the actress placed the glasses on her nose, wiggled them to get them in place, and read the line correctly. The actors continued and after a short scene where the characters went into the basement and were transported in the time machine, the time came for my grand debut. I left my seat and headed downstairs to the floor. On my way to the set, the outside door opened, letting in a flood of sunlight and fresh air. A male page entered and had some words with the AD who then spoke to Royce.

The director said, "Listen, everyone, we have a tour group waiting outside."

Harv was all smiles. "Well, bring them in."

"Not until everyone stops snapping at each other."

Normally directors are the calm center in the stormy process of filmmaking, but Royce sounded as if he was ready to rip into some jugulars himself.

"We'll behave," said Joseph. "Won't we, Elsie?"

She eyed him with contempt.

Harv stepped up to me. "I like having the tours to come in and watch us work. God knows we need the publicity to keep the show alive. Do you mind?"

"No, that's fine with me."

When I started with *Buddy Brave,* I was self-conscious about my performance, but I soon got used to having people watching me work: friends of the studio suits, teen magazine reporters, fans who sneaked past the guards, and a crew of fifty or more eyeing my every move from behind the camera. I could easily put up with a small mob of tourists.

Harv gave Royce a thumbs up, who then nodded to the PA, who passed on the okay to the page who hurried out the door. Dottie wasn't in this scene, so she wandered offstage. Harv, Joseph and Elsie moved to a newly built set beside the master set. Sammy Shovel's "office," at this point, consisted of three canvas walls, some folding chairs and a desk—the set designer hadn't brought in the furniture and set dressings. In this scene, Harv et al asked the PI's help in finding the missing trophies. I took my place behind the office door for my entrance. The actors turned their pages while the tour group quietly walked in and sat in the front row bleacher seats. With an audience present, Harv seemed more animated. He played to the crowd, casting them side-glances and hamming up his role. He needed the public as much as they needed him. I don't blame him; I'm the same way. When I gave concerts in front of thousands of screaming fans, I lit up like a Christmas tree.

When my cue came, I opened the door on the set, stepped onstage and heard squeals of delight from the tour group; inadvertently I smiled at the unexpected response. I sat behind the PI's desk and we continued. I enjoyed the scene. Harv and I bounced off each other, and I tried not to let Elsie's bad acting annoy me. Royce stopped the scene halfway through so we could practice my bit with the dog. Frances entered from backstage and fussed with the dog. During the lull, Harv walked to the edge of the set and thanked the tourists for stopping by. One woman in the tour group caught my eye. She looked familiar—someone I never expected to see in Los Angeles.

I crossed over to Harv and looked at the visitors. "Bunny, is that you?"

Chapter 4: Bad Blood

"Hi, Sandy!" In the bleachers, a plump, late-twenty-something fan with short frizzy brown hair and rimless glasses waved so hard that I expected her arm to fly off.

"Bunny, what are you doing here?"

"When I heard you were on the show this week I just had to fly out and see you. I took a week's vacation from my job. Some of the other girls from the fan club are here too."

She gestured at the other women in the group, who looked about Bunny's age. They giggled and shyly waved.

I smiled and waved back. "Hi, girls. Welcome to L.A."

Bunny continued. "Today we're visiting Hollywood and tomorrow we're going to Disneyland and then to Universal Studios on Wednesdays and the Santa Monica pier on Thursday and Friday night we're coming to see the taping of the show!"

"That sounds like fun," I said.

Harv interrupted. "We have to get back to work, but thanks for stopping by. See you all on Friday and be sure to tell your friends back home to watch the show."

The tour guide ushered the group out the door. As the women left, they peeked over their shoulders for one last glimpse of me, and Bunny gave me a good-bye wave.

Harv said to me, "Who was that?"

"Bunny McAllister. She's the president of my biggest fan club, Sandy's Buddies. We met a few weeks ago at a fan convention she hosted at her hometown in Indiana."

"You're lucky. My fan club disbanded some years ago."

"Sorry to hear that."

No wonder Harv was willing to sign on for this awful show—it gave him one last chance to revitalize his fan base and get back in the limelight.

Frances came on the set with Scruffy. She unhooked the leash from the dog's collar and explained the action to me. Scruffy would enter the office along with Harv and the others. On her cue, the animal actor would jump on the desk and "kiss" me. She took a small, round tin from her fanny pack and popped off the lid. With two fingers she scooped some brown mashed-up goo from the tin and smeared it on my right upstage (away from the audience) cheek. I was used to the makeup people messing with my face but this stuff stank.

"What's that?" I said.

"Liver pate'. Scruffy loves it. The smell will attract him to the spot where he's to kiss you."

If I smelled something like that, I'd run in the opposite direction, but I guess animals have a different sensibility. Frances put a plastic lid on the tin and stepped off to the side of the set, out of camera range but where the dog could see her hand cues. We moved back into our positions at the top of the scene and restarted. Harv, Elsie and Joseph entered the office with Scruffy tottering at their heels. I made my entrance, a little disappointed that my adoring audience was gone. I sat at the desk and we said our lines. Frances motioned and Scruffy jumped up on the desk, panted and stared at me.

I turned to the trainer. "Isn't this where Scruffy's suppose to kiss me?"

Frances picked up the dog, placed him on the floor,

and stepped offstage. We ran the scene again. On my line and her cue, Scruffy jumped, put his paws on my chest and licked the pate' off my cheek. Actually, the mutt slobbered all over my face. His fat tongue jabbed my eyeball. Dog drool ran down my cheek. I couldn't breathe with his paws crushing my rib cage. I nearly passed out from his doggie breath.

Anyone who thinks acting is glamorous is out of his mind.

I grabbed the dog and pulled him off before he drowned me in spit. I was so flustered I quipped an ad-lib. "I haven't been kissed like that since I went out with Rita Hayworth."

Harv and Joseph howled with laughter.

"Sandy, what are you doing?" Royce asked.

"I made a joke. You know what a joke is, don't you, Royce? It's what this script needs."

"I love it," said Harv. "I think we should keep it."

Royce wanted me to stick to the script, but Harv and Joseph persuaded him to leave in the line. Elsie complained but only because nobody was looking at her for the moment. As for me, I was pleased. After being away from show biz for so long, my creative juices were starting to flow. Scruffy jumped off the desk and we finished the scene, none too soon for my comfort. As soon as Royce called "cut," I stood, yanked the handkerchief from my pocket and wiped my face. The tiny piece of cloth wasn't enough to mop up the ocean of drool.

"Can I wash my face?" I said.

Francis asked, "Are you allergic to dogs?"

"No, no. Scruffy was just a little enthusiastic with his kiss, that's all."

I didn't want to trudge all the way to my trailer to clean up, so Royce sent one of the PAs to fetch a damp towel. He then called for a short break while he argued with the crew foreman about something. The builders kept on building a new set and the actors clustered around the craft services table for a mid-afternoon pick-me-up. Frances left, probably so Scruffy could do his business. The PA returned with a wet towel and I wiped my face.

Meanwhile, Carl was talking on the telephone that was set on a mobile stand so the crew could push it across the floor as need. After he hung up he said, "Sandy, wardrobe needs you for a costume fitting. Why don't you go over there now? We won't need you for a while."

He offered to have a PA drive me, but I said I'd walk. I'd been to wardrobe enough times to remember the location and a brisk walk might help burn a few calories so I'd fit into the costume. Just as I was about to open the stage door, though, someone called to me.

"Wait for me!" Elsie ran to catch up with me. "Where ya goin'?"

"To wardrobe."

"That's cool. I'm headed that way too. I'll tag along." Notice she didn't ask *if* she could come with me. "Oh, silly me, I forgot my purse." She grabbed my arm. "Sandy, be a sweetie and get my purse, will you?"

Did she actually want me to touch that horrific-looking handbag? I'd have to put on plastic gloves first.

"Where is it?"

"In my dressing room and I don't want to have to walk all the way back there." She stretched the word "all" into three long syllables.

Her dressing room was not that far away. She was just toying with me. But playing along with her foolishness might be easier than dealing with her temper if I didn't. I agreed and she told me which dressing room belonged to her.

"And while you're there, can you pleasy-weasy get a

bottle of my veggie juice? I'm so thirsty. Don't get me one from the shelf. I want a cold one from the fridge."

"Why don't you get a soda from craft services?"

She scrunched up her face in a gesture of disgust. "All that artificial gunk will kill you. My veggie juices are natural and pure."

I had a snappy comeback ready but wisely held my tongue. I made the short trek behind the set. Elsie's dressing room wasn't locked so I slipped in and closed the door behind me. The dressing rooms stayed unlocked during the day so the actors could move in quickly to change and so wardrobe could drop off and pick up costumes. When I played Buddy Brave, I left my room unlocked simply because I couldn't have crammed a key into the pocket of my skin-tight bell-bottoms. Elsie's room was smaller than my former dressing room but still bigger than my trailer and far more comfortable, except for the dire threat in black letters scrawled across the mirror: YOU'RE GONNA DIE YOU SHREW along with a drawing of a prone stick figure with a knife drawn through its torso. Black and red crepe paper streamers hung from the ceiling.

Either Elsie was auditioning for the role of Elvira with this macabre décor or someone was playing one mean prank.

I gingerly touched one of the letters on the glass. I'd been around enough women to recognize this gooey stuff: black lipstick. I grabbed a tissue from the makeup table and wiped off my fingers. Then I examined the rest of the room. Elsie must have thought the show would be on the air for six years instead of six weeks because she had the place decorated like a penthouse suite: stuffed animals, embroidered pillows, vases of fresh flowers, a stash of cassette tapes and a portable stereo, enough cosmetics to open a boutique and a pile of unopened mail. Various pieces of feminine lingerie were also strewn about. Either she'd had some good times with Troy in here or else she was untidy when changing clothes.

I found the purse easily enough, atop the makeup table. I opened the small refrigerator, which was crammed with plastic bottles full of some kind of reddish-orange liquid as well as veggie sandwiches wrapped in cellophane. As I took one of the bottles I smelled grilled onions and hamburger. I sniffed around until I pinpointed the source: a metal waste can on the floor. I set down the bottle and from the waste can removed a wadded-up square of waxy paper slick with cooked grease. The wrapper bore the logo of Rico's, a hamburger joint just outside the studio walls. The food wasn't great but the late-working studio employees often patronized Rico's after the commissary closed for the day. On days when I finished shooting *Buddy Brave* and had to dash over to a music studio for a late-night recording session, I often swung through Rico's drive-through for an order of fatty fries and grease-bomb burgers to eat on the way.

Why would a dedicated vegetarian have a hamburger wrapper in her dressing room? This room contained more mysteries than a season of *Murder, She Wrote*.

I dropped the wrapper back into the bin, picked up the juice bottle and purse, and met up with Elsie at the stage door. The actress took the items off my hands and we headed out into the street. I put on my aviator-style sunglasses and draped my jacket over one arm.

"Let's take a cart," she said.

"It's a nice day for a walk," I said. "Besides, I don't see any carts handy."

To save time in traveling across the 50-acre lot, employees used modified electric golf carts to get around. Each show in production had a few carts with the program's name on the side. I picked up the pace and Elsie kept up with me, swinging that monstrosity of a purse in wide arcs. Her breasts, unencumbered by a bra, likewise bounced with each step.

I had to find out if she had seen that warning on her mirror. "Say, Elsie, when I was in your dressing room I noticed something really odd."

"You saw my undies, didn't you?"

"Yes, but that isn't what I—"

"I forgot! I left my Victoria's Secrets out where everybody could see them. I'm such a naughty girl." She giggled. "Where are my manners! I forgot to tell you, if you wanted a bottle of my veggie juice, you could have taken one when you were in my room."

"What is it?"

"It's a carrot, green bean and beet energy drink." She waved the plastic bottle in front of my face. "Want some?"

"No, thank you." To me, the only way to eat veggies is piled high on a salad drenched in Thousand Island dressing and not smooshed into something trying to pass itself off as a milkshake.

"You'll be sorry. This stuff makes me feel alive. You don't like me, do you?"

I definitely liked the view of her chestal area but I kept my eyes focused on her face instead. "What makes you say that?"

"Nobody on the show likes me." She tried to make a sexy pout by puffing out her embellished lips but instead she looked like someone suffering from gas. If Elise was trying to channel Marilyn Monroe, she'd tapped into Marjorie Main instead. "They're just jealous. Everyone thinks I got the part because of daddy."

"I didn't know your father was in show business."

"Of course he is, silly." She gave my arm a playful squeeze. "He runs the studio."

Stunned, I stopped in my tracks. "Leo Constantine is your father? I thought Ivan was his only child."

She held a slender finger to her lips. "Shhh, don't spread it around. Daddy doesn't want anyone to know."

To reach the wardrobe department we cut through the back lot, several blocks of scaled-down replicas of New York City buildings used for exterior shots. The brownstones were not actual buildings but just facades, walls held up by girders, with nothing inside but stairwells and ledges where actors could look out the windows. Apparently a shot had just wrapped as some crewmen were loading camera equipment into a van. Elsie called and waved at the young male workers. Didn't the girl ever stop flirting? They waved back, possibly thinking she must be a star (real celebrities don't call attention to themselves. We get enough notoriety without asking for it). Then the guys went back to their work and didn't give her a second glance.

I continued, "So Bloom is a stage name?"

"Nope, that's my real name." She tossed her head, flinging her long hair around like a flag. "Bloom's my mom's name. Daddy met mom when she was working as an usher at a movie theater. I was conceived during an afternoon double feature." She giggled again. "Daddy's married to some old crone who pretends I don't exist, but Consty's nice to me and he gets me jobs and there's nothing that old biddy can do about it."

If her father was giving her jobs like *Off-Kelter*, he must not like her that much.

She covered her mouth with her hand and gave me a startled look. "Why Sandy Fairfax! I barely know you and you got me tattling all of my secrets!"

"Do you want to hear some of mine?"

"You don't have any secrets. I know *all* about you." She ran a finger down my bare arm. "I hear you're quite a lady's man. Maybe we can get together some night and, you know, talk shop."

I've never met anyone who could make such innocent words sound so dirty.

"I hate to disappoint you, Elsie, but I don't have any pull in the business. Sleeping with me won't help you get a job."

"I'm not looking for a casting couch. Just a little recreation."

We turned the corner onto another back lot street. Truth be told, I wouldn't mind a romp in the sack with this temptress. But I was here to work, not to play around, and shacking up with the illegitimate daughter of a studio executive would jeopardize my career worse than a bad review in the *Daily Variety*.

"Sorry, Elsie, but my dance card is full."

In a flash she transformed into a tiger. Her plump lips pressed together in a frown. She dug her fingernails into my arm. "I can have you fired from the show!"

"All right, goodbye, then. My bike's parked over there. I'll head on home."

She threw back her head and laughed. Then she looked at me with a distressed expression. This girl switched moods faster than my ex-wife changed shoes.

"That's what I mean. Nobody takes me seriously. People think I'm a ditz 'cause I'm pretty. But I'm not dumb. I'm a good actress but I keep getting rotten roles. I need a good part so I can show off my talent." Elsie seemed unaware that she had no talent to display. "This sitcom doesn't give me a chance to show my range. And everyone on the show is so mean to me."

"Elsie, can I offer a suggestion? Why don't you act nicer to your co-stars? They'll treat you better in return."

She stopped walking, right in front of a huge, three-story, official-looking façade often used in shows for a courthouse or governmental offices. She dug a bottle of eye drops out of her purse and uncapped the bottle. "This sun is murder on my contacts." She tilted her head back and squeezed liquid into her eyes. Elsie blinked, capped the bottle and returned it to her purse. "There. That's better." She snapped shut the metal purse closure. Then she uncapped the bottle and took a big gulp of the oddball veggie juice.

We started walking again but we never reached the costume department.

"What about Troy?" I said. "How serious are you two?"

"He wants to get engaged but I don't know. He's sweet, but not too bright. All brawn and no brains, you know what I mean?" She sighed. "Some day I'd like to find a decent guy who loves me for *me*, not just the sex. Although the sex is nice." She laughed. "I'm gonna talk to daddy tonight and tell him I want a good role. A great part that will make me a big star. Daddy better do that because if he doesn't, I'll tell everyone his secret."

"Oh? What secret is that?"

She spun around on her heels, swinging her purse by the strap. "He and the studio will be in such deep doo-doo if I tattle. I'll tell everybody that—"

I never learned the secret, because Elsie stopped and gasped for air. He face flushed as she grasped her chest. "I can't breath," she whispered.

"Elsie? What's wrong?"

She collapsed, unconscious, at my feet.

Chapter 5: Dying of a Broken Heart

I dropped to one knee, placed my jacket on the ground, and turned Elsie over, face up. I called her name but she didn't respond. Her limbs twitched and her chest heaved, fighting for air. I glanced around for someone to assist me; the crewmen on the other street would be long gone. I grabbed Elsie by the shoulders and gently shook her because that's what Buddy Brave did whenever someone fainted or got knocked out on the show. Then I realized if a person were in pain, jerking them around wouldn't help. Another reason why people shouldn't take TV seriously.

A cart, one of the larger ones with three rows of seating, came down the street. A young page was driving a well-dressed woman and two men in suits. I stood and shouted at the driver to stop. When he didn't slow down, I ran along side the cart, waving my arms and yelling for help. The driver swerved to avoid me but I grabbed one of the roof posts and jumped onto the left-hand-side running board.

"Stop! Help! I need somebody!" I shouted.

"Get off!" the driver yelled.

I wrapped one arm around the post to keep my balance. With my other hand I grabbed the steering wheel. The cart spun wildly. The driver stomped on the brake and the cart skidded to an abrupt halt. I gripped the post to keep from falling off.

"What's the meaning of this intrusion?" said the lady, who sat in the front passenger seat. "We paid for a private tour."

One of the men in the back seat said, "He's a stunt man, Hazel. This is all part of the movie studio experience."

"I see, Desmond." She fanned herself with a folded Hollywood-map-of-the-stars. "How amusing."

I read the page's name off the name badge pinned on his chest. "Mark, I need a ride to the infirmary. It's urgent." The driver looked confused. "Look, I'm working in one of the shows on the lot and I desperately need your help."

He replied, "I guess I could drop you off at the end of the tour. If you want to get in the back seat—"

"Here! He can't ride with us!" the second man said. "He didn't pay for the tour!"

"This isn't for me." I pointed to Elsie, still sprawled on the pavement. "She needs medical attention."

The driver turned and looked at the victim. "What's wrong with her?"

"I don't know! I'm an actor, not a doctor!"

Desmond craned his neck to look around. "Are we being filmed? Is this some kind of prank TV show?"

"Really now, we must get going," Hazel fumed. "We have dinner reservations at—"

I shouted at her, "I don't care!" To Mark I said, "Either you help me now or I'll report you to your boss as endangering a guest's life." I had no idea who was in charge of the pages, but I figured the threat might motivate the guy.

Mark set the parking brake, apologized to his passengers for the delay, and got out of the vehicle. I picked up my jacket from where I'd dropped it and put it on to leave my hands free. I gently picked up Elsie by the shoulders. Mark lifted her by the legs and together we carried her to the cart. I told Hazel to move out of the front seat. She protested, of course, until I threatened to leave her behind to finish the tour on foot.

With a good deal of grumbling, and moving in slow motion, she squeezed in beside the two men instead of sitting in the unused third row seat. I sat shotgun beside Mark and placed Elsie next to me with her head nestled on my shoulder. I ordered Mark to drive to the infirmary as fast as he could, which in a modified tour cart is only about 14 miles per hour. You'd think that in a deadline-driven business like movie making someone would invent a faster form of studio transportation.

As the cart puttered along, the woman tapped me on the shoulder. "Say, I know who you are. You were on that TV show about the boy detective."

Normally I'm flattered when fans recognize me, but couldn't this idiot see I had a dying woman on my lap? I wanted to ignore her, but in the close quarters I couldn't.

I peered over my shoulder at her. "Yes, that's right."

"I knew it! I loved that show! Here." She shoved her map-of-the-stars at me. "Sign this."

"I don't have a pen."

I never have a writing implement on me. With all that I deal with each day, it's one of those things that slips my mind. Some mornings I'm lucky to remember to put on my pants.

The woman turned to her companions. "Who has a pen?"

The man in the end seat took an expensive-looking fountain pen from his jacket and reached across the poor guy in the middle. The woman snatched the pen from him and handed it to me just as the car hit a bump in the road, nearing ramming the pen into my eye.

"And I loved your records!" she said.

"Really?" I said absently as I checked on Elsie, who hadn't moved in several minutes.

"Oh, yes. 'Doo Ron Ron.' 'Do You Believe in Magic'?"

I looked at the woman. "Wait a minute; I never sang—"

She patted my shoulder with her well-manicured hand as if we were now bosom buddies. "And whatever became of that dark-haired kid who played your brother on the show, you know, Frank Hardy? What was his name?"

If she was such a huge fan, how could she get me mixed up with another TV show?

The cart pulled up in front the infirmary. Mark slammed on the brake and we all lurched forward. Out of spite, I signed the map as "Shaun Cassidy" and returned both the autograph and pen to the lady. After thanking Mark for the lift, I picked up Elsie in my arms and carried her up the steps into the small building.

All the large studios had an on-site hospital, staffed by registered nurses with a doctor on call. The clinic treated actors, stunt people and crews for the various minor aliments of the trade: cuts, scratches, concussions, broken bones, heat stroke, exhaustion and exposure to the chemicals in the studio mill. Broken hearts and bruised egos were not covered. On my show I spent many a day in the clinic, thanks to my insistence on doing my own stunts. Eventually, to save time, a nurse with a medical kit hung out on the set to treat me on the spot and get me back up in front of the camera.

The tiny clinic had a lobby with reception desk, an examination room, supply closet and a couple of private rooms with beds. The two nurses on duty helped me place Elsie into a bed. I tried to explain what had happened. While the nurses tended to the stricken actress I waited in the lobby. I removed my jacket and sat on the same brown vinyl-covered couch that had been here since the '70s. Some things in Hollywood never change. The second hand on the wall clock loudly ticked off the minutes.

After what seemed like forever the nurses came out of Elsie's room, visibly shaken. One of them sat behind the reception desk and dialed the telephone.

I asked the other nurse, "How is she?"

"I'm sorry, sir. Your friend is dead."

Dead? I was so shocked that all I could do say was, "Are you sure?"

"We tried to revive her but she didn't respond. Was Miss Bloom a friend of yours?"

"Not really; I hardly knew her. We're doing a show together. *Were* doing a show together. What happened? How did she die? She was fine just a few minutes ago."

The nurse with the phone finished her call. "The doctor's on his way. He'll be able to tell you more."

I closed my eyes for a moment and put my face in my hands. Dead! Only moments ago she was laughing and flirting and full of life. How could this happen? Only a few weeks ago I had my first encounter with a corpse, a person who traveled into the Great Beyond while in my arms. Now once again the Grim Reaper was dogging my heels and I didn't like it. I put my hands down and opened my eyes. I had to break the news to Royce. He would not take this well.

"Thanks for your help. I need to call someone." I nodded at the phone on the desk. "May I?"

"Yes, of course."

The nurses retreated into Elsie's room to give me some privacy. I sat atop the desk, turned the phone around to face me, and picked up the receiver. I didn't know the number to Stage 14 so I dialed the studio switchboard and the operator transferred the call. The phone rang several times before someone picked up.

"Stage 14, Carl McIntire speaking."

"It's Sandy Fairfax. I need to speak to Royce."

"Hi, Sandy. Royce is busy, but I can help you."

"No, I have to speak with him directly. It's an

emergency."

"Emergency? What kind of emergency?"

"It's complicated. I don't have time to explain."

"I can have him call you back."

I was losing my patience; dead bodies get me unnerved. "I don't care if he's signing a deal with Steven Spielberg. Tell him to drop whatever he's doing and get his rump over to the phone *now*."

"All right, Sandy, hold on. I'll see what I can do."

I traced my finger along the wood grain in the desk as I waited. Royce finally came on the line with his usual grumpy disposition.

"Fairfax, where the blazes are you? Wardrobe called and said you never showed up. Did you stop at a bar for a drink?"

"No, Royce. I don't drink any more and I didn't make it to wardrobe because something came up." I took a deep breath. "I don't know how to break this to you but...Elsie's dead."

"If this is a joke, it's in poor taste."

I stood and yelled into the receiver. "Royce, I don't joke about things like that! Elsie's dead! As in not breathing! As in not living anymore! She fell down in the middle of the street and I brought her to the infirmary and she'd dead!" A long pause on the other end. "Royce? Are you still there?"

"Are you saying she's passed out?"

"She's passed *on*! That's what I'm trying to tell you! Do you want to come over here and take her pulse to make sure?"

"What did you do to her, Sandy?"

"Nothing! Don't blame me! I didn't even touch her! She fell down and stopped breathing. Her skin's a weird shade of pink. I don't know what happened but she's dead."

Another pause. When Royce spoke again, he

sounded worried. "Where are you now?"

"The infirmary."

"All right, here's what you do. Stay put. Don't move. I'll send one of the PAs to pick you up. And Sandy?"

"Yes, Royce?"

"Keep your mouth shut. Don't say a word to anyone until we figure out what happened. Got that? If what you say is true we need to keep a lid on this."

"Sure, Royce. Whatever you say."

I hung up the phone. But despite the commandant's orders, I was too keyed up to sit still. I picked up my jacket and started walking back to Stage 14. The fresh air might help settle my nerves. The lot was empty so I didn't have to deal with gawking tour groups. I retraced my steps and found myself in the back lot again at the scene of the crime, so to speak. I felt uneasy, all alone on the deserted street where she had fallen. I spotted a colorful object on the ground—Elsie's handbag. Mark and I had missed it when we moved her. I picked up the purse; I'm not sure why I did that. At the time the only thing on my mind was that I needed to get this ugly thing off the street in case someone wanted to shoot here. I also spotted the veggie juice bottle, now empty, a few yards down the street where it had rolled away and left a thin line of liquid along the pavement. I kicked the bottle to the curb.

"Sandy!"

The sudden noise startled me. I turned around. Bunny waved at me from the far end of the street. That girl had a knack of showing up at the strangest times. She ran to me, that is, as fast as anyone can run with both arms wrapped around a large brown paper shopping bag and with a suitcase-sized Yellow Submarine tote bag hanging from one shoulder.

"Sandy! Wow! I didn't expect to see you twice in

one day!"

I was surprised too. "I though your tour would be over by now."

"Yeah, we finished ages ago. The tour was amazing. We got to see the room where they store all the fake monster heads and alien outfits used in *Space Posse*. The actors sure look different with that stuff on. Could be anyone under all that makeup. Anyway, after we finished the tour, the guide said we could have lunch in the commissary, so we did. I thought we might see some movie stars in there, but nobody important showed up. What have you got in your hand?"

I didn't want to try and explain why a big strong man was carrying a fuzzy pink girl's purse, so I wrapped my jacket around it and tucked the parcel under one arm.

"Nothing. Just a prop for the show."

Bunny began chattering away. My thoughts were elsewhere, but I didn't have the heart to tell her to shut up.

"So after we got through eating, me and the girls went over to the studio gift shop and I bought all kinds of stuff to take home to show my friends. See?" She tipped the paper bag, emblazed with the studio logo on one side, so I could see inside. "I bought a studio T-shirt and a jacket and postcards and books about old TV shows." She set the bag on the ground, dug around, and removed a box of videos, which she handed to me. "And look what I found! They have your show on tape and it comes with an information booklet!"

"The Best of *Buddy Brave*" set had ten episodes on five videocassettes in a colorful box covered with shrink-wrap. An impressive looking package. Would have been nice of the studio to tell me this was on the market. In spite of my distress I made a mental note to call my agent and make sure the studio was paying me royalties from the sales. I returned the videos to Bunny, which she replaced in the shopping bag.

"The other girls left the store before I did and I lost them and now I'm all turned around. All these soundstages look alike to me. Can you tell me how to get to the main gate?"

The gate was in the opposite direction from my destination. I could have given her directions and gone on my way, but at the moment I was glad to have someone to talk to. After our previous encounter at the fan convention, Bunny had earned my trust, something that I bestow only upon a few people.

"Let me walk you out."

Bunny picked up her purchases and we were on our way. "The tour guide said Buddy Brave shot on Stage 14 and 15."

"That's right."

"Wow. I'm glad I took a picture of it."

I glanced at her and, sure enough, her trusty camera pouch was hanging from a belt around her waist. That camera came in hand when she and I solved a murder together.

I said, "Did the tour guide tell you about the Stage 14 ghost?"

Chapter 6: Only You Know and I Know

Her thick glasses magnified her wide eyes. "A ghost?"

"Back in the silent era, a young actress named Freda Brenton died while making a horror movie. Someone substituted a real knife for the rubber prop knife and she was stabbed during shooting."

"How awful."

"Now Freda haunts the stage. It's true. Weird stuff happened during my show. Sometimes a spotlight came on all by itself and shone on the spot where she died. Sometimes at night when I was alone on the stage, I felt a hand on my shoulder and I heard a woman moaning."

"Really? Were you frightened?"

"No, I just said, 'Hello, Freda, how are you doing tonight?' and the moaning stopped. I think she just wanted people to remembered her."

"I'd be scared silly if that happened to me."

"The backlog's haunted too. Sometimes the security guys see a man in a trench coat walking through the back lot at night. When the guards approach him, he disappears. It's true."

All this talk about supernatural spirits made me think of Elsie and I shuddered. Was her ghost going to haunt the lot? Heaven help us.

"Bunny, how long will you be in town?"

"I'm flying home Saturday morning. Why?"

"I may need your help"

She looked at me quizzically. "My help?"

"When I was at your convention, you helped me

catch a murderer. Remember?"

"Yeah, that was kinda fun." She stopped walking. "Has there been another murder?" She sounded eager to investigate.

"I'm not sure. Something strange happened this afternoon. How can I get in touch with you? What's your hotel?"

"Hotels are too expensive. The girls and me, we're staying at Charlotte's apartment in Canoga Park. She's a member of the fan club and one of the pages here. We're camping out on her floor, like a big slumber party. She's got an answering machine if you want to leave me a message."

"I have a better idea. Why don't you come back to the lot in a couple of days and we'll talk? I'll arrange a pass for you at the front gate so you can get in."

"Would you, Sandy? Wow, that's nice of you. Thanks. Maybe Charlotte can help too."

"I need you to keep this between us."

"I have to tell Charlotte, 'cause she's my chauffer for the week. You won't catch me driving on those crazy freeways. Those drivers are maniacs."

An *Off-Kelter* cart, driven by a panicked-looking young woman, turned the corner at the far end of the street. She must be the PA that Royce sent to fetch me.

"Bunny, I have to go now. I'll see you soon. In the meantime, ask your friend Charlotte to find out anything she can about an actress named Elsie Bloom and the studio chief, Leo Constantine."

"Sure, Sandy, will do. This is great! I love working with you on mysteries!"

We were only a few yards from the front gate, so I pointed Bunny in the right direction. We said our goodbyes and she walked away just as the cart pulled up to the curb.

"Mr. Fairfax! Wait!" The PA driving the cart looked

exasperated. "I've been driving all over the lot looking for you!"

"Don't worry, it's not your fault. If Royce gives you a hard time, have him talk to me."

I stepped into the cart's front seat and before my butt hit the seat, the PA floored the pedal and twisted the cart into a hard U-turn. Those unwieldy crates can't make tight turns. I grabbed the roof post to stay inside. When we reached my trailer, I asked her to drop me off. I got out, thanked her for the ride and told her to inform Royce I'd be in shortly. As she sped away I hung the jacket in the trailer closet and stuffed the purse into my gym bag. Not only did I not want the guys ribbing me about carrying a woman's handbag but I was afraid the purse might disappear. I had a bad habit of not hanging onto things. In less than a day I'd already misplaced my script twice. If guitars didn't come with straps, I'd have lost mine in the middle of a concert.

Inside Stage 14 the *Off-Kelter* cast was gathered around the craft services table, snacking and chatting, apparently oblivious to the fact that the show was permanently minus one actor. The crew was diligently working on a new swing set. Business as usual. But in a far corner stood a tight huddle comprised of Royce, Troy and two men whom everyone in town knew and feared: Leo and Ivan Constantine.

As always, Leo was impeccably dressed in a tailored suit and tie. His beady eyes and no-nonsense mug topped with a brown toupee frequently graced the pages of the *L.A. Times* and the industry trades. The elder Constantine had come to power in the early '70s when Mammoth nearly went belly up from a string of flop films and bad investments. While everyone predicted that the grand old studio was finished, Leo rolled up his stylish sleeves and saved the day. He sold the offsite properties, trimmed the budget fat, streamlined operations, and moved the focus from big-budget movies to lowbrow and crowd pleasing TV shows. Leo cranked out a full slate of successful series—including mine—that transformed the studio's gloom into gold.

While I'm grateful to Leo for green lighting *Buddy Brave*, he never liked the show, which he described in an interview as "a ridiculous, brainless spy romp for girls too young to know any better." To him, I was "little more than a big toothy smile and a cute face that warbles well." But since my show made money hand over fist, Leo tolerated the shenanigans in Stages 14 and 15.

Ivan, with his dark completion and handsome Latino features, resembled his mother more than his dad. The two Constantines had little in common, either in looks or tastes. Ivan had on a cheap-looking sports coat and open neck shirt with no tie. His black hair was natural but thinning on top. His eyes seemed locked in a perpetual squint, due to either the SoCal sun or his rumored shifty business dealings.

I approached the group, stopped, and listened. To my surprise the quartet wasn't discussing Elsie's demise.

"But Mr. Constantine, you promised I could direct an episode," Troy begged.

"You're not ready," said Leo.

"I'm doing great in my film classes at USC."

"Every schmuck in L.A. is taking film classes at USC," said Ivan. "That doesn't mean they should all direct a network program."

Leo raised a hand. "Ivan, please."

"I'm the producer," the son continued. "I hire the directors."

"I'm sure Mr. Rawlins will do a fine job," the elder Constantine said, "but he needs a little more experience."

"My shows are not classroom assignments for

amateurs," said Ivan.

"Mr. Constantine, will you at least look at my student film?" I expected Troy to get on his knees and grovel.

"Of course, Mr. Rawlins. If it's adequate and if *Off-Kelter* is renewed and if you can work around your role on *Space Posse*, I'll consider recommending you as a second assistant director."

"An assistant! I'm overqualified as an assistant."

"If you do well you can move up."

"Don't I have a say in this?" Ivan interjected.

Leo turned to Royce. "Would you be willing to take on Mr. Rawlins as an assistant?"

"Yes, Mr. Constantine," Royce said, which is the answer everyone gives the studio boss.

Ivan said to Troy, "Shouldn't you get back to filming your show?"

"Yeah, sure. Thank you, Mr. Constantine."

After Troy departed, Ivan again spoke to his dad. "If this kid wants to direct, why doesn't he first direct an episode of *Space Posse*? And why did you renew that turkey for another year? Nobody watches that idiot show. *Star Trek: The Next Generation* is killing us in the ratings."

"*Space Posse* has a loyal audience."

Ivan glowered at his father. "I hope Troy Rawlins is a better director than he is an actor."

"Excuse me, Mr. Constantine." Both men looked at Royce. "Are we finishing the show for this week?"

"Miss Bloom's incapacitation certainly comes at a bad time," said Leo.

I'm sure Elsie would have agreed with that statement.

"I don't see where there's a problem," said Ivan. "Things like this happen all the time. The writers can work around it. They can say the character went off to visit her mother or something."

Apparently Royce had called the Constantines immediately after I'd finished relaying the bad news. Surprisingly, Ivan didn't seem upset that an actor on one of his shows had died. But I could understand Leo's reaction. And as the studio chief, he couldn't afford sentimental feelings about his workers, even the ones he might have fathered.

I approached them. "Mr. Constantine, can I speak with you?"

Royce frowned. "Sandy, can't you see we're busy here."

Leo glared at me. "Who are you?"

He didn't recognize me? "Sandy Fairfax. I was one of Mammoth's biggest moneymakers in the 1970s." I thought that glib remark might thaw the ice. I was wrong. Leo still looked unhappy. I tried a more humble approach. "I'm the guest star on *Off-Kelter*." I held out my hand for him to shake but he didn't take it.

"What is it that you want?"

"I just wanted to express my sympathy for the loss of your daughter."

"My what?"

"Elsie Bloom. She told me she was your daughter."

Leo's face turned red. "That's a lie!"

"Sandy, do you mind?" Royce's voice was sharp enough to slice through the canvas on the set walls.

"I'm sorry, I just assumed—"

"We're in a jam here, thanks to you."

"Me? What did I do? It's not my fault that Elsie di–"

Royce made a frantic gesture, moving his fingers cross his throat in a "cut" motion and then jerking his head toward the actors.

"You haven't told them?" I asked, incredulous.

"I said she was in the infirmary. I didn't say for what."

"Royce! They need to know!"

"Know what? Nobody seems to know what happened. Do you want to start a panic?"

"Am I supposed to pretend that nothing unusual happened this afternoon?"

Leo said, "Sandy, let me have a word with you."

He took my arm—his sweaty hand felt clammy against my skin—and pulled me into the shadows beside the wall. His temper must have abated because he put his arm around my shoulder. I can't say I liked the gesture. Leo talked softly in my ear so that no one would overhear us. Matter of fact, I couldn't hear him either.

"Excuse me, Mr. Constantine, but I'm hard of hearing in that ear. Can you please speak up so I can hear you?"

He moved to my other side, put his other arm around my shoulder, and held me close so I couldn't escape. I should have said that I was deaf in both ears so he'd leave me alone.

"Royce tells me that you were with Elsie this afternoon when the incident happened." His breath smelled like a two-martini lunch. "Now the studio doesn't want anyone spreading a lot of speculation. People might get confused if they hear the news from someone other than an authorized source."

Seeing as how I was the one who was with Elsie when she made her final exit, I would be the one best "authorized" in the matter. But I let Leo ramble.

"I'm sure I can count on your discretion. I'd appreciate it if you would talk to no one about Miss Bloom's demise. I mean *no one*. No friends, no family, no press, no media. "

"You can't keep this a secret. People are going to find out—"

Leo poked a finger into my chest. "But not from

you."

"Do you plan on notifying her next of kin right away?"

"Don't worry, my boy." He patted me on the back, no doubt looking for a place to stick a knife later on. "The studio will release a statement at the appropriate time."

Translation: *We'll break the news after I consult with my lawyers on how to keep Elsie's family from suing Mammoth.*

"What about an autopsy? I'd really like to know how she died."

"Don't fret about that, son. I'm sorry you got involved but it's best just to forget this happened and let the studio handle the situation."

His attitude infuriated me. I slipped out from under his arm.

"There's something peculiar about this. Why would a healthy young woman collapse in the middle of the street?"

Leo's eyes burned and his voice dripped venom. "Mr. Fairfax, if you'd rather not cooperate, you're free to leave the show."

Translation: *Keep your big mouth shut or you'll never step foot on this lot again.*

I was temped to go and blab the story to the tabloids out of sheer stubbornness but Elsie's death bothered me. I had what Buddy Brave would call "a really good hunch that something bad was going on." If Leo was behind Elsie's departure to the Great Soundstage in the Sky, he had the power and money to block an investigation. As much as I disliked Elsie, I hated Leo's slimy attitude even more. And what was the big secret that the recently departed claimed she knew? The only way I could find out was to stay with the show, which meant I had until *Off-Kelter* taped on Friday night to find out what happened to Elsie.

"All right, Mr. Constantine. I'll do as you say."

"Thanks, Sandy." He pounded me on the back. "I knew I could count on you." Leo flashed me a smile as phony as the prosthetics used in *The Elephant Man*.

He strutted out of the building; Ivan had already left. Royce shot me a dirty look. I slinked away to the craft services table. In times of stress, nothing beats comfort food. Forget my diet. I loaded up a plastic plate with chips and cookies (still no brownies! How would I survive this week?).

"All right, everyone," Royce called. "Gather around, I have an announcement to make."

Was our fearless leader going to spill the beans? The actors sat on the living room set while the crew guys put down their tools. I remained off stage so I could eat and not get crumbs on the set. Royce faced the cast and the ever-faithful AD took his place beside the director.

"What's up, Royce?" Harv asked.

Joseph said, "The show's cancelled, right? Why else would big cheese Constantine show up?"

Royce said, "It seems Elsie has taken ill and will be out for the rest of the week." More like for the rest of eternity. "Ivan and I discussed whether or not to go ahead with the show." The actors took in a deep breath and held it. "But at the risk of disappointing the loyal viewers of *Off-Kelter*—"all five of them—"we're going to finish this episode." The cast released a collective sigh of relief. "We don't have time to find another actress, so Elsie's character will be written out of the show and some of her lines will go to Dottie."

The grande dame grinned. Nothing pleases an actor more than additional screen time.

"Now wait a minute!" Mrs. Jones shouted. "Why can't my girls get the extra lines?"

Missy and Molly both rolled their eyes.

"The role of Miss Tucker isn't suited for a young actress," Royce said. "As it is, we'll have to totally revamp the cold opening. But we'll try to give the girls a little extra something to do. The writers are working on a new script and you'll get fresh pages in the morning. That's it for today, but tomorrow's call times stay the same. Have a good evening, everyone."

The actors stood, all smiles at the prospect of receiving at least one more paycheck.

Before I could leave, Carl intercepted me. "Don't head out to the sunset, yet, Sandy. You've got a dance rehearsal."

"Right now?"

"Since we're finishing early, we bumped up your appointment. When that's over, you're free to leave." He scrutinized my face. "Are you feeling up to it?"

"What?"

"You look a little flustered."

Maybe that's because I watched a woman die today. "I'm feeling a little overwhelmed, first day of rehearsal and all."

As the AD walked away I tossed my plate into the trashcan and met up with the actors. The twins were long gone, no doubt in a hurry to hit the mall. Harv, Dottie and Joseph were still standing around. The crew had gone back to work on the set so I had to shout over the din of the hammers and buzz saws.

"Excuse me," I said, "Does anyone know if Elsie had—has any health problems or chronic conditions?"

"Naw, she's a real healthy girl." Joseph leered and waggled his eyebrows suggestively. Maybe Elsie was right about his propensity of peeking up her petticoat.

"She'd never had a sick day on the show," Harv said. "She sounded okay at the read through. I can't imagine how she got sick all of a sudden."

"Maybe she partied a little too hardy over the

weekend," Dottie scoffed.

"Sandy, you were with Elsie this afternoon," Harv said. "I saw the two of you walking across the lot. Did she seem all right to you?"

I nearly bit my tongue in half to keep from telling the truth. "She fainted and I took her to the infirmary." I couldn't lie about that. The page and his guests were witnesses to that fact.

"She had heat stroke?" Harv said.

"That must be it," I said a little too quickly. "Might have been heat stroke."

"Nonsense. The weather's nice today," Dottie said. "And I don't see why anyone would be out a entire week for heat stroke."

The AD waved to catch my eye and then pointed to his wristwatch. "Sandy! We're waiting on you!"

As much as I wanted to pick the brains of Elsie's co-workers, duty called. I excused myself and headed outside. Carl caught up with me and said that Royce told him to personally drive me to my dance rehearsal. I guess the director didn't want me stumbling over any more dead bodies along the way. The two of us left in a show cart, with a quick stop at my trailer for me to pick up my helmet, jacket and gym bag. What a dope! Forgot my script again! Carl said not to worry; with all the new changes I'd be better off picking up a new set of pages in the morning. During our short drive I nodded absently as Carl chatted, my mind on other things.

I wasn't in the mood for a dance lesson, but then again, a little exercise might take my mind off the day's tragedy. Music had a way of pumping up my spirits. No matter how cross I was during my concert tours, once my feet hit the stage I felt great. And fortunately, even with the loss of Elsie, my dance scene hadn't been cut. While I was growing up, Gary Cooper and Henry

Fonda westerns entertained my friends but Gene Kelly entranced me. Kelly proved that guys who danced were not sissies and that one could win the girl with the right steps. Dancing was always a big part of my live shows. And every time Buddy Brave danced on the show, the ratings shot up and the fan mail poured in.

We stopped in front of one of the older three-story brick buildings, built during the 1940s but since retrofitted to withstand earthquakes. I thanked Carl for the ride, grabbed my stuff and entered. In the hallway, a hideous maroon carpet hid the beautiful hardwood floor, the result of the misguided remodeling efforts of the 1980s. The practice room was at the end of the first floor hallway. On my way I wondered what kind of dance coach the studio had hired. Years ago my teachers were elderly matrons with their gray hair pulled up in a bun. They made dancing as exciting as laying wet cement in 90-degree weather.

Framed still photos from some of Mammoth's hit shows lined the hallways. I found a photo of Buddy Brave dressed as a Spanish matador and doing the tango with a sweet young senorita in "The Sizzling Salsa Caper." As I recall, that particular actress was a hot tamale offstage as well. I opened the door of the dance studio, hoping the rehearsal wouldn't take long so I could head home.

Beside one wall stood The Most Beautiful Girl In The World.

Chapter 7: Green Eyed Lady

The slim vixen with the gorgeous tan looked to be in her early 30s. Her raven black hair was tied back in a single long braid. Long black lashes framed her huge green eyes. The low cut, long-sleeved black leotard showed off a nice set of breasts. As for those long, muscular legs clad in white tights and leg warmers—a man could die looking at those exquisite legs. Like an idiot, I stood staring with my mouth open while my pheromones kicked into red alert.

She changed tapes in a cassette player (part of the music center built into one wall) and turned to face me. She put her hands on her slender hips and started to speak. I could hardly wait to hear the golden words that would pour out of that beautiful mouth.

"You're late!"

Her rude greeting knocked me out of my trance. How dare she speak like that to a star!

"Do you know who I am?"

"Yes, you're the world's most tardy boy sleuth. I have a tight schedule to keep."

"I'll have you know I've had a stressful day."

"I've been on my feet dancing since seven-thirty this morning, mister, so don't cry to me. So are you going to dance or do you plan to stand there gawking?"

I set my jacket, helmet and gym bag on the wooden bench that ran along one wall. As I sat and replaced the boots with my tan, soft-soled dance shoes, I tried to guess if she was really mad or just teasing me.

She stood beside me as I tied the shoelaces. "Just so

you're not calling me 'ma'am' all day, my name is Cinnamon Love."

I glanced up at her. "You're kidding. That can't be your real name."

"My first name is for a maiden aunt who loved to cook. My last name is really Lovett but another dancer named Lovett joined the union before I did."

Finished with my shoes, I stood up. She was tall—her head was level with my shoulders. "That makes sense. No serious performer would dream up a goofy stage name like that."

Her green eyes flashed. "When it comes to unusual names, you have no room to criticize, Mr. Stanford Ernest Farmington."

I had to top her. "That's Stanford Ernest Farmington *Junior*."

Among family and close friends I go by Ernest because my father is Stanford and I'd never dare to compete with him. My former manager dreamed up my stage name because he said nobody would buy records from someone named Ernest Farmington. Apparently he'd never heard of Engelbert Humperdinck.

She said, "So should I call you Sandy, Stanford, Junior, Buddy Brave or Hey You?"

"Sandy's fine."

"All right, Sandy. Let's get to work."

She grabbed my hand and dragged me to the center of the wooden floor. I studied my reflection in the floor-to-ceiling mirrors. Standing beside this trim angel, I looked fat and dumpy. Time to get serious about dieting. I wanted to gaze into those hypnotic green eyes but Cinnamon got down to business and walked through the steps. I hadn't danced in ages and I struggled to keep up with the one-two-three, hop-step, turn-leap-pivot. I tried to wrap my mind around the complicated footing but I was distracted. Every time she drew close I thought I felt a tingle; no, that was just a blast of cool air from the ceiling vents. I glanced at the third finger on her left hand—no ring! She wasn't married or engaged. But many actors and dancers removed their jewelry when they worked. What was I doing? After a painful divorce and a series of neurotic girlfriends, I had no business falling for another femme fatale. My last relationship, Helen Wheeler, was a psychotic wreck. She would have turned me into an alcoholic if I hadn't been halfway there already. The last thing I needed was an involvement with another woman.

I turned left instead of right and slammed right into Cinnamon.

"Sorry, excuse me." I stepped back and grabbed her shoulders to keep her from falling. She raised a perfectly arched eyebrow at me. "Sorry. I'm having trouble concentrating."

"I can tell. Try to stay focused, okay? We have a lot to cover and not much time." She eyed me until I (reluctantly) took my hands off her shoulders. "Okay, let's pick up from bar eight. Two-three-four . . ."

After a couple more run-throughs she punched the "play" button on the tape player. This time we put the steps to the music, a happy tune that sounded similar to "Singin' in the Rain" but different enough so the studio could avoid paying royalties.

After a few more minutes I dropped onto the bench. "Let's take a break. These steps are too hard."

"No, they're not. You're just out of shape. When was the last time you danced?"

"Recently."

"I mean professionally."

"Not so recently."

"I thought so."

She sat beside me. The perspiration on her skin

glistened under the bright ceiling lights and the musky cologne she wore nearly drove me crazy

Cinnamon asked, "Do you recognize the choreography?"

"Should I?"

"It's based on a scene from your first Buddy Brave movie."

"You saw that flick?"

"Of course I did. I always customize my choreography to the performer's strengths."

"So you didn't watch the movie just because you liked it?"

"I didn't say that. Buddy Brave is an entertaining character." She cocked her head and eyed me coyly. "But I don't know anything about this Sandy Fairfax person."

I could have sworn she was flirting with me but before I could make a snappy comeback she had me back on my feet again. We ran through the piece several more times before a timer beeped.

She grabbed a towel from a shelf and tossed it to me. "That was good work, Sandy." Cinnamon mopped her face with her own towel. "For someone who's been out of the business for a while, you picked it up quickly."

I wiped the back of my sweaty neck with the towel and glanced at the wall clock. Time to leave already? So soon?

"We should run through this again. I'm not sure I remember the steps."

She took a sheet of paper and a cassette tape from a shelf and handed both to me. "I wrote down the steps for you to practice on your own. And here's a tape of the music."

That woman thought of everything! I dropped the items into my gym bag and dumped my damp towel into a wicker hamper. "Thanks, Cinnamon, but I still feel a little rusty. Can I come back for another lesson tomorrow?"

She held the door open for me to leave. "Of course, Sandy. Anytime."

I was so excited at the prospect of seeing her again that I left without removing my dance shoes. Halfway down the block I realized I was still carrying my boots. I sat on a sidewalk bench and switched footwear. When I reached my bike, a 1968 Shovelhead. I squeezed the bag in the storage compartment over the rear wheel, put on my helmet and jacket and started up. I took the surface streets through Hollywood to my house in the hills.

When I bought my house back in 1975, areas such as Tarzana, Studio City and Sherman Oaks had some of the most exclusive neighborhoods but at the time I wanted a fast commute to the studio. After working late and partying even later, the next day I generally didn't wake up until just a few minutes before my set call. At the studio I could shower, shave, and eat, so when the alarm clock went off I just rolled out of bed, threw on the first clothes I could grab, and dashed off. The guards at the studio gate couldn't understand how a teenage millionaire managed to show up for work looking like a sleepy tramp.

I took the narrow street up the hill to the security gate (a precaution against overzealous fans). I grabbed the mail out of the mailbox, buzzed myself through the gate and zipped up the long driveway. I parked the Harley in the garage and went inside. I left my stuff strewn across the living room; bachelors don't care about tidiness. In the kitchen I dumped the mail on the counter and rummaged through the refrigerator for something to eat, until I found a container of leftover spaghetti and meatballs that didn't look moldy. While the food heated in the microwave, I scrounged up enough unwilted lettuce and a few unspoiled veggies for a quick side salad. I quenched my thirst with a cold bottle of O'Doul's. What I really needed was something stiffer to get me through the next unpleasant task. I stood by the kitchen wall phone and dialed my ex-wife. The phone rang three times. My stomach knotted as it usually did whenever I talked to her. Hard to believe that two people who had once been so madly in love were now simply mad at each other.

Just when I thought the answering machine would pick up, a 13-year-old boy said, "Hello?"

What luck! "Hi Chip, it's your dad."

"Oh, hi. Do you want to speak to mom?"

Not if I can help it. I want to talk to my son. "In a minute. How have you been?"

"Fine."

"How's school?"

"Okay."

"What have you been doing in school?"

"Stuff."

Prying information out of a teenager is harder that making a movie starlet admit to her real age. "So what classes are you taking this year?"

"The usual. Uh, mom's here. She wants to talk to you."

Some fumbling on the other end as he handed off the receiver. "Hello, Ernest. We're in the middle of dinner. Did you want something?"

"Hello to you too, Becka. Can't I talk to my son?"

"You could if you called at a more convenient time. I have a hard enough time getting him to eat his vegetables without you interrupting."

"How am I supposed to know what you're doing over there? Next time I'll send over a private eye to spy on you. Look, I was busy all day and just got home from work. You said I could see the kids again if I was sober and working. So I've been dry and I have a job."

"Good for you."

"I have a guest spot on a sitcom. I can bring in guests to watch the taping this Friday night. I'd love to have the kids come and watch."

She asked the name of the show and I told her. "*Off-Kelter?* I saw that once and it's dreadful."

"It'll be better this week, I promise. What do you say, Becka? The kids will get a kick out of it."

"This Friday?"

"Yeah, at Mammoth Picture Studio in Hollywood. The taping starts at seven o'clock and they should be here by six-thirty."

"We're busy this Friday."

"You're just saying that."

"No, honest. Robin has her dance recital."

What rotten timing. "Can't she move it to another day?"

Now she sounded testy. "Of course not. Her recital's been on the schedule for months. I suppose this means you won't be here to watch her perform, as usual."

"Becka! That isn't fair! You know I'd be there if I didn't have this show. And I might add that most of my paycheck from this week will go to child support, although I don't know why. Franklin earns more than enough to pay for that swanky private school you send them to."

"Ernest! That's enough!"

I'd pushed one button too many so I backed down. "Can you at least tell the kids I'll be on the show? It'll go on the air in about four weeks. You'll let them watch it, won't you? I really want them to see the show." And see that their old man wasn't a failure.

"Of course we'll watch. Look, I have to go now, Ernest. We're in the middle of dinner."

"Tell the kids that I love them, will you?"

"Yes, Ernest, I will. And I'm glad you got the job. By the way, your show's on now."

"Is it?"

"Yes, on Nickelodeon. Sometimes the kids watch it when we eat late."

She said goodbye and hung up. Overall, the call went better than I expected.

I switched on the kitchen TV and flipped through the channels until I hit Nick at Night. I settled on one of the barstools at the center island and ate my sad little salad and warmed-over spaghetti as my alter ego kept me company. *Buddy Brave,* produced during television's grand era of secret agent spoofs, featured high-tech gadgets, gorgeous girls, bizarre villains and enough "camp" to entice viewers to set up a pup tent in front of their TV. Every episode found the intrepid boy spy and the lovely girl-guest-star-of-the-week ensnared in some life-or-death situation. In this one, "The Scary Skyscraper Caper," they were trapped on the top floor of a high-rise that the bad guys had set on fire. While the girl panicked, Buddy calmly recited his famous catchphrase, "Don't worry, I'll think of something." Instead of calling for help on the telephone (the phone operators had gone on strike; reality was never the show's strong suit), Buddy recklessly climbed down the side of the building with the girl on his back.

When I did the stunt, I discovered I had a selective fear of heights. I could ride to the top of the highest roller coaster with no problem—I'm a sucker for theme parks—but looking down from the top of a tall building gave me the willies. Before shooting the scene I was in my trailer smoking a joint, just enough to calm my nerves. Why didn't I use a double, you ask? Doubles were too obvious to spot and besides, this particular feat wasn't as horrifying as it appeared.

We shot the scene using a forced perspective similar

to the technique in the classic silent comedy "Safety Last" in which Harold Lloyd hung from the hands of a giant clock atop a tall building. My crew built a building façade on the roof of a skyscraper in downtown L.A. along with a camera tower, just like the Lloyd movie. The shot was framed to show the traffic on the street below but not the building's roof, only a few yards below us. The crew set up a safety net on the roof below (it didn't look safe and I wasn't about to test it). For the close-ups, the crew recreated the skyscraper wall inside Soundstage 15 where I could safely dangle inches above the floor.

When Buddy and the girl were safely on the ground and had the bad guys tied up, I switched off the TV and stuck the dirty dishes in the dishwasher. I was tired from the busy day but I had one more obligation before turning in. I brushed my teeth (plenty of garlic and onion in that spaghetti sauce) and headed out to the garage where I kept my 1964 two-door, poppy red Mustang convertible with the palomino interior, bucket seats and spoke wheels. I drove across town to Beverly Hills for my AA group, made up of industry professionals and a couple of big-name actors you'd recognize. With the stress of a new job, a suspicious death and dealing with my ex, I needed all the help I could get to stay sober—at least for one more week.

I arrived late, but I still had a good group. When I returned home my legs began to feel the effects of the dance lesson. I had neglected to properly stretch and warm up before dancing and my unused muscles were screaming in pain. Tomorrow morning I'd be lucky if I could walk.

In the upstairs master suite I switched on the bedroom TV to catch the local late news as I changed into my pajamas.

The top story of the night was Elsie's death.

I stared at the TV, dumbfounded. The story didn't say much; only that one of the stars of *Off-Kelter* had "collapsed" at Mammoth and was "declared dead" at the hospital with "cause of death unknown" (translation: *Nobody at the studio is talking at this time*). Fortunately my name was not in the story. Good. The segment ended without a comment from either Constantine, so obviously the studio had not released the story. A reporter or paparazzo must have been hanging around the hospital when Elsie's body was brought in.

In the morning Leo was going to have my hide for breakfast.

TUESDAY: REHEARSAL
Chapter 8: The Show Must Go On

The next morning after shaving I threw on my swim trunks so I could spend several minutes soaking in the hot tub. To avoid having to drag my aching legs back up the stairs to dress, I carried my shirt, pants and boots downstairs. The tub's warm, rushing water felt fantastic and helped to ease my sore muscles. I showered in the downstairs bathroom, dressed, grabbed my gym bag (still in the same place I had left it the night before), put on my helmet and jacket, and sped to the studio in record time. I left my stuff in the dressing trailer and headed to Stage 14 where some of the crew members had already gathered for breakfast around the craft services table. First I found Carl and asked him to arrange for both a lot pass for Bunny and another dance rehearsal with Cinnamon. Then I got down to the serious business of the morning—toasting a bagel for breakfast. That's when Royce got in my face.

"Fairfax! You were ordered not to speak to the media!"

I was tempted to attack him with the butter knife in my hand but the plastic blade would only break against his thick skin. "Royce, the only people I talked to last night were my ex and my AA group and I'm positive I didn't discuss a dead actress with either of them."

"Then who told the press? Nobody else knew about Elsie."

The toaster popped up my bagel. With the knife I angrily slapped a glob of cream cheese onto the warm bun. "Nobody except the people I met in the tour cart and the infirmary nurses and the paramedics in the ambulance and the doctors at the hospital and the morgue attendant and Elsie's next of kin and, gee whiz, Royce, looks like lots of people knew about her."

Dottie entered the room, her eyes red from crying. She waved a frilly white handkerchief. "Royce, is it true? Is Elsie really dead?"

As if he had flipped a switch, Royce instantly morphed into protective father mode. He put his arm around her shoulders and spoke softly. "Yes, it's true. I'm sorry, Dottie. It's a big loss, I know."

The diva turned her grief into a theatrical spectacular. She blew her nose and wiped her eyes, smearing her mascara while belting loud sobs. She threw her arms in the air. "How could this happen? Yesterday she was so vibrant, so lively."

"Why don't you sit down?" Royce asked. "Do you want some coffee?" He guided the weeping actress to the AD's canvas chair. After she sat, Royce nestled beside her in his chair. While he played the knight errant, I poured a cup of coffee and put the bagel on a paper plate. A PA gave me a new script. To keep track of the frequent revisions, each new set of pages was printed on a different color of paper. I sat in a folding chair, placed the plate and cup on the floor, and like most actors, scanned the pages to find my lines. Early in the show, Joseph's character stated that Miss Tucker went off to Las Vegas on a gambling spree. As good as any way to explain Elsie's absence. Joseph would relish saying those lines. Grandma—Dottie's character—had taken over most of Miss Tucker's lines. That made me happy. Dottie played her role over the top but she had spunk, and I'd enjoy acting with her instead of Elsie Dullsville.

Joseph stood beside me. With me seated we could at

last see eye-to-eye. "It is true? Is Elsie really dead?" When I nodded, he sang a chorus of "Ding Dong the Witch is Dead."

"Is that any way to treat the dead?" Harv scolded. At the craft services table, he filled a plastic bowl with cold cereal.

"Excuse me for not bursting into tears," Joseph said, "but you can't say she added much to the show."

Harv picked up a carton of cold milk. "She was still a human being."

"Are you sure about that?"

Harv handed the milk and cereal to the craft services guy. "Here, I'm sorry. I don't feel like eating right now."

Joseph said, "Anyone hear what she died of? Royce! What did Elsie die of?"

The reply was, "Hasn't been determined yet."

Harv shrugged. "That's that then. With Elsie gone, the show's over."

"I don't know about that," I said. "Plenty of shows keep going even after an actor dies or leaves."

"How true," Joseph said. "Actors are replaceable. We're the most disposable commodities in showbiz."

The twins entered with the ever-vigilant Mrs. Jones. While the girls tried to sneak an illicit doughnut, mama marched over to Royce. "I heard that Elsie Bloom died." The woman didn't mince words. And did I hear a trace of joy in that statement?

Royce gave her a look of disgust. "Good morning, Mrs. Jones. Yes, that's right."

"I looked over the new script and my girls have even fewer lines than before."

He stood to confront her. "Most of their scenes were with Miss Tucker so there wasn't a good way to integrate them into the rest of the show."

"The writers are just lazy. They could write a better

script if they tried. They hate my girls!"

"That isn't true and you know it. Let's just get through this week, shall we? If the show's renewed then we'll take a look at the girls and see about revamping their roles."

Mrs. Jones looked as if she wanted to rip off Royce's head but before she could do so, Troy, dressed in his space alien makeup and costume, rushed in. "I won't believe it! I can't believe it!"

"You mean about Elsie?" Harv asked.

Troy collapsed in a folding chair and burst into tears. "My little Elsie's dead!"

I've traveled around the world and witnessed some amazing sights, but I'd never seen a grown Gorgandian commander cry.

Between sobs, Troy said, "How did it happen?"

"Sandy might know," said Harv. "He was with Elsie yesterday afternoon. You took her to the infirmary, didn't you?"

"Yeah, I did."

Troy looked at me, or at least I assumed he did. With that grasshopper-like head, I couldn't tell where his eyes focused. "So how did she die?"

I briefly described how Elsie stopped breathing and fell down. I didn't speculate on what might have caused her demise. At that point the two Constantines made an appearance. For the studio head to visit a set not once but twice in two days meant something big must be in the air. The family duo pulled Royce aside. They kept their backs turned and their voices low, so I couldn't hear what they said.

Ivan looked at Troy, who was still blubbering. "Who's that making all that ruckus?"

"Troy Rawlins was Elsie's boyfriend," said Harv.

Ivan walked over to the actor. "What are you doing here? Shouldn't you be next door shooting?"

Troy wiped his tears off his fake head with the back of a scaly green hand. "Yes, sir."

"We're busy rehearsing in here."

The actor stood, picked up his fake tail, and lumbered to the door.

"Mr. Rawlins," Leo called. Troy stopped and turned. "Please accept my condolences."

"Thank you, sir." Troy beat a hasty retreat.

Royce ordered the cast and crew to gather on the set. When we settled in, Ivan orated an on-with-the-show, never-say-die speech that sounded like something a studio publicist had scripted. By now I had recovered from the initial shock of Elsie's death but the rest of the cast still looked stunned. A smart producer might have given his performers some time to process their grief, but Ivan wasn't that bright. We put away our coffee cups, picked up our scripts and reluctantly went to work.

Harv said to the AD, "Keep the tour groups out today, Carl. I don't feel up to it."

Carl nodded. "I understand. We're all pretty stunned."

While the others geared up for act one, scene one, I intercepted Leo on his way to the door (Ivan had already disappeared). "Excuse me, Mr. Constantine."

He stopped and turned. "Yes?" From the tone of his voice, he clearly didn't like dealing with anyone less than a current A-list superstar.

"I'm Sandy Fairfax. We met yesterday."

"Yes, I remember you." He didn't recall me with fondness.

"I'm curious; has Elsie's cause of death been determined yet?"

"The investigation's still pending." He snapped off the words a little too quickly.

"Leo, I think I can help," I said. "I believe Elsie met

with foul play."

His face didn't change expression. "What makes you say that?"

"Somebody left a threatening message in her dressing room. They wrote 'you're going to die' on her mirror with lipstick."

"She told you about this?"

"No, I was in the room yesterday and saw it for myself."

Royce interrupted. "Sandy, stop bothering Mr. Constantine. I need you on the set."

Leo said, "Mr. Fairfax tells me that someone left a death threat for Miss Bloom in her dressing room."

The director glared at me. "Sandy, really. Where did you get a stupid idea like that?"

"It's true," I said. "I'll show you. Follow me."

I rushed down the hallway and the other two tried to keep up. I flung open the door to Elsie's dressing room and we stepped inside to view the macabre display— only it wasn't there. The mirror was shiny and clean. The crepe streamers were gone. Even the waste can— where I had found the hamburger wrapper—was empty. And the room smelled like ammonia, not cooked beef.

"Well, Mr. Fairfax?" Leo said. "Where's this death threat?"

Dumbfounded, I stared at the pristine room. "I don't understand. This isn't how the room looked yesterday. I saw writing on the mirror, I swear it!"

Royce frowned. "Sandy, how many beers did you have this morning?"

"I'm on the wagon, Royce. I'm not drunk."

"If you're going to make up crazy stories, you better first join the Writers' Guild."

The antiseptic odor jogged my memory. Years ago my own dressing room often smelled like this first thing in the morning.

"The custodians!" I said. "They came in last night to clean up! They destroyed the evidence!"

"I'm sorry we bothered you, Mr. Constantine," Royce said. "It won't happen again."

I grabbed Leo's arm. "You've got to believe me—"

He pulled away and those dark eyes bore right through me. "Mr. Fairfax, don't play detective. I don't need a ham actor to poke around in something that doesn't concern him."

Ham actor! How dare he criticize my performance on *Buddy Brave*! Anyone who can say lines like, "If the drapery store blows up, it's curtains for all of us!" and "I can defuse the bomb if I don't confuse my calculations. All I have to do is isolate the isotrometer and trap the trigger mechanism," with a straight face deserves some respect.

Leo fled the scene and Royce tagged along, apologizing to the boss for wasting his time. I hung back and inspected the room one more time as if I'd overlooked something so obvious as black letters on a mirror. I peeked in the drawers in hopes that the cleaning crew had simply hidden the crepe steamers. I didn't worry about leaving fingerprints, which were already splattered over the soundstage. I found nothing unusual in the drawers, just a stack of mail and a pocket calendar. I flipped through the little notebook but saw nothing peculiar, just a list of audition appointments, call times, dates with Troy and weekend parties. The envelopes had return addresses from a management agency, Screen Actors Guild, a tax accountant—the usual paperwork for a working artist—as well as bills from clothing stores, a hair stylist and a nail salon. Some of the envelopes had ominous "past due" warnings in red letters. Elsie had trouble paying her bills, a typical situation for many young actors.

The drawer also contained a letter and a ripped-opened envelope with only Elsie's name, no return address. The note, dated two days ago, was written in block print with black ink.

"My dearest sweetums, Must talk to you tonight. Don't tell anyone else what you know. What you told me is dynamite and you'll get burned if the wrong people hear this. Our usual place, nine o'clock. Love and kisses."

Did Troy write this or another lover? Who were "the wrong people"? Before I had a chance to ponder, someone shouted at me.

"Sandy, what are you doing in here?"

I spun around; Carl was standing in the doorway. "Nothing." My voice went up an octave. I stood in front of the drawer, blocking Carl's view, and as unobtrusively as possible, reached behind my back and stuffed the letter into the drawer.

"Are you looking through Elsie's things?"

I shut the drawer quietly. "Yesterday she said she had a book of poems that I could have it." What a lie. I'd rather fall into the ocean than read poetry, and I couldn't imagine Elsie owning any reading material more demanding than *The National Inquirer*.

"Royce wants you out front. I can have one of the PAs find the book for you."

"No, don't bother. It wasn't that important."

After we stepped into the hallway, Carl locked the door behind us. I had no way of searching the room again and the suspicious letter was out of my reach.

A note of warning, death threats and Elsie's sudden demise. Coincidence?

Chapter 9: What Kind of Girl

I retreated to the bleachers to study my lines while the others rehearsed. As the scenes rolled along, the other actors seemed sluggish and listless. Even though nobody liked Elsie, her tragic death put a damper on everyone. Time came for my first entrance and I got in place. Harv, Joseph and now Dottie, taking Elsie's place, met me inside the office of Sammy Shovel, P.I. The script stated that as the other characters introduced themselves, I was to shake their hands.

"Royce, I have a suggestion," I said.

"You do, do you?" Apparently, Royce hadn't forgotten how I used to yell at him about the badly written scripts on my show.

"This bit with me shaking hands, it isn't interesting business and it isn't funny."

"That's the sort of thing most people do when they're introduced. Do you have a better idea?"

"How about this. Instead of me bending down to shake Joseph's hand, Harv picks up him? I mean, with our height difference, we can get some mileage out of that."

"Sure, why not?" the dwarf said. "That's what I'm here for, the cheap laughs."

I added, "And I should do something special when I meet Dottie as well."

"Royce, darling, that's an excellent idea," she said. "Sandy could kiss my hand."

Hot dog! Now we're talking! I'm not much of an actor but at smooching, I'm a champion. If the

Academy gave Emmys for Best Kisser, I'd have a shelf full of trophies. I had so much practice kissing the girl guest stars on my show that I could have requested workers' comp for chapped lips.

"That's good, Dottie." Of course Royce liked any suggestion as long as it didn't come from me. "Sandy, what do you think of Dottie's idea?"

I gave her a sly grin. "I think I can handle that."

We started the scene again. After I shook Harv's hand, he slipped his hands beneath Joseph's armpits and raised him level with my face.

As I reached out my hand, Joseph joked, "Hey, you're not so big after all."

I doubled over with laughter. Harv guffawed so hard he almost dropped Joseph. Dottie tried to hold in her giggles but they leaked out anyway.

I turned to Royce. "We're definitely keeping that line!"

After we got out the chuckles and composed ourselves, we restarted the scene yet again. This time we were all prepared for Joseph's ad lib. Then Dottie held out her hand for me to kiss. I glanced at her hand and then at her face. Despite her age, she still glowed with the confidence of inner beauty. What a shame to waste such an opportunity.

Time for some mischief.

I took her hand, but instead of kissing it I pulled her close to me, grabbed her in a clinch, tipped her backwards and planted an unforgettable smooch on her lips (ummmm, cherry-flavored lipstick, nice). After I worked my magic, I stepped back and let her come up for air. Harv applauded and Joseph let out some wolf whistles.

Dottie gasped and fanned her face with her hand. "You rambunctious boy!" She slapped my arm and then grinned.

I always leave my ladies satisfied.

I glanced at Royce for his reaction. He leaned back in his canvas chair with his arms crossed and the script open on his lap. "If you're finished pawing the actors, we need to keep going."

Dottie straightened her blouse. "No, wait, we're not ready."

"What's wrong, Dottie?" Royce asked.

"Sandy has lipstick all over his mouth."

This remark drew the largest laughs of the day. Embarrassed, I turned my head away but Dottie grabbed my chin and wiped my face with her lacy hanky. Between Scruffy's slobber and Dottie's lipstick, by Friday night I was going to look a mess. When the actress finished mopping up, I asked if she wanted to go over that last bit again to make sure we had it right.

"No!" Royce shouted. "We're moving on! Harv, your line, 'Mr. Shovel, you're the only one who can dig us out of this predicament.'"

What a party spoiler. But the silliness and the laughter helped to get our minds off Elsie and we finished the scene with more pep and higher spirits.

When I made my exit, I kept going right out the stage door. I get itchy when I'm cooped up inside a windowless soundstage for too long. Next to the stage door stood three white plastic chairs and a matching patio table with an umbrella where the actors could take a break. Joseph occupied one of the chairs (he'd left the stage a few minutes prior). A PA on a bicycle stopped long enough to hand him a Rico's take-out bag. I asked Joseph if I could join him and he nodded at one of the empty chairs. I sat as he took a burger from the bag and unwrapped it.

"I see you're a Rico's fan," I said.

"Hate standing in line at the commissary." As Joseph ate the burger, the condiments and juice dripped onto the table. "People cut in front and pretend they don't see me. So the PAs pick me up lunch from Rico's. Best burgers in town. I love these things."

"Anybody else on the show eat at Rico's?"

He gobbled the last bite of the meat feast and licked his fingers. "Elsie did. She liked the grilled cheese sandwiches." Joseph pulled an enormous cigar from his jacket pocket. "Would you like one?"

I held up a hand. "No, thanks, you go ahead." Years ago I quit a brief cigarette habit after the smoke affected my singing. Took me many more years before I gave up smoking pot as well.

"Suit yourself, but you're missing a good thing."

Joseph took a metal cigar clipper and a lighter from his jacket pocket. He snipped off the end of the stogie and then lit the other end. He took a deep puff and exhaled a smoke plume.

"That smells like a premium brand," I said.

"The best there is. Direct from Havana. Illegal but worth it. It'll be our secret. So, Sandy, are you having a good time with our little Kelter family? The rest of the week should be a breeze with the battle-axe gone."

"How well did you know Elsie Bloom?"

The actor eyed me through a haze of smoke. "I tried to ignore her. But what does it matter now?"

"There's something's odd about her death."

"Odd in what way?"

"Odd in that it didn't seem natural. Healthy people don't suddenly collapse in the middle of the street."

"You think she was murdered?"

"I didn't say that."

He took a long, meditative puff and blew it out slowly. "I'm not surprised."

"Do you know someone who might want to kill her?"

"You can start with the entire SAG roster."

The Screen Actors Guild is the official union for TV and film performers. I was required to join when I was cast on *Buddy Brave*. Fortunately my agent kept my dues up-to-date over the years in case another acting gig came along.

He continued. "There isn't an actor around she didn't sleep with, flirt with, or insult. There isn't an actresses around who doesn't hate her for stealing a boyfriend." He tapped his cigar and the ashes fell on the ground. "If someone killed Elsie, I'd lay my money on one of her boyfriends."

"You mean Troy?"

"Naw. She liked Troy. They were crazy about each other."

"Was Leo Constantine her father?"

The dwarf tossed back his head and laughed. "Where did you hear that load of malarkey?"

"That's what Elsie told me."

"That girl was the biggest liar in town. Every day she'd come up with some new tale. Said she was related to Judy Garland. She was going out with Tim Allen. She was set to make a picture with Tom Cruise. Elsie was always spinning a yarn to make herself sound good. If Leo's her dad, then Wilt Chamberlain's my old man."

"Why would she lie to me?"

"Elsie was just a crazy kid from the Valley. Came from a broken family, poor as church mice. She didn't have any smarts or an ounce of talent but she wanted to be a star so everyone would think she was something special." He placed his half-smoked cigar in an ashtray on the table and sat back. "Why the questions? What's in it for you?"

"I was with Elsie when she died."

"That doesn't mean you're responsible for her."

"I'm surprised the police haven't shown up asking

questions."

"Leo has the cops on a tight leash. He makes sure any nasty business stays in the lot and out of the papers."

I was going to interrogate Joseph some more, but no such luck.

"There you are!" One of the PAs approached me. "Mr. Fairfax, Royce asked me to drive you to wardrobe for your fitting."

I said to Joseph, "Excuse me, but duty calls. We'll talk some more later."

He nodded and resumed smoking as the PA and I headed out in one of the company carts. As we sped along I pondered why Royce wanted me escorted across the lot; when he directed on *Buddy Brave* he never ordered a chauffer for me. Was he afraid I'd trip over another dead body? Or did he fear I'd wander off limits and ask questions about Elsie? Earlier, Royce seemed anxious to get me out of Elsie's dressing room. Did he think I'd find something incriminating? When we reached the wardrobe building, the PA informed me that her orders were to wait and bring me straight back when I'd finished. I resented Royce's overprotective manner but I didn't want to get the PA fired, so I agreed to a return trip.

The wardrobe department always fascinated me. The nondescript building was basically a huge warehouse filled with endless rows of racks crammed with colorful clothes and unlimited imagination. Since Buddy Brave mostly worked undercover, he wore a variety of fantasy costumes, such as a pirate, cowboy, business tycoon, Middle East sheik and even a monster. I loved dressing up as the different characters; I felt like a kid getting paid to play "let's pretend."

An assistant named Edith helped me. She pulled my costume off the rack and pointed me to the dressing room. I liked the outfit: a navy blue pinstripe jacket with wide lapels and broad shoulders along with a white shirt so starched it could stand up on its own. Instead of a tie, Edith gave me a blue ascot, "because it looks like the scarf you always wore as Buddy Brave." So much for typecasting. People still wanted me to dress like that kid dick. While filming the first episode of my show I was out in the sun for too long, so the costume mistress tied a scarf around my neck to hide the sunburn. The producers loved the look so much that they made me wear that goofy scarf every day after.

As the ceiling fan attempted to create a breeze in the windowless room, Edith had me stand in front of a mirror and turn around for her inspection. She stuck safety pins in the areas that needed tucking in or letting out (mostly letting out). As a one-time guest star I wasn't getting a custom made suit but something recycled from past shows. She asked if I was going to cut off my ponytail and I said no. Long hair wasn't vintage 1940s but I didn't care; I wasn't shearing my locks for one show. She handed me some fedoras to try on and eventually we found a white one that fit my large head (no, I do not have a swelled head. Not usually). She found some black leather shoes, which she promised to polish before show time, and I agreed to bring my own black socks (did I have any clean socks? I hadn't done laundry in ages).

In the dressing room I changed back into my regular clothes and then handed off the costume to Edith for alterations. Outside, my ride was patiently waiting, no doubt dreaming of the day when she could be the one giving orders to the lowly PAs. We arrived at Stage 14 just as Dottie was leaving for lunch. I agreed to join her. Not only would I have an attractive dining companion but she might tell me more about the recently dearly departed. I dismissed the PA, scooted over into the driver's seat, and offered Dottie a ride to the commissary. For lunch I purchased a bag of Fritos, a Mountain Dew and a grilled chicken sandwich slathered with mayo and stacked with lettuce and sliced tomatoes. Dottie picked up a chef's salad with a side of cottage cheese along with bottled water. We settled at a small table in a corner of the bustling dining room.

After some small talk, I said, "How well did you know Elsie?"

She stirred the contents of her salad bowl with a fork. Her hand trembled slightly. "Elsie? What a curious lunchtime topic."

"I suppose we could talk about the weather, but that stays pretty much the same year round."

She laughed. "Stanley, you are a card."

"Sandy. My name is Sandy."

She stopped mixing her salad. "That's what I said. Sandy."

I didn't bother to correct her. "Anyway, what can you tell me about Elsie?"

Dottie shrugged, chewed and swallowed a bite of greens. "Thankfully, very little. She was unprofessional on stage and I didn't care to get to know her off stage. But she was a little busy body herself. Always poking her nipped and tucked nose into everyone's business."

"What makes you say that?"

"She loved to dig up dirt. Always prying into my personal life. First she made a fuss about my second husband and his affairs. Goodness, that's public knowledge. I've always been forthright about Harold's shortcomings and I've made my peace about it. Then she threatened to tell people about some silly film I made decades ago."

"What film was that?"

She dismissed my question with a wave of the hand. "I don't remember the title. Just a little non-union thing when I was starting out in the business." The utensil slipped from her fingers and clattered when it hit the floor. "My, I'm all butterfingers today. Excuse me."

Dottie stood and so did I. As I sat, she walked to the silverware rack with grace and carriage, always "on stage" even in the commissary. As I crunched on my corn chips something jogged my memory. I had some vague recollection of a movie I saw years ago with an actress who resembled a much-younger Dottie but I didn't remember the title, either. All that alcohol I swilled over the years must have killed some memory cells.

Dottie returned with a fresh fork and sat down. I continued the line of questioning.

"Did anyone in the cast or crew want to hurt Elsie?"

"You mean kill her?" The actress picked at her food. "Hardly. What would be the point? I'm sure that in another year the girl would finally realize that she was wasting her time in an occupation in which she had absolutely no skill and she'd leave and find work as a waitress or a receptionist."

"Do you think someone she worked with in another movie might have wanted her dead?"

She laid a manicured hand on my wrist. "Please, let's not talk about Elsie any more. I'm sorry she's gone, but heavens, let's not get morbid!"

Dottie launched into the latest bit of studio gossip and I let her ramble as I finished my food. After lunch I drove Dottie back to Stage 14 but I didn't park the cart. Instead, I made a U-turn for a side trip of my own to the other side of the lot. As the old saying goes, if you want to know how to murder someone and get away with it, go ask a mystery writer. And I was on my way to see one of the best scribblers in the business.

Chapter 10: I'm Telling You Now

Matt Sterling cut his show biz teeth writing scripts for *Buddy Brave* and kept working steadily afterwards, crafting scripts for numerous TV mysteries throughout the '80s. I had read in the trades that my old buddy was hard at working on a new fall series, *The Sexy Sleuth Sisters,* about a pair of 20-something sibs in a Beverly Hills detective agency who solved crimes in between mall shopping and manicures. The show filmed on the Mammoth lot so perhaps my pal was still in his old office. Back in the 1930s when studios hired screenwriters to crank out scripts tailored for the movie stars under contract, Mammoth build a two-story block of writers' offices at the western end of the lot, far away from the administrative offices in an effort to keep those pesky wordsmiths out of the producers' thinning hair.

I recognized Matt's office from the haze of cigarette smoke lingering outside. Despite the no smoking rule on the lot, the security guards held their noses and turned a blind eye toward the executives and certain other individuals who puffed away inside their private offices. I parked the cart along the curb, climbed the outdoor staircase to the second level and rapped on the door's glass panel. I cracked opened the door and peered inside. A haze of smoke surrounded a middle-aged man who sat hunched over an electric typewriter, using the index finger of each hand to play whack-a-mole with the keys. The machine's print ball slammed against the ribbon and paper in a staccato rhythm. The man had one long bushy eyebrow, a crop of unruly black hair and a cigarette hanging from his mouth.

"Hello, Matt." I had to shout so he could hear me over the clanking of the typewriter and the wheeze of the old air conditioning unit in the window.

His hands froze in mid-air above the keyboard as he raised his head. "Son of a gun, if it isn't the boy sleuth all grown up! Sandy! Long time, no see! How the heck are you?"

"I'm fine. Can't the studio afford to buy you a computer?"

"Computers! Hate them! Despise them! Can't figure out how to get 'em to work! Too many buttons to push! I can't write with a friggin' cursor blinking at me like a stuck traffic light. I wrote all of my scripts on this baby"—he fondly patted the IBM Selectric—"so why mess with success?"

"Are you busy?"

He stuffed out his cigarette in an ashtray overflowing with butts. "What kind of a question is that to ask a writer? Of course I'm busy! Writers are always busy! If we don't write, we don't eat! Gotta polish a script from a freelancer, make changes in the script they're filming now, and take a meeting with the producers which is as much fun as taking hemorrhoid medicine and far less useful. So come on in! Have a seat!"

He wriggled out of his armless secretary's chair (how did he fit his oversized bulk onto that little seat?) and moved a pile of scripts off the room's only other chair. Matt jerked his head at the coffeemaker atop a filing cabinet and offered me a cup. I'm a big caffeine fan, but the dark sludge caked inside the glass carafe appeared more suited for the inside of a car engine than my stomach. I declined, sat and waved aside the smoke.

"Sorry about that. Nasty habit of mine. Bad for the

lungs." He coughed. "Really ought to give it up."
Edwards lit a fresh cigarette, sat in his squeaky office
chair, and turned off the typewriter. "You look great,
Sandy. So's how life treating you? I haven't seen you in
any movies lately. What have you been doing with
yourself?"

I didn't have the heart to tell him that I'd been
drowning in a sea of alcohol. "I'm just waiting for the
right role to come along."

"Is that what brings you back to Mammoth?"

"Yeah, a guest shot with *Off-Kelter*."

"You call *that* the right role? Sandy, Sandy." He
shook his head and leaned back in his chair. I thought
he was going to topple backwards but he stayed
balanced. "You're a good actor, Sandy. I knew it when
I first saw you on *Buddy Brave*. I loved writing for you
'cause you had class and you were smart. I'd throw any
stunt at you and you'd do it without a whimper. Not
like the spoiled brats I write for on *The Stupid Sisters*."
He gave a snort. "All they want to do is preen for the
camera. Ask them to learn a line of more than five
words, or take a fall, or actually show some emotion,
and they whine. I expected big things of you, Sandy.
After *Buddy Brave* I thought you'd jump right into
some films."

"You know how the business is, Matt." I glanced at
his three Emmys for outstanding writing, displayed on
one shelf of the floor-to-ceiling bookcase that covered
one wall. "You've done pretty good for yourself."

"You mean my gold-plated paperweights?" He
chuckled. "Three Emmys and I'm writing for *The Stink
Sisters*. What does that tell ya?" He sighed. "But I guess
it doesn't matter. Once this show's done I don't expect
to be around much longer."

That didn't sound good. "Are you sick?"

"Sick of the business. Do you want to know my

secret is for staying in TV for so long? Not my talent. Not my connections." He opened a desk drawer, removed a bottle of Clairol For Men hair coloring, and plunked it down beside the typewriter. "Once a writer hits forty, he's washed up. With all of his years of experience and craftsmanship he's suddenly 'too old' to write. Soon as the *Sisters* producers figure out my real age, I'm a goner. I don't list *Buddy Brave* on my resume because it makes me look old. That's a shame. I'm proud of the work I did for you." Matt stuck the bottle back in the drawer and slammed it shut. "So what can I do for you, Sandy? Please say that you want me to write a movie for you."

"Sorry, Matt. If I had an offer you'd be the first writer I'd ask. But what I need from you now is some information about murder."

"Murder?" His dark eyes lit up and he leaned forward, resting his elbows on the typewriter keys. "You want to knock somebody off? I can name a few producers that you can practice on."

"No, it's about somebody already dead. Elsie Bloom. The actress from *Off-Kelter*. Did you hear about her death?"

"Just a paragraph in the *Daily Variety*. What about her?"

"I was with Elsie when she died and I'm trying to figure out the cause of death."

"Ah ha!" He straightened up and smiled. "The boy detective is sniffing around! Tell me what happened, every little detail."

As I retold the events of yesterday, Matt leaned back, laced his fingers over his gut, and listened intently, gently rocking in his chair. He interrupted a couple of times to ask for more information. After I finished my spiel, he crossed to the bookcase—three shelves were crammed with books on weapons, police techniques and forensics—and removed a volume on poisons. He put on a pair of store-bought reading glasses, consulted the book's index, thumbed to a page, read silently and nodded.

"I can't be absolutely sure without a toxicology report but the symptoms you described sound like cyanide poisoning."

"Cyanide? You must be joking!"

He read from the book. "'Symptoms are rapid breathing, shortness of breath, dizziness, loss of consciousness. This happens quickly in a matter of minutes. The victim would perhaps clutch at his chest, collapse to the floor and die.'" He removed the glasses, set them on a shelf, and shut the book.

"That's exactly what happened. But how did the poison get to her?"

"It's easy to hide. Just mix it with water or any type of liquid. Dissolves quickly and doesn't leave a trace."

"Elsie was drinking veggie juice when she was with me. Maybe someone sneaked into her dressing room and doctored the drink. But how could someone put poison inside a sealed bottle?"

He shrugged and replaced the book on the shelf. "I'm just telling you the probable cause of death. You'll have to figure out the rest for yourself."

I stared at the typewriter in a daze. "Poison—if I had known—maybe I could have done something to save her. At least tell the nurses so they could—"

Allen put a large hairy hand on my shoulder. "The poison shuts down the cell function instantly. Once cyanide gets cookin,' it's over in a flash. She was probably dead when she hit the ground. There's nothing you could have done, Sandy."

"Thanks, Matt. But where would somebody get cyanide? You can't pick it up at the pharmacy."

The office chair groaned as the writer sat down. "It's

not as rare as you might think. You can buy the stuff from a chemical supply company. It's also used to electroplate metals, like jewelry. I wrote cyanide into a couple of shows. One time I had a college professor order it along with the regular supplies for his chemistry lab."

"So I'm looking for a chemist or a jewelry maker."

"You know, Sandy, I bet you could find cyanide here at the Mammoth mill where they make the metal props." He flipped the Selectric's 'on' switch and the machine hummed to life. "I hate to end this fascinating conversation but I need to finish these pages toot sweet. My boy's got a ball game tonight."

"A boy? When did that happen? When you worked on my show, you were a bachelor."

"What can I say? Twelve years ago I went to a book signing, fell in love with the author, and married her. You got any kids, Sandy?"

"Two. A boy and a girl."

"That's marvelous."

"My ex has custody."

"That stinks. Let me tell ya something." He leaned over the typewriter and shook a stubby finger at me. "Spend all the time you can with those kids. I worked too many late nights and now I regret it. Once you miss a milestone, it's a goner. That's my quote of the day."

I rose to leave. "Thanks, Matt. I'll remember that."

"One more thing, Sandy. If you come in contact with cyanide, don't touch it with your bare hands or get any on your skin or you'll end up like Elsie."

I thanked Matt for his time but he probably didn't hear me. His two fingers were already pounding out golden words on the paper in the roller. I closed the door behind me as I left the room and hoped that the afternoon breeze might fumigate the smoke from my clothes. I hopped in the cart and arrived at the set just in time to run through my scenes. I couldn't find my script (where *did* I leave it?) but no matter, the writers had a fresh batch of revised pages. The only decent new jokes were the lines we had ad libbed earlier. During my kiss with Dottie, she gave me an aggressive pucker that nearly bit off my lip. She seemed more angry than seductive. Did my lunchtime chat upset her? Scruffy drenched my face again but this time I was prepared; I told a PA to stand ready with a towel.

Royce called for a break and I approached the twins, who were stuffing themselves with protein bars from the craft services table.

"Didn't you kids have lunch?"

"Yeah," said Molly, between bites. "But that was so way long ago and I'm hungry."

"You girls got a minute?"

"For what?"

"I just want to talk."

The girls looked at each other and shrugged. "Yeah, whatever," said Missy.

We sat at the plastic table outside. Molly tilted back on the chair's back legs and propped her heels on the table. Missy took a compact and tube out of her purse and applied lipstick on her mouth—black lipstick.

"Are you into goth fashion?"

"What?"

"Your lipstick. It's black. Most girls wear red lipstick."

"Oh, that." Missy quickly recapped the tube and shoved it into her purse. "Mom doesn't like us wearing weird colors or glitter stuff. I use it just to make her mad."

"Have you girls been in acting for a long time?"

"Yeah, we did commercials when we were babies," Molly said. "Baby foods, toys, diapers."

"Like it was so embarrassing," Missy quipped.

"Strangers used to come up to me and said, 'I saw the ad where you were a baby sitting on the toilet.' I could just die. Totally gross."

I asked if they liked acting.

"It's a bummer," Missy said. "I can't stay up late 'cause I got an early call. Gotta watch my weight. Can't eat chocolate 'cause it makes my face breaks out. Can't go to the beach 'cause my skin burns."

Her sister added, "We can't go on dates 'cause mom's afraid the boys will get us preggers. She says boys only want us for our money."

"As if," Missy said. "Our money's locked up in a trust fund until we're eighteen. We're broke all the time. When we go to the mall we have to bum money off our friends so we can buy clothes. That really sucks."

"Are you going to keep acting after you're eighteen?"

Molly shook her head and her hair swung around like a golden tetherball. "No way. Shooting is, like, so boring. You sit around for hours so you can go on camera for thirty seconds. All we get are bit parts. Mom tried to get us leads in movies, but the producers say twin acts are so yesterday."

"We talked it over, Molly and me, and we're going to use our trust fund to pay for college. We want to study fashion designing. We love clothes."

"We're looking at East Coast schools," Molly chimed in, "so we can get away from mom and she won't be pushing us into auditions."

"We didn't want to do this stupid show but mom made us. Maybe with Elsie gone the show will get cancelled. I hope so."

"You didn't like Elsie Bloom, did you?"

The twins told me exactly what they thought of the late actress. They hated Elsie because she was mean to them, so the girls retaliated by playing pranks on the actress, such as dropping insects down the back of her blouse or taking photos of her making out with Troy and then hanging the prints around the set.

"Someone played a mean trick on Elsie the day she died." I described the threatening setup I had found inside the woman's dressing room. "Do either of you know who might have done something like that?"

They both glanced at each other and shook their heads. "No, we don't know anything about that," said Molly.

From the look on her face and the tone of her voice, I knew she was lying. "The letters on the mirror were written in black lipstick, just like Missy's."

"Anyone can go to a store and buy black lipstick," said the sister.

"Did you perhaps loan your lipstick to someone?"

"No freakin' way!" Missy shouted. "Like I want someone else's grotty mouth on my makeup? Ewwwww!"

"Yesterday after the table read I overheard you two talking about doing something to Elsie. And you had plenty of time during the lunch break to sneak into her dressing room."

"Well, all right, yeah, we wrote that stuff on the mirror," said Molly. "And hung some streamers we found in the prop closet. But that was just to make her mad. We didn't kill her!"

"Did you see anyone else go in or out of Elsie's dressing room during lunch?"

"Nope, nobody." Molly was livid. "Just 'cause we hated the slut doesn't mean we did anything bad. Don't go saying we killed her 'cause we didn't!"

A new voice piped in, shrill and harsh. "What are you saying about my girls?" Mrs. Jones stood by me, looking as if she wanted to tear my head off.

I stood. "Hello, I don't believe we've met. I'm Sandy Fairfax."

"Yes, I know who you are. The girls have to leave. It's time for their studies."

Molly and Missy moaned as they got on their feet.

"Come along, girls, don't dawdle. The teacher's waiting."

"Nice meeting you," I said to the twins.

The girls mumbled a goodbye of sorts and plodded down the street. State law required all child actors to spend several hours a day with a tutor to keep up with their education (that didn't affect me during my show because I'd already finished high school).

"Did I hear you accuse my daughters of killing that actress?" Mrs. Jones knew how to get right to the point.

"Of course not. You've got a couple of good kids. But if Elsie Bloom was murdered, then your daughters might not be safe."

"Of course they're safe. I watch out for them." In the event of a confrontation with a killer, I'd lay my money on the mom. "And who said anything about that Bloom girl getting murdered?"

"I'm just saying that her death looks suspicious."

"Nonsense. All of that fast living finally caught up with her. Drinking, carousing, it's bound to take a toll. I'm not sorry to see her go, not at all. That woman was a bad influence on my girls. Always trying to get them to do something nasty. Shameful!"

"I don't presume to tell you how to raise your children," I said, "but I think they could use a break from acting."

Mrs. Jones narrowed her eyes at me. "What have they been saying?"

"They said acting isn't their passion."

"Ungrateful kids. They don't appreciate the sacrifices I've made for the. Driving them to auditions and rehearsals every day and night. Spending all my money on their acting lessons and clothes and makeup. Never taking a vacation or buying things for myself. Taking them to parties where they can meet the right people. When they're older they'll thank me."

"Maybe they need a break."

"To do what? Watch TV or hang out with bums? When I was their age I wanted to be an actress but my father said no. I've hated him for that ever since. I'm making sure my girls will achieve something they can be proud of. When they're married and stuck in the house all day with their babies, I don't want them looking back on a childhood of broken dreams and wasted years."

"I think you should let your girls decide on their own dreams."

"You mean let them make mistakes and ruin their lives? Not if I can help it."

The AD came to fetch me for rehearsal. I bid goodbye to Mrs. Jones; I was grateful for an excuse to escape. As I stopped by the crafts services table for a cold Mountain Dew, a PA showed up with two large, empty cardboard boxes. Carl told him to take the boxes to Elsie's dressing room.

"What's going on there?" I asked.

"Elsie's mother is collecting her things," Carl replied.

I glanced at the soda can in my hand and an ugly thought popped into my head. I set down my soda and ran down the hall, nearly knocking over a crew guy in my way. Inside the dressing room, a middle-aged woman in a blouse and slacks was removing the bottles of veggie juice from the fridge and putting them into a box.

"Don't touch those!" I shouted.

The woman looked at me. "Who are you?"

"My name's Sandy Fairfax. Please, leave those bottles alone. They might be poisoned."

"Poisoned?" Royce stood in the doorway. In his hand was an open, half empty bottle of Elsie's veggie juice "Sandy, why are you here? Why are you bothering this nice woman?"

I stared at the bottle in shock. "Royce! Where did you get that bottle?"

"Why, do you want one?" He gestured at the refrigerator. "Mrs. Bloom doesn't drink this stuff. She's giving it away to anyone who wants it."

"You drank it?" As much as I disliked the man, the thought of another person falling down dead in front of me spun me into a panic. "Don't drink any more! Call the hospital! It's poisoned!"

Royce grabbed my arm and dragged me into the hallway. "Fairfax, what's eating you? Elsie's mom is quite upset and I won't have you bothering her with crazy talk about poison."

"I'm sure Elsie was murdered. Right before she died she was drinking from a bottle of veggie juice I'd taken from her fridge. Just like the bottle you have. Someone must have slipped poison into it."

"Is that so?" Royce waggled the bottle at me. "I've been guzzling this stuff for twenty minutes and I feel fine. Several of the crew members have been drinking it too and nobody's puked or turned purple or fainted or died."

I took the bottle from him and sniffed the juice. I didn't detect any poison but then again, I had no idea what cyanide smelled like. Besides, the pungent carrot, celery and onion blend was strong enough to knock out an elephant without the aid of any drugs.

"Maybe the cyanide takes a long time to work."

Royce yanked the bottle away from me. "Cyanide? Where did you come up with that crap?"

"Matt Sterling told me. He's a mystery writer."

He jabbed his finger into my chest. "Now get this straight, Fairfax. Let the poor girl rest in peace. If you say one more word about poison or murder or Elsie Bloom, I'm pulling you off this show."

I stood nose to nose with the man. "You don't have enough time to replace me."

"Really? In this town, pretty boys like you are a dime a dozen."

"Is there something about Elsie's death you don't want me to know?"

"It's for your own safety. You start asking too many questions about killers and somebody might take a pot shot at *you*."

Before Royce and I had a chance to launch into another one of our marathon shouting matches, Mrs. Bloom joined us in the hallway.

"Mr. Jobbe, can someone please carry the refrigerator to my car? It's too heavy for me to move."

Just then Mrs. Jones walked down the hallway. "I can help with that." She stepped into the dressing room, wrapped her fat arms around the fridge and easily lifted it. I was impressed at her generosity in helping out until she added, "Soon as we get rid of Elsie's junk I can put Molly in here."

"Excuse me?" Royce said.

"The girls' dressing room is too small for two people. Now that this room's open—"

"Hold on, Mrs. Jones, we're not moving anyone around."

"But none of the other actors has to share a—"

"The girls can stay put for now. If the show's renewed, then maybe we'll reconsider the room assignments." To Mrs. Bloom he said cordially, "I'm terribly sorry about this, I'll send in a PA right away to help you." He scowled at the stage mom. "Your assistance isn't needed here."

Mrs. Jones set down the fridge and stormed away.

Royce turned his displeasure back toward me. "Are you still here?"

"Apparently so."

Royce shot me a killer look. "I mean it, Fairfax. Shut up about the murder talk or you're history."

"Is that a threat?"

Just before Royce walked away he slammed the juice bottle against my chest. "Here, finish this. It'll keep you healthy."

Chapter 11: Forget That Girl

I assumed Mrs. Bloom wasn't in the mood to tell me if her daughter had any enemies, so I didn't bother to question her; I only offered her my condolences and returned to the set. I took a sip of the veggie juice that Royce had given me and nearly threw up, not from any poison but from the vile taste. I dropped the bottle into the recycling bin near the craft services table, retrieved my can of Mountain Dew, and took a long swig. Now *that's* refreshment.

After running through my final scene in the show I was dismissed for the day. I carried my replacement script to my trailer and shoved it into my gym bag so I wouldn't lose it. I eyed myself in the mirror long enough to comb back that stray lock of hair that constantly fell into my eyes. I gathered up my things, put on my sunglasses, and headed outside. As I passed by Stage 12, some of the *Space Posse* cast was leaving as well. I caught up with one particular actor.

"Troy! I almost didn't recognize you without your makeup!"

"I know we've met. You're Sandy Fairfax, right?"

"That's right. I'm guesting on *Off-Kelter* this week." I asked where he was headed (to the parking lot) and said I was going that way too. We talked as we walked.

"I wanted to say how sorry I am about Elsie's death," I said.

"Thanks."

"I'm surprised you're back at work so soon."

"Staying busy keeps me from falling apart. Everyone

on the show has been so nice about what's happened. It's weird, you know, some days I'm on Planet Gorgan more than I'm on Earth. The show feels more real than reality. You know how in science fiction nobody really dies, they just come back to life in a different form? I keep expecting the scriptwriters to say, 'We wrote in a scene where Elsie shows up alive.' She was a lovely girl and I miss her terribly."

"Do you know why she might have suddenly collapsed?"

"No idea. Maybe she had a heart condition. She never talked about her health."

"Do you think she might have been poisoned?"

"Poisoned? That's ridiculous. Why would someone want to poison her? She wasn't a big star. She wasn't a threat to anyone. Sure, she rubbed people the wrong way, but when you got to know her she was really a kind soul."

"Maybe I shouldn't bring this up, but I heard that Elsie was seeing other men."

Troy glared at me. "So what?"

"You knew about them?"

"Of course I did. Elsie told me. She didn't keep secrets from me. She didn't love those jerks; that was just business, she said. Anyway, she'd stopped all of that. She was tired of the way those idiots treated her."

"Maybe one of her old boyfriends was angry at getting dumped."

His voice took on a sharper tone. "Did you ever think that maybe Elsie committed suicide? It's possible, you know."

I stopped in my tracks and nearly dropped my bag. "Suicide? How do you figure that?"

"Did you know she was bi-polar?" I stared at Troy. "I thought not. Elsie had these mood swings. When she was depressed she talked about killing herself so people would fuss over her at the funeral. But then she'd cheer up. She'd slip in and out of the dumps just like that." He snapped his fingers.

"I was with Elsie when she died and she didn't seem suicidal to me."

His voice rose. "You didn't know Missy Poo like I knew her. She might have poisoned herself. Did you ever think of that? Did you?"

"Missy Poo?"

Troy looked startled. He turned his head away. "We had pet names for each other. It's nothing."

We reached the parking lot. Troy stopped beside a Honda and took the keys out of his pocket. "Elsie's gone and let's leave it at that. Stop trying to turn her death into something ugly."

"I don't mean anything by it, Troy. I only want to help if I can. By the way, before Elsie died she told me she had a big secret that would ruin the studio."

"I suppose we'll never know what it is, will we?"

"Was she the daughter of Leo Constantine?"

He shot me a look that could burn the polish right off my bike. "You're nuts!"

Troy unlocked his car with the remote, got in and slammed the door in my face. As he backed out, he floored the pedal and nearly ran me over. I jumped aside as the Honda sped away, tires screeching on the hot pavement.

I kept walking. I didn't buy the suicide verdict or the bi-polar diagnosis. When I last saw Elsie, she was cheery, bubbly and—pardon the pun—full of life, not despondent. Why wouldn't Troy at least consider the possibility of murder? Maybe he wanted her dead, but if so, why? Those two were crazy about each other. Besides, Troy had an alibi: he'd been on Stage 12 filming *Space Posse*. But when I reached my destination I forgot about angry men and their dead girlfriends. My heart beat just a little bit faster as I rushed down the hallway to the dance studio. That morning I'd asked the AD if I could have another session with Cinnamon. I told him I was having trouble with the footwork, which wasn't true. I only wanted an excuse to see her again.

Through the closed door I heard music. Apparently she was busy with another dancer. When the music stopped I opened the door quietly and peeked in. Cinnamon was talking to a young woman in a loose-fitting top and sweatpants. Cinnamon wore a dark green leotard that set off those gorgeous eyes. Black tights caressed those luscious legs. Forget dancing; I'd just stand here. Now I know what they mean by a "room with a view."

She glanced in my direction and gave a nod. While she gave the pupil some last minute instructions, I sat on the bench and changed shoes. After the student left, Cinnamon stood over me with her hands on her hips.

I jerked my head towards the door. "Was that another one of your victims?"

"I see you're back for more punishment."

I finished tying my shoelaces and grinned at her. "Your inspirational teaching motivates me to excel to my fullest potential."

She rolled those big eyes and sighed. Cinnamon changed tape cassettes and started the music for my song. After I ran through the piece on my own she helped me polish the steps. I hardly noticed the time pass when a pesky buzzer sounded.

"That's all?" I said. "Can't I stay a little longer?"

"Sorry. That's all the time the producer is paying for."

"Can't you toss in an extra ten minutes pro bono?"

"And what makes you think that you're so special?"

"I thought that was obvious."

"I see, it must be your humility."

A young man holding a pair of tap shoes stood in the doorway. Cinnamon told him to come in while I, frustrated, changed shoes. As I started out the door, Cinnamon asked when my dance scene was shooting. I told her filming was tomorrow morning in the back lot.

"I'll be there," she said.

I nearly floated out of the room.

*****

When I arrived home I found a familiar black Lexus parked in my driveway. My agent was one of the few people who had a house key and the security gate pass code. During my divorce, when he was new to the business, he came by my house to talk about new headshots and we ended up looking through my old photo albums of the kids. Instead of giving me work, he offered me a shoulder to cry on. During my drinking days he let himself in to pick up the pieces and put me to bed. Marshall still came around to mooch my food, although he earned enough off his other clients to stock his own supermarket. I stowed my things in the hall closet and switched on the intercom system that played classical music throughout the house. I liked having the background noise to cover up the loneliness. I ran upstairs to my bedroom just long enough to empty out my pockets and put on slippers; after a day of running around the lot, my dogs were beat. Downstairs I found Marshall, as usual, in my kitchen. He was dressed, as usual, in an expensive suit and tie.

Marshall, with his head in the depths of my fridge, greeted me in his usual manner. "Don't you ever go shopping? Your refrigerator is a disgrace."

"And I suppose you're helping by cleaning it out?" I sat on a stool beside the island. "I had a hard day at the studio and I'm starved. As long as you're here you can fix me some steak and potatoes."

He turned from the fridge and poked me in the gut. "If you're serious about making a comeback, Ernest, stick with the salads. That's my professional advice. Nobody likes a fat entertainer."

"What about Jonathan Winters? William Conrad? Victor Buono?"

"I don't manage them."

He removed his jacket and handed it to me (since when did I become his butler?) while he rolled up his spotless white shirtsleeves. He tucked the end of his tie into his shirtfront. I draped the jacket over a dining room chair while he played chef. I didn't mind because he's the better cook and I was grateful for the company. Marshall rounded up some chicken breasts to bake. He started a pan of water boiling to steam the rice and vegetables.

"What kind of dinner is that?" I said. "Can't you at least fry that chicken and put some sauce on the veggies?"

"Lean meat makes a man lean. Remember that."

"I see what you're doing. If I die of starvation, you can knock me off your client roster."

"How about a fruit salad for dessert?"

"How about that chocolate cake I bought at Gelson's?"

The bananas and peaches that Marshall found were rotted, so he tossed them in the trash bin. "Honestly, Ernest, how do you survive? There's hardly any edible food in this place. You need a wife to take care of you."

"Every time I find a woman, she's a nut case."

"Now that you're sober, I should think you'd be more discriminating."

He set placemats and ceramic plates on the dining room table.

"What are you doing? We can use paper plates."

"Ernest, when was the last time you ate like a

civilized man?"

"Never. I throw the food into a trough and gobble it up with my bare hands."

Marshall ordered me to set the table—with real silverware, not plastic forks—while he finished cooking. After my divorce I rarely used the dining room, which held too many memories of the parties Becka and I used to throw. Besides, the space seemed overwhelming for one person. After I set the table I made a pot of coffee and Marshall made a fuss about the contacts he was making to find me work, no doubt a ploy to keep me from firing him for the *Off-Kelter* gig. When the food was ready, we filled up our plates and sat across the table from each other. Marshall placed a cloth napkin on his lap. I didn't bother with a napkin; I grabbed a fork and dug in. The spices he had added to the chicken and veggies actually made the meal palatable.

Marshall asked how the job was going. But instead of talking about the show, I told him all about Elsie's death.

"Ernest, what are you doing? If the actress was murdered, you need to let the police handle it."

"You mean the way the police handled the shooting at that fan convention by blaming me."

"Maybe Elsie had a heart attack. People do, you know."

"But Matt said—"

"Matt's a writer. It's his job to look for the dramatic in mundane life. Remember the last time you played boy sleuth? The killer almost silenced you as well."

"This is different. Elsie was poisoned, not shot."

He took another bite of his dinner. "So you're going to involve yourself with the criminal element until someone poisons your food."

"I've been eating at the studio commissary. If that

drek doesn't kill me, nothing will."

"Ernest, I won't have you blowing this job. Forget about the actress and focus on the show."

I rested my elbows on the table, stared off at the wall and pouted. I don't know why I did that. I used to use that technique with my parents and it didn't work with them either.

"Come on, Ernest, eat your food and stop acting so blue."

If my life were a cartoon (and sometimes I think it must be), a light bulb would switch on over my head. I stared at Marshall, clapped my hands together, and grinned.

"Blue! That's it! That's where I've seen Dottie before!"

His fork paused in mid-air. "Excuse me?"

"At lunch today Dottie told me she had appeared in a film a long time ago that she didn't remember. I think I know what movie she's talking about. Years ago"—I named a certain well-known rock star—"used to invite me to his house for his big weekend parties. After dark he'd set up a screen and a projector on his patio and show blue movies. I remember one of them, 'Frontier Frolics.' Dottie played an Indian squaw who showed the cowboys how to have a good time. She wore Indian war makeup and an awful wig with long black braids. That's why I didn't recognize her at the time."

"Are you sure it was Dottie?"

I chuckled. "Believe me, Marshall, it was. And Elsie found out. Maybe she was planning to tell the news hounds that the celebrated actress had made a skin flick. That gives Dottie a motive for murder."

"Not likely, Ernest. Dottie isn't the first actress who did an occasional adult movie to pay the bills. Besides, the way some of these 'R' rated films steam up, that sort of thing is hardly scandalous nowadays."

"All I'm saying is that Dottie has something to hide."

"Ernest, listen to me. You're on a sitcom, not a cop show. Keep your mind on your acting. You need to do well so I can get you another job."

"Really, Marshall, if I mess up on *Off-Kelter,* who's going to see it?"

We finished eating. I filled up the dishwasher with the dirty dishes and took the cake out of the fridge. I was about to cut a huge chunk when Marshall glared at me. I ended up with just a sliver. Marshall scrubbed the pots and pans while I ate my dessert and then we took our coffee cups into the living room. I flipped on the wall switch and he sat in the recliner chair. Marshall offered to help me run lines so I took the gym bag out of the closet and parked myself on the sofa. I put the bag on the coffee table and opened it to take out the script. Instead, I removed Elsie's purse. Marshall stared at the pink monstrosity and then arched his eyebrows at me.

"It isn't mine. It's Elsie's. She dropped it when she died."

"You've been carrying it around for two days as a souvenir?"

"I'm going to give it back to her family but I haven't had the time."

"Do you know where her next of kin lives?"

"No, but maybe I can find an address in here."

I opened the purse, turned it over, and dumped the contents onto the coffee table. I've been around women enough to know about the luggage they haul around with them, but how did Elsie managed to cram so much stuff into the bag? If we men put that much junk in our pockets, the sheer weight would keep us from standing. Marshall set his cup atop a coaster on the table and leaned closer. I spread the doodads across the table.

Amid the cosmetics and trinkets, I found the bottle of eye drops for her contact lens. I held up the bottle to the ceiling light.

Right before Elsie collapsed she had placed some of these drops into her eyes.

Cyanide is easy to hide. Just mix it with water or any type of liquid. Dissolves quickly and doesn't leave a trace.

I screamed, dropped the bottle, and sprang to my feet.

"Ernest! What on earth is wrong with you!"

"Don't touch that thing!" I pointed a shaky finger at the bottle. "It's the murder weapon!"

Chapter 12: Tell the Truth

I ran, screaming, into the kitchen. I turned on the kitchen tap, took a bottle of bleach from under the sink, poured the cleanser on my hands and scrubbed. Marshall followed, probably thinking that now was the right time to commit me to the loony bin.

"Ernest! Will you settle down!"

"Gotta get this stuff off my hands!" I rubbed my hands with the dishwashing brush. "If a drop of cyanide gets on me, I'm dead!" I faced Marshall. "Do I look pale? Flushed?"

"No, you look stupid." He turned off the water.

I grabbed the lever and kept the water going. "Marshall! Call 9-1-1! Get me to a hospital!"

He pushed the tap lever down and held it. "Sit down, Ernest."

I slid onto a kitchen stool. I felt my wrist pulse. Fast. That didn't bode well.

"Now tell me why you're acting like a maniac."

I took a deep breath. No chest pains yet. Maybe I had washed off most of the poison. "Elise died of cyanide poisoning. Someone spiked her bottle of eye drops."

"How do you know that without testing the drops for poison?"

He sat on another stool as I shared what Matt had told me about the poison. Elsie's veggie juice wasn't spiked but she'd used the drops minutes before she collapsed. Marshall listened without interrupting.

When I finished he said, "So what are you going to

do?"

"Well, I..." I checked my pulse again. A bit slower. Good. The effects of the cyanide must be wearing off. "I don't know. But the killer must be someone who knew her well. She used her eye drops during the table read and nothing happened. But before Elsie went to lunch on Monday, she left the purse in her dressing room. That's when the killer must have placed the poisoned eye drops in her bag."

"You need to turn this over to the police."

"If the cops were interested, they would have launched an investigation by now."

"What are you going to say when the police ask why you didn't turn in the evidence right away?"

"I was busy with rehearsals."

"You had time to talk to a mystery writer and snoop around in the victim's dressing room."

"Whose side are you on?"

"Ernest, I'm trying to keep you out of jail."

I glared at him. "If I was the killer I wouldn't hand over the murder weapon with my fingerprints all over it, now would I?"

"You have a point there. But what if the bottle isn't poisoned? What if Elsie died of a medical condition?"

I rubbed my eyes, suddenly aware of my fatigue. Too much excitement and too little sleep. "I'm exhausted, Marshall. Let me sleep on it. Maybe I can see things more clearly in the morning."

"Do you still want to run lines?"

"No, forget it. I'll just have another stack of revisions in the morning."

"I still think you should talk to the police. If there's a killer running loose, you're not safe. Don't play the hero."

"Yes, Marshall."

I walked Marshall to the front door and we bid our

goodbyes. He assured me he'd attend the Friday night taping. At least I'd have one friendly face to root me on. After he left I stuck our coffee cups and saucers in the dishwasher and opened a bottle of O'Doul's. I snapped off the kitchen light, and settled in the recliner to look over my lines. But after reading the same paragraph four times I realized I couldn't concentrate, and I tossed the script onto the coffee table. The pages skidded to a halt beside the contents of Elsie's purse, still strewn about. I moved to the sofa and shifted through the contents. I set aside her billfold, address book and a small spiral-bound notebook. I fetched a pair of rubber gloves and a plastic baggie from the laundry room. With my hands protected from any stray cyanide I carefully placed the bottle of eye drops into the baggie and sealed it. Whew! I washed the gloves and my hands again (can't be too careful) before returning the gloves to the cabinet. I placed the bagged eye drops on the kitchen island where I'd see it in the morning.

I sat on the sofa and searched Elsie's billfold, a bright pink number in glossy vinyl (what is it with women and the color pink?) filled with cash, credit cards, SAG card, health insurance card, car registration—nothing suspicious. I thumbed through the address book and the various listings for casting and temp agencies as well as names that looked like friends or family. One entry jumped out: L. Consty. Leo Constantine? The phone number had a 310 area code. The area code for Hollywood is 323, so the number wasn't Leo's studio phone. Beverly Hills and Westwood share the 310 area code. Why would a minor B-list actress have the private home number of a studio boss?

I sat back and stared at Elsie's stuff. What was I doing, going through a dead woman's purse? Why was

I eager to look for a killer ruthless enough to spike a bottle of eye drops? Marshall was right; I should let the cops handle this. But Hollywood was full of unsolved murders and I didn't completely trust the police. Besides, with my presence on the show I had an inside track and if I could find a clue to help the investigation, so much the better.

I thumbed through the wide-ruled pages of the notebook and tried to read the childish scrawl—large, loopy letters adorned with flowers and smiley faces drawn in various ink colors. After reading a few entries, I deduced that Elsie had used this pad to record her jumbled thoughts. Maybe the scribbling helped her make sense of the world. Some pages had questions ("Go with a darker eyeliner?") or observations ("Mrs. Jones—so mean today!") or emotions ("Bombed the audition. Feel like dirt!" along with a frowny face). Maybe she did have mental issues, as Troy had suggested. The boyfriend himself was mentioned numerous times along with kissy-marks. Three-quarters into the book I found her last entry, dated last week. She had written the letters "YT" in purple ink with a huge red "X" over them. At the bottom of the page was the note, "OMG!!! Tell Snooky Doodle!" Who or what was "YT" and "Snooky Doodle?" How do I find out without telling people that I was reading a dead woman's private diary?

When I'm confused I turn to the one thing that calms me down: music. My dance scene was set for tomorrow morning and I needed to practice. I set the memo pad aside, put on my dance shoes, and took Cinnamon's cassette tape and my portable tape player to my poolside patio where I could practice without stumbling into the furniture. I turned on the patio light and pushed the wrought iron table and chairs out of the way. I turned on the tape player and beneath the clear night sky I walked through the steps until I was too tired to go on. I took the tape player inside the house, turned off the outside lights and set the house burglar alarm before I trudged upstairs to my bedroom. One thing about amateur sleuthing—it's tiring.

*****

The next morning found me seated in an office at the Hollywood Community Police Station on Wilcox Avenue. When I told the person at the front desk that I had information about Elsie's Bloom death, she told me to wait in this room. After several minutes of cooling my heels I desperately craved a stiff drink. Stress had triggered much of my drinking and I yearned for a cold one now to calm my nerves.

"Sorry to keep you waiting. I was told you wanted to see me about a possible murder?"

A middle-aged, stocky Latino with short brown hair entered the room. He was carrying a cup of steaming hot, aromatic coffee that he didn't offer to me; instead, he drank it in front of me. This is known as cruel and unusual punishment. He wore civilian clothes instead of a cop uniform. Both of us registered shock as we recognized the other. The man's face broke out in a devilish grin; I wanted to hide under the table.

"Ernest Farmington. I'm surprised to see you. Been keeping out of trouble?"

"I didn't know you worked on murder cases, Officer—" I knew the face but couldn't recall his name.

"Detective Miguel Hernandez. I was promoted and transferred not long after our encounter."

Some encounter. Late one night two years ago, I ended up drunk and angry in a cheap bar somewhere in Reseda (I still can't remember why I went there or how I'd arrived). Some creep recognized me and started tossing insults at me. I responded by throwing punches back at him. The bartender called the fuzz. Hernandez and half the LAPD force stormed in just as I was breaking a chair over the punk's head. Hernandez ordered me to stop and when I didn't, he grabbed me, slammed me face first into the bar, yanked my hands behind my back and cuffed my wrists. All the while my face was bleeding from where my taunter had sliced my left cheek with a broken beer bottle (I still have a faint scar from the cut). After Hernandez hauled me outside, the paparazzi snapped shots of me with beer and blood running down my face. I was booked under my legal name but the press still had fun with headlines like "TV's Boy Sleuth Busted By Real Cop."

"Do you still rough people up when you arrest them? You broke my nose when you smacked me into that bar counter."

"As I recall, Mr. Farmington, you were not cooperating. You're pretty riled up when you're drunk."

"I don't drink any more."

"I'm happy to hear that. Now how may I help you?"

For the third time in as many days, I repeated the tale of how Elsie had met her Maker. I explained my suspicions about poison and presented the bottle of eye drops, still sealed in the baggie. Throughout my story, Hernandez's facial expression alternated between skepticism and amusement. After I finished talking, I sank back into my chair and stared at the coffee cup, hoping Hernandez would take the hint and offer me some. He didn't.

"Mr. Farmington, a few weeks ago in the Midwest, a murder victim died in your arms."

I sat up in the chair. "You know about that?"

"You're a celebrity and word gets around. Now don't you think it's strange that within a month, a second person dies in your presence under mysterious circumstances?"

"I didn't kill Elsie Bloom! Or the other person!"

"Calm down, Mr. Farmington. You're not a suspect." He left the word *yet* unspoken but hanging in the air. He picked up the corner of the baggie and eyed the bottle, clearly humoring me.

"And you say Ms. Bloom was killed by this bottle of eye drops?"

"Go ahead, have your lab boys analyze it. If it has cyanide in it, you'll know I'm right."

"What if it doesn't?"

For a moment I was confounded. I hadn't considered that. What if my overactive imagination, fueled by watching too many TV mysteries, was simply out of control?

"But it has to. That's the only explanation that makes sense."

"Do you have any other evidence that might indicate murder?"

"No, but don't you think it's strange that a healthy young woman just up and dies for no reason?"

"People always die for a reason, but most of the time it's not from murder. We'll know more after the autopsy."

"When's that going to be?"

"I don't know. The coroner's office won't contact us unless the findings look suspicious. Tell you what, Mr. Farmington, we'll check out this bottle and see what's in it. If we have a case, we'll let you know."

"You're not going to lose that, are you? I've heard about the police tampering with evidence or misplacing it or—"

"We don't ruin evidence. The LAPD is not like what you see on TV shows. Especially not *your* show."

Now I was furious. How dare he criticize *Buddy Brave*! I stood. "Thanks for your time," I said with as much irony as I could muster. I headed for the door.

"Mr. Farmington." I stopped and turned. His next sentence sounded more like a warning than a question. "You're not thinking of playing detective and investigating Ms. Bloom's death on your own, are you?"

"Of course not. Buddy Brave is just a TV character. He isn't real."

I made sure I slammed the door on my way out.

WEDNESDAY: PRESHOOT
Chapter 13: Dancing Fool

Not every scene in a sitcom is performed live on taping night. Parts of the script that require special effects or might be dangerous to create in front of an audience, such as the use of smoke or fire, are shot ahead of time and then played back over the monitors Friday night so the audience can follow the story and (hopefully) provide laughter for the audio track. Outdoor scenes are preshot as well. On Wednesday morning, my big dance number was scheduled for filming on the back lot. Personally, I was glad to get the complex routine in the can so I'd have one less thing to worry about on Friday night.

After I left the police station I headed for the studio. Since I had an errand to run after work today, I drove the Mustang. I parked the convertible in a lot close to the back lot and walked to the shooting area, carrying my gym bag. I had no trouble finding the spot—the one street of the brownstone facades that bustled with people and activity. The crew had moved in potted trees and fake lampposts and also painted store names on the windows to give the illusion of a real city street. Despite the sunshine, the lighting guys had set up spotlights to ensure even lighting. Silver-coated umbrella-shaped reflectors aimed the light at the right places. My dressing trailer had been towed and parked next to the site. I've always been amazed at the huge amount of work the crews put in ahead of time to make sure everything is ready on time for the actors.

Beside my trailer stood a wheeled clothes rack that held three sets of my costume in case the clothes were damaged during filming. I took one hanger off the rack and changed inside the trailer. I put on my dance shoes and I was ready to go. Thanks to the alternations, the navy suit fit well, with enough "give" so I could dance without worrying about the pants ripping (Tight pants are sexy but not good for movement. During a concert early in my touring career, the backside of my pants burst open in midsong. I finished the song quickly and hurried offstage—making sure I didn't turn my back to the audience—for an unexpected costume change. From then on, the costume mistress used stronger material for my show pants).

Soon as I stepped out of the trailer the makeup gal grabbed me and stuck me into a canvas chair beside a table with a lighted mirror. She tucked a paper collar around my neck and then cleaned my face with a cotton square moistened with astringent. She applied foundation with a small sponge; fair-skinned people like myself wash out under the camera lights. She used a concealer to hide the scar on my cheek. Sitting in the chair gave me a chance to gobble some breakfast (A PA brought me orange juice and a bagel with cream cheese from craft services) and to think about the Elsie's death. I had a feeling that Hernandez would dismiss my suspicions. If Elsie had been a bigger star, the detective might have shown more interest. The gal brushed my light eyebrows and slightly darkened them with a pencil. She "set" my face with powder and carefully removed the paper collar. The hair stylist combed my hair and retied my ponytail. I studied the results in the mirror. Wow, I looked good! I thanked both the ladies for their work.

The costume mistress handed me the fedora. She'd stuck some double-sided tape inside the brim to make sure the headgear didn't fly off in mid-step. In one *Buddy Brave* episode I had a cap taped on my head during a scene in which I hung upside down from a rope tied around my ankles (when someone tells me they feel like they're at the end of their rope, I can honestly say I've been there). Unfortunately, someone had put too much tape inside the hat and when we finished shooting I had to use every means short of a crowbar to remove that stupid cap.

I made my way to the end of the street. Royce met me with a bullhorn in hand. We hadn't started the first shot of the day and he already looked more frazzled than usual. He grabbed my arm and pulled me aside, out of earshot of the crew.

"Leo Constantine isn't happy today," he said.

"That isn't news."

"A cop from the LAPD called him this morning about Elsie Bloom."

Apparently the early morning visit to my former nemesis had paid off. "So?"

From behind his sunglasses the director's eyes narrowed. "Leo also told me that you've been harassing people about the girl."

"Get this straight, Royce. I don't harass people and even if I did it's none of Leo's business who I talk to. If he has a problem he can talk to me directly.

"Leo isn't happy about your wild accusations."

"Accusations? I have evidence that Elsie didn't die of natural causes." I was bluffing, but I wanted to see Royce's reaction.

For a second he looked worried. "What sort of evidence?"

"I turned it over to the police."

Before we could continue this intriguing conversation, the cinematographer announced that everything was set up and ready to go.

Royce gave me the evil eye and then reverted to his normal I'm-in-charge persona and yelled at the crew though the bullhorn. He showed me where to stand and where I would end the dance sequence. The scene had no dialogue, so the sound guys hadn't rigged up a microphone (even if they had, chances were I'd have to re-record the lines later in a sound booth. Outdoor mics picked up too much ambient noise). Speakers for the music lined the street out of camera range. Down the center of the street ran a miniature railroad track for the camera dolly. A crew guy stood by to push the dolly as the camera followed me. We did a walk-through for me to get a feel for the space and so the camera guy could practice moving with me. I danced down the length of the sidewalk to the corner where a fake lamppost stood. At the end of the number I jumped onto the base of the post, grabbed the column, held up my arm, and struck a pose.

Royce called for a rehearsal with the music. As the camera reset to the beginning of the track, Cinnamon called my name and ran to me. I hadn't seen her before, but with all the people milling around, it's easy to miss someone.

"Don't you look handsome in that suit!" she said.

"You're looking pretty good yourself."

She wore a loose fitting sweatshirt and sweat pants (I assumed she had on a leotard and tights underneath although I couldn't see. I struggled to keep from thinking about what else was underneath those baggy clothes). Even without makeup she looked gorgeous.

"Now that I see how the routine looks, I have a couple of changes I'd like to make." She looked at Royce. "Do we have time?"

He agreed and went off to shout at someone while Cinnamon smoothed out a couple of difficult areas. What works inside a controlled environment like a rehearsal hall often doesn't carry over to the actual dance surface, like an uneven sidewalk. Her off-the-cuff adjustments improved the sequence. After a couple of practices, I was ready to go. I returned to my starting position and Cinnamon stepped back behind the camera to watch.

When the crew reported in ready, Royce announced, "Playback and action!"

The music blared from the speakers, louder than I expected. I hopped to it, so to speak, dancing down the street with the camera rolling along in tandem. During the second rehearsal I felt confident—and sweaty. If we didn't finish this scene soon, I'd have to change into a clean costume. At the end of the scene I leaped on the lamppost. Even thought Royce stood only a few feet from me, he still used the bullhorn.

"Hold that pose, Sandy, until the rain stops."

I dropped my raised hand and stared at him. "Rain?"

He lowered the bullhorn. "Yes, Sandy, rain. The dance is a parody of 'Singin' in the Rain.' We can't do the song without rain."

"That means I'm going to get wet?"

"That's right."

Overhead a metal pipe that ran the length of the street provided rain and snow effects. Working with effects usually didn't bother me. On *Buddy Brave* I was nearly drowned in a flood, burned by the sun, frozen in a blizzard, and swept away by a tornado, but when I signed the *Off-Kelter* contract nobody had warned me about rain. My agent should have asked for more money.

I jumped off the lamppost and the makeup gal dabbed the sweat off my face. As the camera was moving back into place, I spotted a tour group huddled behind some wooden sawhorses set up at the end of the street. Among the tourists was Bunny, with a huge smile on her face. I didn't mind the guests. I work better with an audience, and I couldn't disappoint my biggest fan.

"This is a take!" Royce hollered through the bullhorn. "Playback and action!"

This time I gave a flawless performance as I tripped the light fantastic down the sidewalk. At the end of the number, I leaped onto the lamppost, threw my head back, flashed that famous thousand-watt smile—and was drenched. I expected a gentle mist but apparently the rain machine was set for "typhoon." The water gushed down by the gallon, saturating my suit and permeating every pore. And this wasn't clean water, either—or warm. The studio wasn't about to spend money to heat water for an effect. Out of the corner of my eye, I saw Royce standing safely outside the downpour. He kept the camera rolling forever just to make me suffer. But I wasn't about to give him the satisfaction of a retake. As the deluge fell I kept the smile frozen on my face and my eyes open as much as I could. What a trouper. Some of the water fell into my mouth, nearly choking me. My grip was slipping on the slick lamppost. If I fell, I'd crack open my skull on the cement sidewalk. My muscles started to cramp. I could barely breath under the heavy downpour.

"Cut!"

I stumbled off the lamppost and ran to safety outside the area of the rainfall. I wiped the water out of my eyes and coughed up the vile-tasting stuff. In spite of the warm SoCal sun I shivered. Water ran down my face and ponytail. A group of women swiftly surrounded me. One gal stripped the soggy jacket off my back. The second pried the hat off my wet head, taking a couple of chunks of hair along with it. The costume mistress helped me into a black fleece bathrobe. As I tied the robe's belt, a PA handed me a large white towel. As I wiped my face with the towel, the camera crew applauded. These guys have seen everything, so when they like a performance you know you've done a good job. I gave them a nod of appreciation. The tour group also clapped, and I waved at them. But I wasn't happy when I slogged over to Royce, leaving a trail of wet footprints.

I draped the towel over my wet hair. "What are you trying to do, Royce, kill me?"

"What's the matter, can't you stand a little rain?" he said.

"Rain! That was a friggin' hurricane!"

"Get cleaned up. We're doing another take."

"That take was perfect and you know it!"

"We need the coverage in case the film's bad."

"You just want another chance to drown me!"

He frowned. "Drown you? Don't be ridiculous."

"If you want another take, get a stunt double."

Royce raised the bullhorn and called to the camera operator, "Did you catch all of that?" The guy gave him a thumbs up. Royce glared at me. "All right, I'll let you go. But get changed immediately and report for rehearsal. At four o'clock we have a full run-through for the network brass. And if this footage turns out bad, I'm hauling your butt back here at midnight for a reshoot."

"You're all heart, Royce."

The big guy announced to the crew, "That's a wrap."

The crew immediately started hauling off the fake trees, removing the film reel for processing, and dismantling the camera track. These guys worked faster than NASCAR pit technicians. I asked a PA to bring Bunny over so we could talk. As the gofer walked off, so did Cinnamon. I called to her but she kept going. Didn't she hear me? Was she ignoring me? I wanted to run after her, but not dressed in a bathrobe and dripping water. With the dance scene wrapped up, I had no more excuses to see her in the practice room. Then the PA showed up with Bunny in tow and left us so we could talk.

Bunny was so excited I was afraid she'd faint at my feet. "Sandy! I loved that dance! That was super spectacular! Is that going to be on the show?"

"Yes, you'll see the footage at the taping." I removed the towel from my head and shook the water out of my ear. "I feel like I just shot a scene from *The Poseidon Adventure*. Bunny, what are you doing here? You keep popping up wherever I look."

"Charlotte, that's the page," she pointed to a uniformed woman standing behind the sawhorses, "found out you were shooting this morning so I had to come and watch."

"I thought you were going sightseeing today."

"This was way better than Universal City! Besides, I have that information you asked for."

Before Bunny could share her knowledge, Royce interrupted. He told me to stop the chatter and get my tail back to the soundstage (or words to that effect).

After he left, I said to Bunny, "I need to get to rehearsal. Can you come back and we'll talk this afternoon?"

"Sure, Sandy, no problem."

"And here's something you can do for me in the meantime. Find out what you can about a choreographer named Cinnamon Love."

"Why do you want to know about her?"

"No reason."

Bunny rejoined Charlotte as I retreated to my trailer. I shed the clammy clothes and warmed up with a hot shower. I dried off, changed into my street clothes, and left the wet costume on the trailer floor for wardrobe to collect and clean. A PA drove me to Stage 14 where the

AD had been rehearsing the other actors. I'd worked up an appetite dancing so I headed to the craft services table for a calorie-loaded pick-me-up. Despite my diet, I was going to eat whatever looked good. At the edge of the table sat a pan of yummy-looking brownies baked to perfection. It was about time my favorite snack appeared on the scene. I grabbed a plastic fork and dug out a square. I held the brownie between my fingers and prepared my taste buds for a moment of pleasure. But as I brought the goodie to my mouth, I noticed a peculiar odor.

"Hey!" I yelled at anybody within range. "Who brought in these hash brownies?"

Chapter 14: Inside Out

Carl hurried toward me. "What's the commotion, Sandy?"

I placed the offensive brownie on a paper plate and shoved it in his face. "This brownie is loaded with pot!"

"That's not true. We'd never serve anything like that." The craft services attendant looked worried.

"I've eaten enough of these babies to know what I'm talking about."

"I didn't bring in that pan. I saw it there a few minutes ago when I came back from the bathroom, but I assumed it came from the cast or crew. You know, people are always bringing in treats for birthdays or anniversaries. I swear I don't know anything about it."

I believed him. These guys are pros and rely on word-of-mouth for business. Something like this, even as a joke, would get them banned from most shows. I asked the crowd standing around if anyone had seen the brownies.

Harv said, "I was the first one here this morning. I didn't see the pan when I arrived."

"Maybe you missed it?" Carl asked.

"I don't see how. I toasted some cinnamon bread and if the brownies had been there I'd have had to reach over them"—he demonstrated—"to get the butter. I'd have seen it."

The others present denied bringing in the pot brownies, so either they were all innocent or excellent liars. Nobody recalled seeing any strangers loitering around the set that morning, but that didn't mean much.

The craft services table was tucked behind the set and a person could easily sneak in through the unlocked stage door while the cast and crew were busy on stage.

The attendant covered the pan with some clear cling wrap. "I'm sorry, Sandy. I'll dispose of this."

"I think you should take it to security."

Carl looked at me quizzically. "Why?"

I'm sure whoever cooked up the pot brownies wanted to render me too sick to continue my investigation. My love of sweets was no secret. But with Leo and Royce annoyed at my sleuthing—and both in a position to end my career—I figured I'd better keep quiet about my suspicions.

"Never mind. Maybe it's just a prank and someone delivered it to the wrong stage."

As the attendant left with the suspicious brownies (I hoped he wasn't planning to take the tainted treats home for himself), Carl called for an early lunch break. I asked Harv if he had plans for lunch and, fortunately, he was free to join me.

"Before we go, Harv, I have a favor to ask. Can I use your phone? My trailer doesn't have one."

"Sure, no problem. Just dial 'nine' for an outside line."

He chatted with Dottie as I made my way to my former haunt, now in use as Harv's dressing room. The place looked much the same as when I called this room home except for the new furniture, new wall paint and a pushbutton phone instead of a black rotary. I found the spot where I had carved my name in the door mantel, my attempt at posterity. If these walls could talk, I'd rather keep some of the stories unspoken. When I shot the *Buddy Brave* pilot I was a hot-blooded eighteen-year-old overwhelmed by instant fame and wealth. So many beautiful women passed through my dressing room that the crew nicknamed me "Randy Sandy." I didn't snoop in Harv's things, as I had no reason to suspect America's most loveable dad of any dark deeds. I punched "nine" and Becka's number into the phone pad and waited. A man's voice answered. My stomach twisted into a knot.

"Hello, Franklin, it's Ernest. Is Becka there?'

"I'll see if she's available."

My encounters with my ex's husband had been, thankfully, infrequent. He worked in show biz as a lawyer in the unglamorous world of movie contracts and legal clearances. He didn't hobnob with celebrities or attend big shindigs, which suited Becka just fine. She'd had more than enough wild parties during our marriage. Franklin was a dull man but a decent stepfather who treated my kids well, for which I was grateful. During my visits to their house he stayed out of my way but made it clear I wasn't welcomed.

After an agonizingly long pause, Becka finally came on the line. "Yes, Ernest?"

"Let me guess. This time I'm interrupting your lunch instead of dinner."

"No, Franklin and I are busy with the interior designer."

"What designer?"

"We're fixing up the kids' rooms. They're growing up and they don't want unicorns and space ships on the walls anymore."

When did my kids grow up? Did I miss something? "I hope you're not going to throw out the things I gave them. What about that big stuffed unicorn Robin keeps on her bed? You're going to keep that, right?"

"Of course we'll keep it, but we're putting some of their things in the attic."

"If you're going to hide it to where they can't find it, you might as well toss it."

"Ernest, this isn't about you personally. The kids are

getting older. They have other interests now."

"You shouldn't get rid of their toys. They might still want to play with them."

Translation: The next time I visit *I* might want to play Unicorn Hunter and Spaceman. I wasn't ready for my kids to desert their dear old dad for prom dates and soccer leagues.

Becka gave an exasperated sigh, not a good sign. "Did you want something?"

"I have an idea about Friday night. I know Robin has her recital, but what's Chip doing? I can't image he wants to watch his sister dance."

"No, Chip isn't going to the recital."

"So why can't Chip come by himself to see my show? Marshall can pick him up and take him home so Franklin doesn't have to drive into town."

"Chip's going to a movie with his friends."

"He can hang out with his buddies any time. He needs to spend time with his dad. Let me speak with him."

"He's in school right now."

I knew that. I don't think straight when I'm angry. "Tell him to change his plans."

"I can *ask* him but I'm not going to *tell* him."

"What kind of mother are you if you can't control your kids?"

I shouldn't have said that. The coldness in Becka's voice nearly froze the phone line. "I really have to go now. The designer's waiting."

"Promise me you'll ask Chip about Friday?"

"All right." She didn't sound convincing.

"It'd mean the world to me if he came to the show."

"Bye, Ernest." She hung up before I got in another word.

I've never understood women. I thought my sobriety would improve my relationship with Becka, but ironically drying out only seemed to make matters worse. Since she'd taken care of the kids for so many years, now that I wanted more involvement, she wasn't ready to share the load. But I couldn't keep Harv waiting while I wallowed in my problems, so I put the phone call out of my mind and met my fellow actor outside the stage door. Harv was chatting with Troy, the Gorgandian. I said hello to Troy; with the alien makeup I couldn't read his expression.

"Hi, how are you doing?" he replied. He didn't sound angry. Maybe Troy had forgotten about our talk yesterday.

Harv commandeered one of the show carts and drove us to the commissary. We bypassed the cafeteria line for the executive dining room in the rear of the building. The feeding grounds for the exclusive hadn't been remodeled since it was build in the 1930s. I'd eaten in here a few times when the time came to renew my contract for each season of *Buddy Brave*. Jarvis dragged me here to wine and dine the network suits before he began negotiations. At the time, I thought the room and the company were both stuffy and unbearable, but today, under more relaxed circumstances, the place didn't seem as threatening. Still, the dark paneled walls and mahogany furniture reeked of power and prestige. Framed portraits of the past Mammoth studio chiefs lined the walls so the old guard could peer down on their successors. Unlike the noisy cafeteria, in this room the mostly older male diners hunched over their china plates and conversed in low tones. As Harv and I passed by the tables, Ivan Constantine glanced up from his linguini long enough to shoot me a dirty look. We sat in a padded booth along a back wall and a waiter brought us leather-bound menus and water glasses. Certainly a lot of pomp for a mere French dip roast beef sandwich, potato salad, cherry pie and large Mountain Dew. Harv ordered the same, substituting Diet Coke for his drink.

"Great minds think alike," I joked.

"It's a quirk of mine," Harv said. "Whenever I eat out, I always order the same as my dining partner. Otherwise I spend the whole time thinking that their food looks better than mine."

"What if they order something you don't like?"

"I'll eat anything. I learned to make do during my years as a starving actor. Back then I mooched a ton of meals off friends."

"I'm sure you didn't have to beg for meals during *Anyone Home*?"

"No. That's when people mooched off *me*."

I had the same problem during my days of fame, of strangers emerging from the woodwork to claim they were my best friend in third grade and in need of a handout. We discussed our common experiences until the waiter brought our food and set the china dishes and metal cutlery on the white tablecloth. We placed cloth napkins on our laps and tucked into our meals. I cut up my sandwich into bite-sized pieces. The French bread and the piled-high meat oozed with too much beef juice to pick up—just the way I liked it. As we ate, I eased the conversation toward a certain topic.

"Did you know Elsie Bloom well?"

"Well enough to know what kind of person she was."

"Which was?"

"A scumbag."

"What about that nice tribute you gave her on the Channel Seven news?"

"Oh, that." Harv removed the paper cover from the end of the straw and sipped his soda. "That was just Hollywood talk. I won't bash another actor in public. Not good for the image. You know how that goes."

I finished my potato salad and launched my next attack. "During the Monday read through, I heard Elsie say she had a secret about you."

Harv shot me a look of sheer terror, then ducked his head and crammed a couple of bites of sandwich into his mouth. After he chewed and swallowed he glared at me.

"What about it?"

"Sounded like blackmail to me."

"She's dead now so it doesn't matter."

"I don't mean to pry—"of course I did—"but are you in some kind of trouble?"

"No, not at all." Harv worked intently on his food.

"Why would Elsie be threatening you? Were you one of her lovers?"

His face reddened. "No," he said emphatically. "We were never lovers."

"What, a beautiful woman like that? The way she flirted with everyone? You never went out with her even once?"

He glanced around to make sure nobody was listening. Harv took a deep breath, leaned over the table, and whispered, "I don't date women."

If the back wall of the booth hadn't been supporting me, I would have fallen over in astonishment. "You're gay?"

"Shut up!" Harv moved his hands up and down in a "keep it down" gesture.

I looked around. The guests at the other tables were still engaged in their own conversations, so apparently no one had heard us.

"You're gay?" I repeated softly.

He nodded and took another sip of his soda. "You probably know I was married to Susan for a while but we both figured out pretty quickly that wasn't going to work out. I figured out who I really was and she respected me enough not to blab to the media. We get along better as friends than spouses. As for my love life, let's just say there's a bar in West Hollywood that's very discreet about my business. You're shocked, aren't you?"

"I have nothing against gays, it's just that I never expected—"

"—that America's most lovable dad batted for the other team, right? I'm not ashamed of who I am but I don't need to plaster it on a billboard."

"Don't you feel you're being dishonest with your fans?"

"We're actors, Sandy. We give people the image that they want to see. Hollywood is all about fantasy. When I'm working, I'm the All-American, traditional daddy. When I'm off the clock, I love men. I'm quiet about it and I'm not hurting anyone."

"I take it nobody in the cast knows."

He nodded. "The only reason Elsie found out was that she slept with one of my former acquaintances. That loudmouth moron told her about me and ever since she's used it as leverage to get whatever she wanted on the show."

"Why didn't you call her bluff? Plenty of actors have come out."

He finished eating and pushed his plate away. "As they say in the business, Sandy, timing is everything. I'm not ready for the backlash, and I'm not interested in crusading for a cause. Maybe I will when I'm old and gray and retired. Certainly not while I'm the spokesman for the American Family Foundation."

"No doubt they pay you a good honorarium."

"Yes, they do, but this isn't about the money. I love the foundation. They do good work and they're wonderful people. My contract with them is up in three years. I plan to bow out gracefully at that time. I'd rather leave with dignity than have the foundation drop me like a leper."

I finished the last of my pie. "I guess your secret's safe now that Elsie's gone."

He eyed me. "But you know."

"Let me assure you, Harv, you have nothing to worry about. What you do for recreation is none of my business."

He sat back and his shoulders sagged in relief. "Thanks, Sandy. I appreciate that."

The waiter showed up with our bills (the studio should be arrested for what it charged for a sandwich and a soda). Harv offered to pick up my tab and in return I insisted on covering the tip. He signed off on the receipts while I dug some bills from my wallet. After the waiter left, Harv rested his forearms on the table and leaned toward me.

"Can I tell you something, Sandy?"

I tucked my wallet back into my pants pocket. "Sure, what is it?"

"When I was a boy, I had a terrible crush on you. Does that embarrass you?"

"No. I appreciate the support of all my fans."

His hand started creeping across the table toward me.

I added with a smile, "But I only date women."

He pulled his hand back, cleared his throat, and spoke in a loud, jovial voice. "We'd better get back to the set. Gotta be ready for the network guys at four, right, Sandy?"

Harv seemed happy as he drove the cart back to Stage 14, perhaps feeling better for having shared his secret with someone. On the way, he jabbered about an upcoming audition for a father role in a movie by a major family-oriented film company. I wasn't listening. I couldn't help thinking that he had an excellent motive for killing Elsie.

In a few minutes I'd learn that Harv wasn't the only one who hated the deceased actress.

Chapter 15: Remember

At Stage 14 the stagehands were scrambling to finish the swing sets as the lighting guys adjusted the Fresnel spots overhead and the set decorator put up the various curtains, photos and knickknacks that made the fake walls look like real rooms. Royce was in his usual blither about something but he wasn't angry with me, so I was content. Frances brought in Scruffy. The dog sat on his haunches as I chatted with his owner.

"It's a shame about Elsie, isn't it?" Frankly, I was getting sick of that line, but it seemed like a good conversation starter.

"No, not at all," the trainer shot back.

"Why's that?"

"She hated Scruffy. She teased him until he turned angry. One day she kicked him. I told her I'd call the Humane Society and she just laughed at me."

"Why didn't you call?"

She hesitated before answering. "Work is hard to find. The producers are scared of lawsuits if an animal is hurt. More studios are using special effects instead of real creatures."

"I'm sorry to hear that."

"But the other actors are nice to Scruffy. I will like working on the show with Elsie gone."

The AD told me I had some visitors. My scene wasn't up for a while so I went outside to meet my guests: Bunny, along with Charlotte, still in her page uniform. Bunny introduced us and I shook the woman's hand.

"Nice to meet you, Charlotte. I'm glad you're taking good care of Bunny this week."

"Hi, Sandy."

Charlotte gazed at me with big brown puppy eyes and nearly melted into a puddle. I have that effect on fans. Before she fainted, I suggested we sit around the plastic table, which we did, with Bunny to my right and Charlotte beside her.

"Now, what can I do for you ladies?"

"We got some information for you." Bunny nudged her friend. "Tell Sandy what you told me."

"There's rumors that the studio might close," said Charlotte.

"That's hardly news," I replied. "That tale was going around back when I worked here. Mammoth's always been one picture away from bankruptcy. I think the suits say that just to keep everyone scared and working harder."

"This time it's serious. In the last couple of months a bunch of employees sent out their resumes and some of the older ones took early retirement so they wouldn't lose their pensions."

"Has Leo—Mr. Constantine—said anything about selling? Has anyone asked him directly?"

"The company newsletter says things are great."

"That's not surprising. Leo would insist that the Titanic was watertight even as it was going down." A lowly page wouldn't know about the closed-door inner workings of the executive suite, so I changed the topic. "Do the letters 'YT' mean anything to you? Maybe a person?"

This time Bunny answered. "Leo Constantine's first wife was named Yolanda Torres."

"No, she wasn't," I said. "He was married to Linda Thomas. Back in '78 or so, I met her at a studio holiday party."

"That wasn't her real name." Bunny pulled a fat hardcover book from the depths of her Yellow Submarine tote bag. "I read about it in here. After the studio tour on Monday I bought this at Larry Edmunds."

She had named a well-known bookstore in Hollywood that specialized in movie posters and film books, a cineophile's dream spot. The book was titled *Mammoth: Big Scandals at a Small Studio*. The author was an entertainment journalist known for dishing out celebrity secrets. I took the book and skimmed through the pages

"So that's the book!" Charlotte exclaimed. "The tour guests ask about it all the time but the studio store doesn't sell it."

"I can see why," I said. "This writer doesn't say one nice word about Mammoth."

"Last night I skipped ahead and read the chapter about the Constantines." Bunny sounded eager to impart her knowledge to me. "Yolanda grew up in Madrid. Leo met her when he was in Spain on business. When Leo brought her to American he told her to change her name so people wouldn't know she was Spanish. Yolanda died when she and Leo were on vacation in Spain. He buried her over there 'cause Leo said she wanted to be laid to rest in her hometown. The writer of the book thinks Leo didn't bring back the body to America 'cause he was hiding something."

"Like maybe Yolanda didn't die of natural causes?" I suggested.

"The book says Leo and Yolanda didn't get along. He had an affair while they were still married. Soon as Leo got back from Spain, he and his mistress got hitched."

"That must be the current Mrs. Constantine."

"So Mr. Constantine maybe killed his first wife so

he could marry someone else?" Charlotte asked.

Bunny nodded. "That's what the book says."

"Didn't the cops investigate the death?" I asked.

"The Spanish police didn't find anything suspicious," Bunny said.

"Smart move on Leo's part," I commented. "If Leo intended to bump off his wife, he'd do so in a place where the LAPD couldn't nose around. So it's possible that Elsie found proof that Leo killed his first wife, or arranged to have her killed, and she threatened to blackmail him with the information." Maybe the letter I had found in Elsie's dressing room was referring to Leo or his goon squad.

"How would Mr. Constantine know what Elsie knew?" Charlotte asked.

"She had his home phone number and maybe she called him. Charlotte, do you know if Leo has other children besides Ivan? Maybe some from other lovers?"

"I haven't heard of any other children," Charlotte added. "But Mr. Constantine doesn't talk about his family."

Bunny interjected, "The book says he did, but didn't give any names."

I asked the page if any employees on the lot went by the nickname of Snooky Doodle. She replied in the negative, but added that Mammoth was a big lot and she didn't know everyone.

"Should we tell the police about Yolanda?" Bunny said.

"Not a chance," I said. "We have no evidence, just wild guesses."

Charlotte said, "Sandy, I almost forgot, I found someone who knows Cinnamon Love."

"What did they say?" I tried not to sound too eager.

"They said she runs a dance studio in Northridge. That's how she supports herself between dancing jobs.

She dances in a lot of music videos. She's divorced and she's a really nice person."

What a coincidence. Northridge was an easy jaunt from my home in the Hollywood Hills.

Carl came to fetch me for rehearsal, just when things were getting interesting.

"Before you go, Sandy," Bunny blurted, "I want you to look at this." She pulled a sketchbook from her tote bag (did she have an entire library tucked inside that satchel?), flipped open the cardboard cover and showed me a page. "I drew this over lunch today."

I took the pad in hand. The page had a pencil sketch of me, in costume, doing my morning rain dance on the back lot. I'd seen Bunny's artwork before, but the quality of this quick sketch amazed me.

"Bunny, this is great. You've improved. You've been taking an art class, haven't you?"

"Yeah, like you told me to, and I love it. I'm putting this drawing in my next club newsletter."

Carl was standing by my elbow, tapping his foot, so I returned the sketchpad to Bunny and thanked the ladies for their information. Charlotte and Bunny left for the front gate while Carl and I entered the soundstage. The set was a hive of activity, preparing for the producers' run-through. The front row bleacher seats held enough suits to start a haberdashery shop. The Constantine dynamic duo was present as well. Leo glanced in my direction, frowned and looked away. Did he suspect that I knew his dirty little secrets, or was he miffed that he was sitting in these bleachers instead of perched on a barstool at a swanky club?

Royce passed me enroute to his director's chair. "Glad to see you finally decided to join us, Fairfax."

"Royce, I wouldn't miss the pleasure of your company for all the world."

He shot me a sour look as he moved on. I

desperately hoped to find evidence that Royce was guilty of some kind of crime, even jaywalking. He'd look good in an orange jumpsuit.

I walked through the set to get my mind off murder and to focus on my work. In the living room I found slips of paper discreetly taped everywhere: on the back of the sofa, on the table beside the phone, atop the TV set. I leaned in for a closer look. The slips were dialogue cut from a script—Dottie's lines. I straightened up; the actress gave me a frightened look. I'd discovered her secret.

"Dottie, why don't you ask Royce for a teleprompter?"

She smiled coyly. "That's such a bother. I don't want to put anyone out."

"Other actors use teleprompters. It's nothing to be ashamed of."

"We never used such gadgets on the live stage. We recited our lines by heart every night."

I said gently, "Dottie, you're not a young ingénue in the theater any more."

She didn't take this observation well. She drew herself up and frowned. "I am an actress! I can still play a role. Just because I use a few memory tricks doesn't mean I should retire!"

"I never implied—"

She turned on her high heels and stormed off. I had suddenly come down with a bad case of foot-in-mouth disease.

The AD called for quiet on the set. Dottie got in position for Scene One in the kitchen, next to the counter that held one of her lifesaving paper slips. Royce and Carl sat in their respective chairs. The other actors took their places and Royce called for action. I sat in a folding chair off to the side. As much as I wanted to stroll around and find some answers about

Elsie and Yolanda, I didn't want to leave and miss my cue. Frances dabbed the liver pate' on my cheek for my kiss from Scruffy. First Royce tried to drown me on the back lot, and now a mutt would douse me with dog drool. There's no business like show business.

The run-through went okay, considering that Leo frequently interrupted with asinine remarks on how to improve the show. Considering that his studio was losing money and prestige over a dud like *Off-Kelter*, I wasn't surprised he was making some effort to plug the leaks on the sinking ship. On the other hand, Ivan, the show's producer, didn't seem to care. He was checking his Daytimer or reading papers from his attaché case. Maybe he wanted the show to fail. During tax season all the studios wrote off the costs of their biggest losers. Perhaps Ivan wanted *Off-Kelter* to fold quickly so he could move a more profitable show into the soundstage or so that the public would soon forget about Elsie Bloom.

I did decent work but not top of my game. It's hard to keep up one's energy during a comedy when the only sounds from the audience are coughs and pager beeps. Executives are notorious for their lack of humor but a few chuckles now and again would have been appreciated. After we finished the show, the suits left their thrones in the bleachers to mingle with the common folk.

One executive gushed as he pumped my hand. "Sandy Fairfax! I'm surprised to see you acting again. I thought you'd retired."

My response was to grin as if I was filming a toothpaste commercial. "No, I'm still in the game. I hope to do more acting in the near future." What a load of hooey. I'd rather sing for pennies on the street corner than get stuck on another show like this one.

After he dismissed the actors and crew, Royce

huddled with the suits. He chatted with Leo but I couldn't hear the conversation. Were they discussing the show—or murder?

As I headed for the door I felt a tug on my pant leg. "Hello, Joseph."

"Hello, yourself. We need to talk."

"About what?"

"About Elsie Bloom."

He looked serious. I doubted he was going to confess to the crime so I made the next plausible assumption. "Do you have some information about her?"

"Maybe." He glanced at the people milling around. "But we can't talk here. You got plans for dinner?"

"I do."

"Tell you what. Meet me tomorrow for a late brunch and we'll talk."

That sounded great. Thursday morning was scheduled for camera blocking, when the camera crew moved in and worked out the placement of their shots. Since this part of the rehearsal process was tedious and time consuming, stand-ins were used, giving the actors free time until the afternoon. The late call would provide a golden opportunity to talk with Joseph and to snoop around the lot as well. We agreed to meet at 10 a.m. at Canter's Deli, a popular restaurant among musicians and show biz folks in Mid-City along Fairfax Avenue. Joseph scooted off before I could quiz him further.

I headed for the parking lot where I'd left my car. Dottie stood at the edge of the lot, one hand shielding her eyes from the setting sun as she scanned the cars. She wore a light jacket and clutched her handbag tightly in the other hand. She looked worried.

"Hi, Dottie," I said. "Is something wrong?"

"Somebody stole my car!" She sounded hysterical.

"I parked right there"—she pointed—"and now it's gone. Somebody took it."

I didn't believe her. Security frequently patrolled the parking lots. Besides, a thief would take one of the Mercedes, not Dottie's old Caddy.

"Are you sure you parked in this lot?"

"Of course I did! I left it here, but now it looks different. Someone changed everything around while I was away!"

"Try to remember, Dottie. Are you certain this is the right lot?"

"No, wait. Maybe it was over there." Her hands fumbled with her purse handle. Her lower lip trembled.

I took her by the arms. "Take it easy, Dottie. Try to think. This morning when you parked, did you notice any landmarks? Were you close to a specific building?"

Her eyes were swollen with tears. "I don't know. I can't remember. I'm just a silly old woman."

"No, you're not. You just have a lot on your mind."

A tear slithered down her cheek. "I'm scared, Sandy. My mind is all muddy these days. What am I going to do?" She turned her face away. "What if I forget everything Friday night? All my blocking, my lines? If I couldn't act any more. . . ."

I took her hands in mine. "It's all right, Dottie. You're okay. You're just tired. Tell you what. Let me drive you home."

She looked at me; thin lines of mascara marred her pretty face. "What about my car?"

"It'll be safe on the lot. Security can look for it in the morning. Can somebody bring you to work tomorrow?"

"I don't know." She bent her head and rummaged around in her purse.

"A friend? A neighbor?"

Dottie took a lace hanky from her handbag and wiped her face. "Mabel. She lives next door. I'll ask her."

"Good. I'll take you home tonight and Mabel can bring you in tomorrow."

She took a moment to check her appearance with a compact mirror before responding. "Really, Sandy, I can't ask you to do that. That must be out of your way."

Yes, the side trip was an inconvenience, but I couldn't let her stand on the streets of a questionable neighborhood at night and wait for a bus. "I don't mind as long as I have a pretty girl in the car beside me."

She smiled as she tucked her stuff back into her purse. "You're such a tease."

"Come on, Dottie, let's go. It's getting late."

She gave me her address and, fortunately, her house in Tarzana wasn't far off my route. I held the passenger door open on the Mustang as she got in. Once she was secured in her seatbelt I started up and took the surface streets north and to the west. On the way my passenger chatted about her garden, bridge games and grandchildren—everything but the misplaced car. In record time I pulled up to her house, not one of the huge glamour estates but a modest home north of Ventura Boulevard. I got out and opened the door for her.

"Thank you, Sammy. I appreciate the ride."

"My name is Sandy."

She gave a nervous giggle. "Yes, I know. You remind me so much of a man I knew named—"

"Dottie, if you don't mind me asking, when was the last time you saw a doctor?"

"A doctor? Why do I need to see a doctor?"

I wanted to discuss her memory loss, but she'd probably forget our conversation the next morning. I simply bid her a good night. Dottie hurried up the front steps and I waited until she was safely inside the house before I left. I revved up the Mustang and headed south to catch the on ramp to the 101 Freeway North (which actually goes west) toward Ventura County. At this time of day most of the rush hour traffic had dissipated, so the lanes moved at a steady pace. With the top down on the convertible, the wind kissing my face and the car radio blasting oldies from KRTH 101.FM, I was in full cruising mode (on the road I stay alert with rock 'n' roll). With my right hand I tapped the downbeat on the gearshift knob and steered with my left. I sang along with the radio. Now only I did know the songs but in days past I'd met the artists as well.

I crossed the L.A./Ventura county line, left the freeway and wound through a semi-rural town. I reached the entrance of a gated community and stopped by the intercom long enough to punch in a familiar pass code. Fortunately, the codes hadn't changed, and the gate swung open. I should have called the occupants and announced I was coming, but thought better of it; I wasn't sure of the reception I'd encounter. I cleared the gate and meandered through the narrow, curvy streets until I found one particular house. I parked in the driveway, took the stone walkway to the front porch, rang the doorbell and fought the temptation to run away.

The door opened. A tall man in his 60s stood in the doorway and studied me with surprise. He was a handsome man with only a few distinguished wrinkles on his lean face and a full head of white hair. He wore a striped shirt, brown slippers and pants; I'd never seen the man in denim.

I cleared my throat. "Hello, father."

Chapter 16: Daddy's Song

"Hello, Ernest. How nice of you to drop by." Even when caught unawares, Stanford Ernest Farmington Sr. was still calm and in control.

"Stanford, who is it?" My mother came from the living room.

Mother, like Dottie, came from that era when ladies carried themselves with elegance and grace. Mother's almost as tall as father. Her short, dyed brown hair was precisely styled and her face still looked young, thanks to spa treatments, an extensive cream regime and good genes. Even at home she dressed sharply. Tonight she wore earrings and jewelry that matched her dress and low-heeled shoes.

"Why, Ernest!" said Opal Farmington. "What a surprise!"

"Hello, mother."

"Stanford, why didn't you tell me our boy was coming?"

My father gave me that look of disapproval. "I wasn't informed."

"I'm sorry," I said. "I should have called ahead. Is this a bad time? I can come back another day."

"Nonsense, come in, don't stand on the porch all day." When I stepped inside and father closed the door, mother held me at arms' length and gave me the once-over twice. "Let's have a look at you." She touched my cheek. "You shaved off your beard."

"Yes, I did."

"And looks a blessed sight better for it." My father

had a way with backhanded compliments. "Your hair can use a trim as well."

I sighed. My long hair had been a source of contention ever since I let it grow after high school.

"I think he looks just fine." Mother always came to my rescue. She took my hands in hers. "How are you, Ernest?"

"I'm fine, mother." She presented her cheek and I dutifully kissed it. "I should have called ahead, but I've been busy working."

"You have a new job? That's nice. Why don't you sit down and tell us all about it?"

"I can't stay long. I only came over to ask a favor."

"Then ask us over dinner. Have you had dinner yet?"

"No, but—"

"Stanford, our boy is joining us for dinner."

"Did Imelda cook enough for three?" That's my father, always practical.

"She always fixes more than we need. I'm sure we'll have enough.

I said, "I hadn't planned—I don't want to intrude."

"Stop it, Ernest. You know you're always welcome. Stanford, be a dear and ask cook to set another place at the table."

"Of course, mother." My father left for the kitchen.

I asked, "Have I come at a bad time?"

"Your father's a bit preoccupied with his work, that's all. Now go wash up, we're ready to sit down."

I'm thirty-eight years old and my mother was still telling me to wash my hands. I obliged and used the downstairs powder room with its monogrammed hand towels and shaped scented soaps. Once relieved and washed I trod through the long hallway. The familiar rooms of my childhood had changed little. In the living room, the vintage furniture and décor were, as always, in immaculate condition. Near the bay window stood the baby grand Steinway where I had spent hours as a youth practicing scales and lessons; my butt had nearly worn a dent in that wooden stool.

In the dining room Stanford had already seated himself at his customary place at the head of the large mahogany table; Mother's place was at the opposite end. No doubt she was responsible for the centerpiece of fresh cut flowers. My brother, Warren, and I used to sit on one side with sister Celeste on the other. Originally, sis and I sat together, but we clowned around so much that father separated us. From habit I went to my old place in the chair closer to mother. As a southpaw, I sat on Warren's left to avoid bumping elbows.

"Should I sit here?" What was I doing, asking my father permission to sit down in my childhood home?

"Yes, that's fine."

I pulled out the wooden chair and sat. We waited as the cook, an elderly Latina in a gray uniform dress, put the place setting in front of me: cloth napkin and placemat, china plates, polished silverware. Dinner was a big occasion with the Farmingtons.

When the cook left I asked, "What happened to Maria?"

"She hasn't been with us for several years now. She moved up north to live with her sister. Imelda is with us now. Has it been that long since you've had dinner with us?"

What could I say? During my drinking days my public antics embarrassed my family so much they nearly disowned me. I didn't visit because I didn't feel welcomed. I'm sure my folks wouldn't have appreciated me stumbling around in a drunken stupor.

"I suppose so. How is the orchestra doing?" Always a safe conversation topic.

Father lived and breathed the Golden Wing

Philharmonic, which he founded and nurtured into a first-rate company. He talked about the schedule for the upcoming season, which included symphonies by Beethoven, Mozart, Haydn and Mendelssohn.

"In the spring we have a guest violinist playing a Paganini Caprice," he said. "You should come and hear him, Ernest. You'd enjoy the piece. I wish you'd stayed with the violin. You could have mastered the instrument if you'd made the effort."

"I never got the hang of the violin."

"Nonsense. You had a gift, Ernest, and I tried to encourage you. It's a pity you squandered your talent."

"I play guitar these days." I propped my elbows on the table. Father shot me a look. I removed my elbows from the table and rested my hands in my lap. "In fact, I played guitar at a concert just a few weeks ago. I only had two days to learn the music but I did it. The fans loved the show, and the band members said I did a great job."

"I'm sure you did. Your brother was invited to perform his new concerto at the Hollywood Bowl next summer. Your mother and I are going. We can arrange a seat for you if you'd like."

Here we go again. Just once I'd like to hold a conversation without the shadow of my spectacular brother, the world's greatest organist and composer, hovering over me.

I fiddled with my silverware. "Warren didn't invite me."

Opal said, "Stanford, dear, why don't you pour Ernest a drink?"

My father stood, picked up a glass decanter from the sideboard, poured some of the red liquid into a small glass and held it out to me. "Sherry?"

My stomach tightened. I hadn't told my family about my recent sobriety. My parents had been social drinkers for years, and much of their work with the orchestra revolved around wine and cheese receptions. They could hold their liquor—but not me.

"No, thank you," I said.

He frowned. "I thought you liked sherry."

"I do, but I don't want any right now."

Mother furrowed her brow. "Ernest, dear, have a drink with us. We can toast this new job of yours."

"I can't have *any* booze, okay?"

My parents stared at me, incredulous. I wanted to hide.

"You needn't raise your voice, Ernest," my father said, more sad than angry.

"Sorry."

"A fine vintage sherry is hardly 'booze.'"

"I'm sorry, but—" I took a deep breath. "I'm an alcoholic and I can't drink."

My mother said, "It's nothing terrible, Ernest. It's just a little glass of sherry."

"I know, mother, but I—if I start on one glass, I can't stop. I can't help myself."

Now she looked confused. "Ernest, you are not an alcoholic. Alcoholics are smelly old bums who live in gutters."

I looked her in the eye. "No, mother, I'm a drunk and I go to AA meetings every week." I softened my voice. "I know you and father mean well, but I can't have sherry tonight or any other night. All right?"

"All right, son. We understand. You don't need to be defensive." Stanford handed the glass to Opal. "Here, mother, you take this."

She set the sherry on the table before her as he poured a glass for himself. He resumed his seat at the table and, fortunately, Imelda's entrance with a serving platter spared me from further discussion. Mother asked the cook to bring me something to drink from the kitchen. I ended up with a glass of fizzy water, which I hated, but at this point I was willing to guzzle castor oil to keep peace in the household. Mother chattered about her latest charity work while she and father finished their drinks; Imelda doled the food onto our plates. She retired to the kitchen and we laid our napkins on our laps. As per the family tradition, we bowed our heads as father recited a table grace from the Book of Common Prayer. The various aromas began tickling my nose, improving both my appetite and disposition. Pork tenderloin, mashed potatoes, steamed broccoli and cauliflower along with Waldorf salad—a feast far better than anything I could have scrounged up at my place tonight.

Stanford opened a bottle of red wine and filled glasses for him and mother. He didn't offer any to me. We ate for a few minutes before mother posed a question.

"So, Ernest, tell us about this job of yours."

I smiled. Maybe I could still redeem myself after the sherry fiasco. "I have a guest spot on a TV show."

"That's wonderful! Did you hear that, Stanford?"

"What show is that?" he asked.

"*Off-Kelter.*"

Stanford lowered his fork. "I don't know that one."

"It's a sitcom, new this season. Comes on Monday nights."

He shook his head as he speared a bite of broccoli. "Never watch sitcoms. Too low brow and ridiculous."

No surprise there. My father's idea of riveting entertainment is a documentary on archeological digs in South America.

Still, I persevered. "This episode has a pretty good script. I have a funny bit with a dog. Harv Brandon and Dottie Hendricks are in it too. They're a couple of old hands and they're great to work with. Today I filmed a dance number on the back lot. I thought it went very well."

Mother asked for the gravy and I handed her the china gravy boat. She carefully ladled the thick brown sauce over her spuds. "That sounds nice. Who was your partner? Some pretty young girl, I imagine."

"No partner. It was a solo number. I got to show off. I had an excellent choreographer who—" Who I wanted to see again in the worst way but had no idea how to contact her and I better not get my hopes up. "Who showed me some new steps." I set down my knife and fork. "Mother, father, I have a big favor to ask both of you."

"Certainly, what is it?" Stanford asked.

"This Friday night is the show taping and I can bring guests. It'd mean a lot to me if you would come and watch."

"Watch what?" For such a brilliant man, my father is terribly obtuse about pop culture, which is why he never understood my teen idol career.

"The sitcom. The show. We tape it live in front of a studio audience. You can see the show as we act it out. I want you to come and watch me. Please?"

Opal looked at Stanford. "What do you think? That sounds interesting."

"We have that dinner date with the Egglesons." He spoke as if this event was an unwelcome chore.

"I thought it was next week. Are you sure it's this Friday?"

"Yes, it is, mother."

"I'm afraid we can't make it, Ernest," said Opal. "We're meeting some people in Westlake Village for dinner."

My hopes plummeted. "Can't you reschedule?"

My father spoke sharply. "They're very busy people. William Eggleson is quite often out of the country on business. I worked with his assistant for several months to set this up."

"So these big wigs are more important than your son?"

"Don't be angry, dear," mother said. "We don't mean to slight you but we can't cancel on such short notice."

"You would if I was playing Hamlet at the Ahmanson Theatre."

Stanford said, "You should have let us know about this show weeks ago, instead of springing it on us at the last minute. That's the trouble, Ernest, you never talk to us. The only way we know what you're doing is when we see something on the evening news about you getting into trouble."

"I didn't think you cared!" Then I bit my lip, ashamed of my outburst.

Mother patted my hand. "Of course we care, dear. We always have. We're simply not free this Friday night. Now, cheer up. We have one of your favorite desserts tonight."

Normally I'm a sweets fiend, but I wasn't interested in eating any more. Still, dinner was almost finished, and I could leave soon. Good thing I'd cleared all the liquor out of my house, or I'd definitely be drowning my sorrows when I got home. Imelda cleared the dishes and brought in small plates of brownies buried under vanilla ice cream and hot fudge sauce. I stuffed down a few bites while we made small talk about something or the other. I can't remember the topic; I was just thankful that the conversation was about something other than my own failings.

After I'd eaten an acceptable amount of dessert, I said, "Thanks for dinner. I really need to go."

"You're welcome to stay the night," mother said. "We can put you up in your old room."

"No, I have an early call in the morning." I hated lying to my parents, but I needed to beat a hasty retreat before the evening slid downhill any further. "If you'd excuse me." I stood.

Mother got up as well. "I'll see you to the door." She called into the kitchen, "Imelda! Be a dear and pack up the leftovers for Ernest to take home."

"Mother! I don't need a doggy bag!"

"Hush, now, it's no bother. Imelda makes too much food for the two of us, and your father doesn't like leftovers. Besides, I'm sure you could use a good meal. Living all alone, it must be hard cooking for one."

"Yes, you're right, mother. Good night, father."

"Ernest?" Was that a touch of gentleness in his eyes?

"Yes, father?"

"I'm sure you'll do well with your show. They're fortunate to have you. I always thought you'd do well if you went into musical theater. I remember when you and your brother put on those funny skits for us on Christmas Eve. You were good at making people laugh."

"Thanks, father."

Imelda met us in the foyer. She handed me a paper sack full of plastic food containers, and returned to the kitchen to clean up.

"Mother, this food isn't necessary."

"Why can't a mother pamper her little boy? Ever since you left home, you won't let me do things for you."

"I can fend for myself."

She fiddled with the buttons on my shirt. "I wish you'd let your father take you to his tailor. He could fix you up with some nice clothes."

"I have plenty of clothes already."

"When are we going to see our grandchildren again?"

"I don't know, mother. It's hard making arrangements with Becka."

"Your brother brings his darlings around nearly every week. They've grown so much."

"I'm not Warren, okay?"

She gave me That Look, the one of supreme martyrdom. "Why must everything be a battle with you?"

"I'm sorry. I spoiled dinner tonight, didn't I?"

"Don't be silly. Of course not. We love you, Ernest. Why can't you see that? We expected great things from you. You're so talented. There's so much you could do if you set your mind to it. Your father and I both want you to be happy. Are you happy, Ernest?"

From the living room came the sounds of Chopin's Revolutionary Etude, Op. 10, No. 12 in C minor. My father always played the piano after dinner as his way to unwind from the day. Judging from the moody piece he played, Stanford seemed troubled.

Opal nodded toward the living room. "Why don't you go in there and play something for your father?"

"No, I couldn't."

"It'd mean so much to him."

"I haven't practiced in years. He'd only pick at my mistakes."

"Why can't you meet your father halfway? He did so much for you when you were a boy. Maybe at the time you didn't appreciate the hard work, but he made you into a fine musician. He deserves your respect."

I shifted the food sack to my other hand. "I really have to go."

"Wait, before you leave." She glanced into the living room and then whispered, "Let's talk outside."

Mother switched on the outside porch light and opened the front door. We stepped out and she shut the door. "I have something to tell you."

"Mother, what is this all about? Why are we out in the dark?"

Indeed, night had fallen in SoCal. The community didn't have streetlights, so the stars shone clearly. The other houses along the street disappeared into an inky void. The sound of crickets filled the night, along with a high-pitched coyote howl in the distant mountains. In the calmness, the bustle of L.A. seemed a million miles away.

"I didn't want to embarrass Stanford, but our dinner engagement on Friday isn't social. Your father is going to ask the Egglesons to underwrite the upcoming season for the philharmonic."

"I see. Eggleson is looking for a tax write-off."

"You don't understand." She sounded desperate. "Without this donation, Golden Wing will fold."

"What? That's not possible. The orchestra's been doing well for years."

"I don't know the details, but symphony is having some financial difficulties. Your father's too proud to talk about it, but I know he's concerned."

"I'm sorry to hear that."

She forced a smile. "I'm sure everything will work out fine."

I saw through her false bravado but didn't let on that I did. "I'm sure it will, mother. Thanks again for dinner. Tell Imelda she did a wonderful job cooking."

"I will. And don't be such a stranger. Come by and see us again soon. Maybe your father will be more relaxed next time."

"You'll be sure and watch my show when it comes on the air, won't you?"

"Of course, dear. Make sure you tell us when it's on. We wouldn't miss it for the world."

"I thought father didn't like sitcoms."

"We'll be sure and catch this one." She kissed my

cheek. "Good luck on Friday night. Love you, Ernest."

"Love you too, mother."

We hugged and I headed across the walkway to my car. I waved until she retreated inside the house. I set the bag of food on the floor of the passenger side, started up, turned on the headlights and backed out of the driveway. Traffic was light on the 101 so I zipped along in the fast lane at 80 mph, the cool night air on my face. Along the way I thought about father and the orchestra. In recent years I'd been too busy with the bottle to follow the family news, but I thought the philharmonic was a success with its rave reviews, packed houses and impressive roster of guest musicians. Father was always frugal with finances, and he kept a keen eye on the day-to-day operations. How could his baby go belly-up?

Back in the Hollywood Hills, I parked the Mustang in the garage. I turned on the kitchen light and stuck the bag of food in the fridge. I was exhausted but too keyed up to sleep. I needed to unwind and forget about sitcoms, parents, orchestras and murders. I popped open a cold O'Doul's. With snacks in hand—a bag of sour cream and onion potato chips and a package of chocolate cookies—I sprawled across the sofa in the den to watch TV. With the remote I flipped through the cable channels in search of something light and entertaining. I stumbled across an old movie starring Elsie Bloom—exactly what I needed for a brainless evening of boob tube.

Yes, there on my TV screen was the murder victim, very much alive and painfully overacting in a spaghetti western. I munched on the goodies as she screamed and ran through the countryside, chased by banditos on horseback; disrobed for a boyfriend in a bedroom; and pranced around on a beach in the world's tiniest bikini. The movie was so unintentionally bad it was funny.

When the film ended I read the credits, as I always do, to see if I recognized anyone I might have worked with. Apparently the movie was filmed in Barcelona. Not a bad deal for Elsie—in exchange for giving a crummy performance, she received a free trip overseas.

I'm glad I had a good laugh that night, because the next day started out badly (and turned progressively worse). The waitress at Canter's Deli asked Joseph if he wanted to order from the kids' menu and if he needed a booster seat. The Fourth of July never shot off such noisy fireworks.

THURSDAY: CAMERA BLOCKING
Chapter 17: Short People

"No!" Joseph shouted. "I'm not a baby and I eat real food! Do I look like I'm still in diapers?"

From the look in her eye, the waitress wanted to toss us both out. But she seated us and scribbled down our orders anyway, although she seemed a bit peeved. After she left our table, Joseph muttered a few derogatory words about her, which I won't repeat.

"Do you get that often?" I asked.

"Only from the idiots."

"Must be tough. I had the opposite problem. I was always tall for my age, even as a kid. I heard all the beanpole jokes. 'How's the air up there?' and 'Watch out for airplanes.' Got old really fast."

"You're lucky. When you're in a store you don't have to ask a stranger to get an item off the top shelf for you. Or you can't see your way out of a crowd."

"True. I can't hide in a crowd at all."

We chatted about this and that until the waitress brought our food. I'd ordered coffee along with lox and cream cheese on a bagel with tomatoes, onions and olives. Joseph went whole hog with orange juice and a three-egg omelet with hearty chili and beans, cheese and onion.

I eyed his food. "You like to live dangerously."

He laughed. He asked me to pass the ketchup. After I obliged, he downed his food with the tomato sauce. I'd finally found someone with worse eating habits than myself.

"My wife's on a health food kick," he said. "Organic, tofu, all that junk. Anything that tastes like cardboard, she serves. I'm gonna start sprouting bean sprouts instead of hair. So when she's not around, I eat what I like."

I cut up my bagel and lox into bite-size pieces. "You're married?"

"Going on ten years. We met at a dance for little people. She's small but a real firecracker, know what I mean?" He gave me a wink.

"And she tolerates your cigars?"

"Naw. She makes me go out in the yard to smoke."

As we ate we discussed wives and ex-wives until the conversation eventually turned to parents. I shared some highlights of last night's dinner with my folks. I took a sip of coffee and concluded with, "My father expected me to eventually take over his orchestra. He doesn't consider my records as real music."

"Parents are like that. Nothin' you do is good enough," Joseph said. "My mom and dad are average people. When I came along, my dad was shocked. First he blamed mom. Then he put me on weird diets and exercise programs to make me grow. He finally hit the road for some bimbo in hopes he'd finally have the big boy he always wanted."

"Did he get one?"

"Yeah, in spades. Last I heard the brat got kicked off a college basketball team for using steroids."

"That's rough about your dad running off."

"But I got my revenge. I became an actor so every time my old man went to the movies or turned on the TV, he'd see me."

The waitress refilled my coffee cup. I asked Joseph why he wanted to see me.

"I hear you're investigating Elsie Bloom's death," he said.

"I'm not investigating anything. I just think her death looks suspicious, and the police aren't moving on it." I eyed him. "I know you didn't like her much."

He leaned back his head and let out a high-pitched laugh. "You think I'm a suspect? That's rich. If I went after everyone who made fun of me, half of L.A. would be six feet under. I didn't kill Elsie. She wasn't worth doing prison time for. Did anyone find out what she died of?"

"I think she was poisoned. What do you know about Leo Constantine? There's a rumor he may have murdered his first wife."

"May have? Of course he did. Doesn't take a private dick to figure that out. Yolanda was a sickly girl. Most people don't know that because she didn't go out much. Leo went to parties without her and ogled all the starlets. Everyone except Yolanda knew that he slept around. Poor kid. If Leo's wife was sick, why did he insist she go halfway around the world with him? He wanted to kill her in Spain where nobody would notice."

"You seem sure about this."

"Back when it happened some inside sources gave me the scoop. But Leo was slick, and nobody could prove it."

"If Leo didn't like his wife, why didn't he divorce her?"

"She was a staunch Catholic and didn't believe in divorce. He converted just long enough to marry her and then went back to his old ways. So what does this have to do with Elsie?"

"I don't know. Maybe nothing. What's your information?"

"I overheard Leo and Elsie talking last week. It didn't sound like any friendly how-do-you-do."

I leaned across the table and whispered so nobody

would overhead us. "You did? Where?"

"I'd finished work one night. On the way to my car I cut through the park, you know, that nice wooded area with the benches. Leo and Elsie were standing by some trees. I hid behind a big tree and listened. They never saw me. See, sometimes being small comes in handy."

"What did they say?"

"I only picked up bits and pieces. Sounded like Elsie was threatening Leo. She said, 'I'll tell everyone' and 'you better be careful.' He brushed her off and said she was mistaken. But when she left, he looked scared."

"Why didn't you tell someone about this?"

"What's to tell? I don't know what they were talking about. I figured Elsie was spouting off another one of her tall tales to make Leo do her a favor."

A well-known rock musician, whom I'll call Robert to avoid disgracing the guilty, and his entourage took the empty table beside us. These shabby dressed guys with unshaven faces looked as if they'd just ended an all-night recording session. Judging from their crude behavior and loud comments, they'd also gotten a head start on the day's drinking.

The rocker stared at Joseph. "Well! Look here, boys! A freak in our midst."

Joseph glared at them and his face reddened. His neck veins bulged.

I said to him, "Just ignore them, they're drunk."

Robert shouted at us, "Hey, shorty, better eat your vegetables so you'll grow up big and strong!"

The dwarf tightened his lips into a thin line. He clenched his fists.

"Let it go, Joseph," I said. "Don't mess with these punks. They'll hurt you."

Robert said to his gang, "You heard the one about the little guy who tried to make love in a snowstorm? He was the midget with the frigit digit."

Before I could stop him, Joseph jumped from his chair and kicked Robert hard on the shin. The rocker yelped in pain and grabbed his sore leg. One of his henchmen stood and swung a fist at Joseph. The dwarf scooted under their table to escape the blow, but another guy (I recognized him as the bass player of the band) picked up Joseph. The dwarf kicked and punched, but the bassist held him just out of reach. The rest of the band circled around the two, flexing their fingers in anticipation of using Joseph as a punching bag.

The other patrons stared as the deli manager hurried towards us. Joseph and I didn't need the publicity of getting tossed out of Canter's. I was taller and more sober than the rocker's pals, so I had the drop on them. I pulled Joseph from the bassist's hands.

"Excuse us, we were just leaving," I said.

I tucked the dwarf under one arm. With my other hand I grabbed my wallet from my pocket, dug out some some bills and dropped them on the table, probably more than what the meal cost but I had no time to stop and count the money. I rushed to the front door with Joseph in hand. Let me tell you, hanging onto a squirming dwarf is no easy task. He screamed for me to put him down. The rocker and his buddies yelled obscenities at us. I resisted the temptation to turn around and take a poke at the imbeciles.

On the sidewalk outside, Joseph was still shouting when I finally sent him down. "Sandy! You moron! I don't need you protecting me!"

"Yes, you do. Those rockers would have mashed you worse than a bag of potatoes."

He straightened his jacket and tie and smoothed his hair. "Running away makes me look like a chicken."

"Yeah, a chicken with his teeth intact and his arms unbroken."

He fished the car keys out of his pocket and clicked the remote to unlock his Jeep Wrangler parked along the curb (how did he find a spot so close to the door?). "How much do I owe you for breakfast?"

"Skip it. My treat."

He climbed into the vehicle, custom modified with extensions on the pedals for his short legs. Joseph shut the door, rolled down the window and stuck out his head, shouting over the traffic noise. "Let me know if you want any help nailing Leo!"

I waved as he pulled into traffic. I walked two blocks to the pay lot where I'd parked the Harley; I seldom left my vehicles unguarded on the street. I headed east on surface streets toward the studio and pondered my next move: getting some hard evidence. Everyone in the *Off-Kelter* cast had a strong motive for murder, but Royce and Leo were the two most ruthless to actually carry it out. If Elsie had scribbled her thoughts in a memo book, perhaps Leo had made notes as well. The big guy bombarded his associates with a constant stream of memos and letters. He claimed he was "preserving his legacy," but in reality Leo was leaving a paper trail to cover his hind end in case of a lawsuit. Maybe I could find a clue in the executive offices. As I idled at a red light, I realized that sneaking into Leo's office might be considered breaking and entering. Technically I wasn't planning to break anything. If I saw something incriminating in the office, I'd tell Detective Hernandez and suggest that he get a warrant.

But I had another job to do before sleuthing. Once on the Mammoth lot, I headed for the studio's floral shop that provided the fake trees, bushes and greenery for the sets. The shop also handled flower deliveries for employees. I ordered the largest "Good Luck" floral arrangement to send to Robin right before her dance recital. I asked them to tuck a small plastic unicorn and a tiny set of silk ballerina slippers among the flowers. I enclosed a note: "Lots of good wishes for your recital tonight, punkin. You'll be super. Wish I were there. Kisses and hugs, your loving dad." No substitute for my presence, but at least I could let my girl know that I was thinking of her.

With that task finished, I headed for the Administration Building where the mucky-mucks held court. As I passed by Stage 12, the *Space Posse* cast was outside on a break. Then I encountered Frances, standing by a tree and waiting for Scruffy to finish his business. She told me that she'd be missing rehearsal this afternoon for personal business, but her assistant would be there with the dog. Frances also handed me a small, oval can of liver pate' to use for later. I'm not sure why I had to handle the can of dog treats instead of the assistant, but at least I didn't have to doggy-sit the mutt. Frances cleaned up after her ward with a small scooper and a plastic bag. I stuck the can of pate' in my back pants pocket and continued on my way.

I timed my arrival at the ad building for a little past one o'clock, after the secretaries and office assistants had left for the one-hour lunch break. With columns framing the front doors and a carved stone façade, the two-story building was the most imposing edifice on the lot. Up the front steps, through the doors and down the parquet hallway. As a former star, my presence on the first floor wouldn't raise an alarm. People would assume I was here to chat about a new project (come to think of it, I'd rather be discussing a job than snooping around for a murder). I took the stairs to the second story, opened the fire door and peeked down the corridor. This was where my sleuthing became dicey. I'd reached the inner sanctum where Leo and his top aides reigned. Nobody came to the second floor without an appointment or a guaranteed blockbuster movie proposal with financial backing in place. Most Mammoth employees never stepped foot on these hallowed grounds.

The door to the executive suite opened, and I ducked back into the stairwell. I opened the door just a crack to peer through. An older woman, smartly dressed in a polyester dress suit—probably the executive secretary for either Leo or Ivan—left the room. She looked rather stern, like someone used to driving away wannabe filmmakers and crazies. After she stepped into the elevator at the far end of the hall, I left my hiding place. Fortunately, the woman hadn't locked the door behind her, so I easily slipped into the executive suite.

The Constantines had some nice digs. The large outer office for the secretaries was tastefully decorated with framed artwork, fresh flowers in vases and comfortable leather chairs where clients could cool their heels. Plush carpeting covered the floor. Along the wall stood a copy machine, fax machine, cappuccino machine, computer printer and all the gizmos that make a modern office run (unless a piece of machinery has something to do with cars or guitars, I have no idea what to do with it). To my left were desks for the two secretaries, each desk with a computer, paper trays and a Rolodex of contacts most producers would kill for. File cabinets lined the walls. I tried opening a couple of drawers, but they were locked. I glanced through the paperwork on the desks, but the pages looked like routine studio business. Of course an efficient secretary would never leave incriminating evidence out in the open. Besides, I doubted that the secretaries had any dirt on Elsie. The wall across from the outer door had the solid wood entrance to Leo's lair; to my right was a similar gateway to Ivan's man cave. What I wanted was inside Leo's office—and that door was locked.

I jiggled the doorknob several times, but it didn't

budge. I could kick the door in, but I'd only get a broken foot for my efforts. I stared at the door and thought: If I was the head man and had locked myself out, what would I do? Leo was too busy to worry about mundane things like keys; he'd throw a fit if he couldn't get to his office immediately. Like most busy men, he probably relied on his secretary to keep track of things. I rummaged through the unlocked drawers of the secretaries' desks until I found a ring of keys. Most of the keys were small, probably the keys for the file cabinets. I tried the larger keys on Leo's door until I found the one that worked. I replaced the key ring where I had found it and closed the drawer. I realized I was leaving fingerprints all over the place. Why didn't I remember to bring gloves?

I entered Leo's office, closed the door behind me, and surveyed his domain. The cavernous room, lined in dark oak paneling, reeked of power and masculinity. Oscars, Emmys and Golden Globes won by the studio filled a glass display case. Framed photos of Leo shaking hands with A-list stars, politicians and millionaires covered the walls (no, I wasn't in the photos). The bookcases had leather-bound books that I'm sure Leo never read. The wall behind the mile-long oak desk featured a huge picture window. The wall decor consisted of mounted fish from his well-publicized Colorado fishing trips.

I'd need more than an hour to dig through the stuff piled on the desk: mountains of scripts, daily show reports, memos, letters, contracts, financial spreadsheets and travel itineraries. I flipped through the pages of his desk calendar. I didn't expect to see Elsie's name—Leo was too smart for that—but perhaps he had a code name for her. I recognized names of various directors and producers. The letters "TY" appeared on a few weekends. Maybe one of Leo's fishing buddies or a mistress?

In a tray marked "for filing" I pawed through photocopies of Leo's memos. An inch or so down I hit pay dirt. The memo, typed on studio letterhead and marked "confidential," was dated a week ago and read as follows:

TO: Royce Jobbe
FROM: Leo Constantine
SUBJECT: Elsie Bloom
It has come to my attention that Miss Bloom is pregnant. Obviously that will present a problem if *Off-Kelter* is renewed for the remainder of the season. I recommend talking with the actress ASAP regarding her options.
Regards, Leo

Elsie was pregnant? Apparently nobody else in the cast knew that. What "options" did Leo mean? Was Elsie carrying Leo's baby? Did he want Royce to get rid of her or the offspring? A week ago—that's when Joseph said he'd heard Elsie and Leo talking in the park. And before the Monday read-through Royce had told the actress he wanted to talk to her about a memo—this must be it. I had to show this paper to the police and urge them to start investigating, but Leo might get suspicious if the memo turned up missing. I'd make a photocopy. That way I wouldn't technically be "stealing."

I stepped into the outer office to use the copier and decided to first nose around in Ivan's office as well. Maybe he had a hand in Elsie's demise as well. I found the office key in the other secretary's desk (honestly, the Constantines needed to beef up their security). His office was smaller than dad's, obviously, but still had space for a fully-stocked wet bar, an oak wardrobe full of expensive suits and cashmere coats, and a door that opened to a fire escape, handy in case Ivan wanted to avoid someone in the outer office. I glanced through his desk calendar. Today's date listed a meeting at eight p.m. with Stifert Development Inc. Where had I heard that name before? The TV news had a recent story about that firm buying up properties around town in order to build luxury condo towers. I checked through the calendar's previous weeks and found several Stifert entries. Why would Ivan be talking to condo developers?

The clock in the outer office chimed one-forty-five. I had to scoot before the secretaries returned. I left Ivan's office, closed the door, and lifted the lid on the humming copy machine to reproduce the Elsie Bloom memo. I laid the paper on the glass, closed the lid and pressed "copy." Unfortunately, to operate the copy machine I had to stand with my back to the outer door. I couldn't see anyone entering from the hall and, with the thick carpeting, couldn't hear footsteps. A movement caught my eye and I turned my head, but not fast enough. Someone had crept up on the side with my bad ear and I didn't hear them. Before I could see their face, the person whacked me on the back of the head with something heavy and knocked me out cold.

When I came to, my head throbbed. I shook my head to clear the fuzziness. I opened my eyes. I tried to rub the sore spot on the back of my head but I couldn't move my hand.

Someone had tied me to a chair.

Chapter 18: Chains

The culprit had lashed me to a sturdy wooden chair with no armrests and a back of horizontal slats. My wrists were tied together behind the chair back; each ankle was bound to a chair leg and a rope across my chest held me in. I tugged on the ropes but they didn't give. I tried to scoot across the floor but the chair was too heavy to budge. My fingers couldn't undo the tight knots on my wrists. Whoever did this knew what he was doing.

I studied my surroundings. I was no longer in the executive suite but inside an empty soundstage, dimly lit by a single work light. The cavernous room had no set, which meant nobody was using the stage. I might have to wait hours—or days—before someone found me. If I missed rehearsal, nobody would think of looking for me here, wherever "here" was. Maybe my assailant planned to return to finish me off, in which case I needed to escape immediately. Fortunately, my attacker hadn't gagged me. I yelled for help until I realized I was wasting my energy—soundstages are soundproof.

These rooms are constructed so filmmakers can shoot without noise leaking in. Likewise, a person standing on the street can't hear, and directors can work in secrecy. I could shout all day—or set off a bomb— and nobody outside would hear me.

This wasn't my first time in this type of predicament. In every episode of *Buddy Brave* I was roped, chained, imprisoned or shackled. Each week the

writers came up with a clever way for me to escape.
Perhaps my most ludicrous escape was in season four's
"The Perilous Pasta Caper." A mad scientist attempted
to infect the nation's food supply with a drug that
would make the public susceptible to the campaign
promises of a evil candidate running for U.S. president
who, when voted into office, would turn the country
into an oppressive dictatorship (the scriptwriter later
became a speechwriter for a politician. Who says life
doesn't imitate art?). The scientist used a chain of
Italian restaurants to administer the drug and, when
Buddy investigated, our malt-shop detective found
himself tied up with miles of cooked spaghetti. To free
himself, the brave boy sleuth simply ate through his
bonds, which sounded far easier on the script than in
filming. Real pasta doesn't hold up under the camera
lights, so in shooting we used dyed twine for the
"spaghetti." I chewed on the ropes through many takes.
Let's just say that episode left a bad taste in my mouth.

Come to think of it, Royce directed that episode.

The ropes were cutting off my circulation, cramping
my arms and turning my legs numb. I had to get out
before my muscles froze. What would Buddy do?
Sometimes the young lawman used a sharp object
hidden on his person to cut through his bonds. No, I
didn't have a knife in my pocket (maybe I should start
carrying one). I didn't have a lighter to burn the ropes
(too bad I'd quit smoking). I rubbed my wrists against
the chair back, but the furniture had no nails or bolts
sticking out for sawing the ropes. Maybe if I
concentrated, I could send a message via mental
telepathy to Matt Sterling, and he'd write a happy
ending to my ordeal. Unless an earthquake hit and
rattled the bonds loose, I was stuck.

In the corner something moved; was it a rat? I was
so dazed from the conk on the head that I was hearing

noises; I thought I heard a dog barking. Wait a minute—I *did* hear a dog barking. Maybe the dog had a person with him who could help. Or maybe my assailant had a pit bull that would finish me off. I could see the headlines: MANACLED MUSICIAN MAULED BY RABID MUTT.

I shouted, "Hey! Is someone out there? Help me!"

Scruffy trotted into view, dragging his leash on the ground. He must have slipped away from Frances. For the first time this week, I was ecstatic to see the mangy cur.

"Scruffy! Come here, boy! Over here!"

The critter sat on his haunches before me, his fat tongue lolling out of his mouth as he panted.

"Scruffy! You remember me, don't you, boy? The man on the show you like to kiss?"

The canine wagged his tail and gave a couple of friendly yaps. As a trained animal actor, maybe he could carry a message for me.

"Scruffy! Listen to me! Go get help! Fetch Frances! Bring your trainer here! Go on, boy! Go! Get Frances!"

The ditzy dog merely stared at me and barked. I repeated the command, but he didn't move. What rotten luck. Just when I needed Lassie to save the day, I was stuck with Scooby-Doo. Then Scruffy recognized me. He jumped up on my lap and started licking my face. The confused cur thought we were filming the show. With my hands tied, I couldn't push him off. I turned my face away from his slobbering tongue. He slurped my ear with gusto.

"Scruffy! Get off! Bad dog! Get down!"

The dog sat in my lap and barked happily in my face. I nearly died of asphyxiation from his doggie breath. But I got an idea. I couldn't eat through these ropes—but Scruffy could. I jiggled my legs until the mutt jumped off. Then I wiggled the chair and twisted my hands enough so I could reach into my back pants pocket. I strained on the ropes, stretching out my fingers until I could just barely grip the can of pate'. I slowly pulled the can from the pocket, careful not to drop it. The bonds dug into my skin and I winched in pain. As a musician, my fingers were pretty agile, so I managed to hook a finger into the pull-tab and peel back the lid (good thing I didn't need a can opener). Holding the can in my right hand, I used two fingers on the left to dig out the pate' and smear it on the wrist ropes. I kept spreading the smelly gunk until the can slipped from my fingers and clattered on the concrete floor. Did I slather on enough stuff to attract the dog? I'd find out soon enough.

"Scruffy! Lookie! Doggie treat! Yum, yum!"

The pooch cocked his head at me. How did Frances ever train such an ignorant animal?

I jerked my head towards my hands. "Pay attention, you silly mutt! Come on, dinner time!"

In the unventilated room, the odor of the pate' filled the space and almost choked me (I'll never eat liver again). Scruffy finally smelled it too. He barked and trotted behind the chair. I felt his wet tongue lapping at the ropes.

"You nutty dog, chew the ropes! Don't lick it, eat it!"

Scruffy bit into the ropes—and my skin as well. I screamed in pain and the chewing stopped. I panicked. I twisted my head and spotted the canine from the corner of my eye. The last thing I wanted was to scare him away.

"Go on, Scruffy, keep eating! Good boy! It's good that you're chewing me!"

The hungry mutt gnawed on the ropes. I felt the bonds loosen. A few more chomps and the ties dropped from my wrists. I brought my hands around and pushed the rope off my chest. My arms and shoulders ached; my wrists had red marks from the ropes as well as teeth marks from the dog. I leaned over and untied the bindings from around my ankles, which was difficult to do as Scruffy kept licking my hands. Free at last! I stood up, a little unsteady from being confined for so long. I checked my watch. I was an hour late for rehearsal, which meant no time to call the police. As much as I wanted to catch my captor, I didn't want to face Royce's fury for my tardiness. But if Royce was the guilty party, I couldn't wait to see his face when I walked in, hale and whole.

I scooped up my four-legged savior and left the building. After sitting in the dark room for so long, the sunlight blinded me for a moment. When my eyes cleared I saw that I was next door to the administration building. The kidnapper hadn't taken me far. An empty cart, with the name of another TV program stenciled on the side, was parked nearby. I set the dog on the front seat with a command to "stay!", got in the driver's seat, released the hand brake, and pulled into the street as a man came out of a nearby building.

"Hey!" he shouted. "That's my cart! Come back here! Thief!"

I floored the pedal and yelled over my shoulder, "It's an emergency! You can pick it up at Stage 14!"

He ran after the cart, shouting at me to stop, but I soon left him behind. Scruffy seemed to enjoy the ride. He stuck his head out the side of the cart and let his mouth hang open as he watched the scenery go by. I drove the cart as I did the Mustang on the freeway, which was pretty scary. I cut the corners, swerved around pedestrians, and never slowed down. I screeched to a stop in front of Stage 14 and set the handbrake. I grabbed the dog and ran inside.

The four cameras were in place. The overhead lights

burned brightly. Camera cables snaked across the floor. Dozens of people scurried around. Little pieces of colored tape covered the floor to mark the positions of the actors and the camera set-ups. A young woman approached me. She wore a polo shirt with the name of Frances' animal business sewn on the left chest.

"Where have you been?" she said. "Everyone's been so worried! Are you all right?"

"Yes, I am. You see—"

But she wasn't listening to me. She grabbed the dog and cuddled him. "Are you all right, boy? Hmmmm? I've been so worried about you. We missed you, yes we did."

She walked away. I called out with all the sarcasm I could muster, "I'm fine too, thanks for asking."

Carl stepped up to me. "Sandy, where have you been? You're holding up the show."

"Sorry I'm late. I was all tied up."

*****

The afternoon rehearsal was rocky. First Royce gave me the hairy eyeball. "So you finally decided to join us, Fairfax. I hope our scheduled rehearsal didn't inconvenience you in any way."

I glared back at him. "I was sitting down with a terrible headache." I waited for his reaction to that loaded remark.

He squinted at me. "Do you want some aspirin?"

"No, now that I'm here my headache is gone."

"Good. Get in position. We're ready for your first scene." Either Royce was innocent or he could pull a convincing poker face.

As I waited by the set for my entrance cue, I rubbed the indentations that the ropes had left on my wrists. With my short-sleeved shirt, the red markings were clearly visible.

"I didn't expect to see you here," Harv said.

I looked at him with surprise. "Why's that?"

"Since you didn't show up, I thought you were sick." He glanced at my hands. "What happened to your wrists?"

"I was doing a costume fitting at wardrobe and the cuffs were too tight."

Harv gave me a look. He obviously didn't believe my story, but he said nothing and walked away. His remarks bothered me. Was he responsible for my afternoon misadventure? I had trouble concentrating and I blew several lines. I was certain that my attacker was in the room; would he try to bump me off again? My scene with Scruffy went well—a little too well, in fact. Scruffy jumped his cue and landed on my desk a line too early. Instead of licking my face, he nibbled my wrists. Some residue from the pate' must have stayed on my hands. After several efforts Scruffy finally got the scene right. After we finished, Royce commented on how well I was getting along with the dog.

I smiled. "Scruffy and I understand each other."

I wasn't in the next scene, so I told Joseph I wanted to talk with him privately. I swung by the craft service table to grab some munchies—thanks to the detour to the empty soundstage, I'd missed lunch—and the two of us hunkered down in Joseph's dressing room. The producers must have thought that a dwarf only needed a small room because this one was cramped, barely room for the two chairs where we sat. In between bites of cookies and chips, I told him about my jaunt to the executive offices and my tribulations in the soundstage. When I finished, he chuckled.

"There's nothing funny about this," I said. "I might have starved to death in that stage."

"I wasn't laughing at you. It proves I'm innocent. There's no way I could have reached up, bonked you, and then carried you out of the office."

"Maybe you were on stilts." This made Joseph roar with laughter. "I guess you're right. You're off my suspect list."

"Whoever clobbered you must be a pretty strong guy."

"Or woman. I saw Mrs. Jones pick up the refrigerator in Elsie's office."

"So whatcha gonna do now, Sherlock? That memo you found is probably shredded by now. And Leo's gonna make darn sure that from now on his door's locked and bolted."

"That's where you come in, Joseph. You're just the right size for the job."

He narrowed his eyes. "What job?"

"Tonight Ivan's meeting with a condo developer. I need you to listen in."

"What's the kid doing with a condo developer?"

"That's what I'm trying to find out. I think he's trying to pull off a real estate scam."

"What do condos have to do with Elsie?"

"I don't know, but if we can't get Ivan on a murder charge, maybe we can at least nail him for a shady business deal."

"What do you mean, *we*? When did *I* get involved in *your* snooping?"

"Since now. Maybe this ties together. Maybe Ivan poisoned Elsie because she'd discovered his scheme."

Joseph clasped his hands. "I think Royce killed her because she was carrying his baby."

"Do you know if Royce and Elsie were—?"

"Screwing? Heck, yeah, everybody on the show knew that. When we shot the first two episodes they were kissing and cooing over each other all day long. Pretty soon Royce's wife found out. I guess she read him the riot act because he started ignoring Elsie, and she went back to lover boy Troy."

"Do you think Troy might have killed Elsie out of jealousy?"

"Naw, the fling didn't last long. I don't think Troy ever found out. He's not the sharpest pencil in the drawer. Royce and Elsie only made out when Troy was off doing his show."

"Did anyone know about Elsie's pregnancy?"

"I don't believe she was really knocked up. Could be another one of her lies so she could blackmail Royce or Leo."

Carl rapped on the door and announced that Joseph was needed on the set.

"Give me a minute," the dwarf shouted.

I said, "Look, Joseph, I need you in Ivan's office tonight to listen in on that meeting."

"Are you nuts? I may be short, but I'm not invisible."

"You can hide in the wardrobe. There's enough space in there to hide a dozen dwarfs."

"What if he gets something out of the closet?"

"It's seventy-nine degrees outside. Ivan is not going to need a coat."

The AD knocked again, more urgently. He opened the door and stuck his head into the room. "Joseph, we need you right now."

The dwarf sighed. "Royce got ants in his pants? I'm coming." Joseph climbed off the chair.

"Please, Joseph, do this for me?" I begged. "For Elsie? For justice? All right then, for revenge."

His eyes brightened and he smiled. "For revenge, you got yourself a deal."

Why did I trust a person who was only motivated by his baser instincts?

Chapter 19: Moonlight Feels Right

After rehearsal wrapped for the day, I grabbed some of the remaining goodies from craft services and rushed outside before anyone waylaid me. I started walking toward the parking lot, but then ducked down a side alley and doubled back to my trailer, now parked down the street from Stage 14. I hide inside the mobile dressing room and ate my impromptu meal. I couldn't go out for dinner; the front gate guard might get curious as to why I wanted back on the lot after the show had finished for the day. But for now, nobody would notice my bike among the other parked vehicles owned by the crew members, usually involved with editing or technical effects, who worked long past sundown. As I ate, I felt a twinge of guilt about Joseph's involvement. Getting myself tied up was one thing, but if anything happened to my partner in crime I'd hate myself. However, my plan looked foolproof. What could go wrong? Of course that's what I thought earlier when I was inside Leo's office.

I took a short nap on the trailer's couch and waited for the lot to close for the day. Under the light of a full moon, I left the trailer and hurried toward the ad building, careful to stay in the shadows of the empty streets. The studio had an eerie feel at night. After the hustle of the daytime activity, the evening's quiet seemed disturbing. The street lamps, humming softly, cast a mellow glow over the lot. A light mist hung in the air. The temperature had cooled, and I shivered in my short sleeves. This was the time of day when the security guards often reported strange happenings on the lot. I expected to see Freda, the Stage 14 ghost, out for a stroll.

I met Joseph in the alley behind the administration building. He was lighting a cigar.

"Put that out!" I said. "Do you want someone to see us?"

"Who's here to watch? Everyone's gone home. That is, anyone with any sense."

I checked my watch. "Okay, let's get you in place before Ivan arrives." And before my unwilling spy changed his mind and left. "Let's go in through the fire door."

With no lights shining from the windows, the ad building resembled a fortress. I reached up and grabbed the chain attached to the lower ladder of the fire escape. The steps pulled down, and I scrambled up. Joseph's ascent was more like a crawl; the steps were set too far apart for his short legs. He had to pull himself up onto one step before tackling the next.

"What if Ivan catches me?" he said as we climbed. "He isn't known for his good nature."

"Don't worry. I'll be here to help you."

"Yeah, just like you helped yourself this afternoon when you were tied up."

I reached the top level and waited for Joseph to catch up. I checked the time: seven-forty. I hadn't counted on my partner taking so long. We were cutting this too close for comfort. I pushed the latch on the fire door—locked. I juggled the latch several times.

"Shouldn't a fire door be unlocked?" I asked.

"Fire doors are for going *out*, not coming *in*. Any more smart ideas, Sherlock?"

Now I was determined to get Joseph inside if only to wipe that smirk off his face. He began his arduous descent down the steps and I followed. Back on the ground, we walked to the building's front door.

"Open sesame!" Joseph pushed the door ajar. "Why did you make me climb those nasty steps when we could have come in this way?"

"We still can't get inside Ivan's office."

At the end of the street three women pushed a large, wheeled canvas bin in our direction. I grabbed Joseph's arm and pulled him behind the hedge that ran along the front of the building. I peered through the greenery.

"What gives?" Joseph did not sound happy.

"Shhh, keep your voice down. The nighttime cleaning crew is here."

"Great. They can clean up and I can go home." He started to move.

"No, wait." I held out my arm to block his departure. "I have an idea. See that cart the ladies are pushing?"

"Yeah, so?"

"Back when I was doing concerts, I had problems getting past the fan mobs. A couple of times I sneaked into a hotel through the service entrance by hiding inside a laundry bin."

"You're suggesting I get inside that crate?"

"That's right. You're just the right size to fit."

"I ain't doin' it."

The three Latinas stopped the cart in front of the ad building and stepped away for a smoke. When they turned their backs, I picked up Joseph under his arms and set him down inside the cart, next to an assortment of spray bottles and jars of cleaners.

He sneezed. "This soap crud is killing my sinuses."

"So stop breathing."

I dumped a handful of clean white rags atop the dwarf to hide him. I ducked behind the hedge again and watched as the women snubbed out their cigarettes and returned. They rolled the cart up the handicapped ramp beside the front steps and inside the building. Moments later, a Porsche pulled into Ivan's reserved parking space, followed by an SUV that parked nearby. Two guys, dressed in suits and ties and carrying large portfolio cases, got out of the SUV. They caught up with Ivan, shook hands all around, and made their way inside. I ran to the back of the building and found a dark spot beside the bushes where I could watch Ivan's window. The only bad part of my plan was if Joseph did get into trouble, I had no way to rescue him. The fire door was locked, and running up the inside stairs would take too long.

Ivan's office lit up. He hadn't drawn the drapes, so I could see the three guys walking around. I wished I'd given Joseph a microphone or a walkie-talkie so I could hear the conversation. Buddy Brave always had some nifty communication gadgets, although in reality the devices were plastic models that didn't work. I watched and waited, checking my watch frequently. I was tired, cold and hungry. What was taking so long?

About forty-five minutes later the office went dark. I watched the fire escape, waiting for Joseph to come down. After five minutes he didn't show up. Ten minutes passed. Was he trapped inside the office? Should I go inside and look for him? What if—?

Something tugged on my pant leg. I screamed and turned around.

Joseph said, "What are you so jumpy about?"

"What are you doing here? You were supposed to come down the fire escape!"

"Forget it! I wasn't about to haul my butt down that contraption again! I nearly broke my neck on it the first time."

"How did you get here?"

"Same way I got in, through the front door. After the kid and his cronies left, I took the elevator." He removed a small bottle from his jacket pocket and started to unscrew the cap.

"What's that?" I asked.

"Some top quality Scotch."

"Have you been carrying that around all night?"

"If you must know, I swiped it from Ivan's bar."

"You—what! What if Ivan finds it missing! He'll know someone was in there! Put it back!"

"He had a dozen of these things. He won't miss one." Joseph took a sip. "Want some?"

"No! So what happened at the meeting?"

"I ain't talkin' on an empty stomach."

I guess paying for dinner was the least I could do for him after he played spy for me. We found our vehicles in the parking lot and headed out. We were both too tired to drive far, so we ended up at Roscoe's House of Chicken and Waffles in Hollywood, open until midnight on weekdays. Not the swankiest of restaurants, but some good ol' Southern comfort food sounded mighty good and filling. Joseph ordered the chicken salad plate and a beer. I opted for one of the house combos of mac and cheese, greens, cornbread and two pieces of chicken.

"I'm parched." He took a long pull on his beer. "Sure you don't want one?"

"No, thanks." I sipped my lemonade. "I quit drinking."

"You don't smoke. You don't drink. Don't you have any vices?"

"I have an image to maintain." We both laughed. I cut my fried chicken off the bone. "So tell me, what happened? Did you have any trouble getting into the office?"

"Of course not. The cleaning ladies let me in."

"You're kidding."

"I kept sneezing from those stinky cleaners, and the gals found me. They asked what I was doing. I said a mean, nasty big person shoved me into their cart against my will." Off my look, he added, "That's true, isn't it?"

I let the insult slide. "Go on, then what?"

"I told them I had an appointment with the young Mr. Constantine. They unlocked his office so I could wait inside."

"They believed that baloney, that Ivan would condescend to take a meeting with a little person?"

He leaned back and preened. "They were overcome by my charm. Women know that great things come in small packages." Joseph had an ego bigger than mine.

"So did you hide in the wardrobe?"

"No, I stood on the desk and pretended I was a table lamp." He chewed a big bite of chicken salad and swallowed. "Of course I hid, you ninny. The door on the wardrobe didn't close tight so I could see and hear everything."

"And—?"

"Will you relax? I'm getting' to it. Long story short, Leo's gonna build condos on the Mammoth lot."

"Office condos?"

"No, goof head. Residential. High-rise luxury towers. Million-dollar flats."

"Where's he going to put these towers? The lot's built out."

"There'll be room once he tears down the buildings."

"Which buildings? They're all in use."

Joseph waggled a finger at me. "Lean over." I did so and he rapped me on my thick skull. "Hello, anyone home in there? What do you think Ivan plans to do? He's going to close the studio and sell the land to the developers so they can put up one of these fancy smancy lifestyle centers. You know, swimming pools and gyms and uppity boutique shops and all that junk for the young money set."

I stopped eating and stared at him in astonishment.

"Sell the studio? He can't do that. What about the board of directors, the stockholders?"

"Ivan told these guys that he's the majority stockholder. He's been buying up stock on the sly under fake names."

"The swine."

"Apparently Ivan's been planning the scheme for years. He was never interested in producing shows. He just wanted access to the lot so he could swing this million-dollar deal."

"If he wants to make a quick buck, why doesn't he just sell Mammoth to one of the major studios?"

"Ivan's in dutch with these condo guys. He's a silent partner. He'll get a percentage of the condo sales and store rentals for years to come."

"What about his dad? Leo won't let Mammoth go without a fight."

"Money's thicker than blood."

"You're certain about this?" I asked.

"Sure I'm sure. Those guys had drawings, blueprints, scale models, the works."

"How soon does Ivan plan to move on this?"

"Next week. Meanwhile, he's keeping this quiet so the historical societies don't step in."

The group called Hollywood Heritage was active in preserving old movie landmarks, such as the Lasky-DeMille Barn on Highland Avenue, but they wouldn't have time to organize a protest if Ivan started tearing down the lot right away. Was the condo deal the secret that Elsie threatened to tell the world about?

My head was swimming. The rich food was making me groggy. I pushed my half-eaten dinner plate away. "I'll go to the police. There must be a way to stop this."

Leo took a swig of his beer. "Whatcha going to tell the cops? Eavesdropping on a private meeting ain't exactly legal."

"You're right."

"If you're thinking of sneaking into his office and grabbing the evidence, forget it. Ivan hid the plans in a wall safe." Joseph finished cleaning his plate. "I'm ready to call it a day. How about you?"

I had to agree. As much as I wanted to stop Ivan's mad scheme, we couldn't do anything tonight. We paid our bills, said our good nights, and headed to our respective homes. I needed a good night's sleep so I'd be in peak performing mode tomorrow when we taped *Off-Kelter* before a live audience. Tomorrow would also be my last day—perhaps ever—on the Mammoth Pictures lot. I had less than twenty-four hours to find Elsie's killer, stop the sale of the studio, and perform in a network TV show.

Not even Buddy Brave could pull off a stunt like that.

FRIDAY: SHOWTIME
Chapter 20: This Just Doesn't Seem to Be My Day

Before the morning run-through, the cast was scheduled for publicity shots. After parking the Mustang on the lot, I detoured to the studio gift store to buy the latest issues of *Daily Variety* and *Hollywood Reporter*. I skimmed the pages but found nothing new about Elsie's death or a hint of Mammoth's possible sale. If Ivan had a plot up his designer sleeves, he knew how to keep it secret. Inside my trailer I found two sets of my costume, cleaned and pressed. I changed clothes, left the magazines in the trailer, and reported to the set. As a teen idol, I was an old hand at photo shoots, so I put on my smile and went through the paces. The photographer captured shots of me solo, with the cast, and posed in various scenes on the sets. Harv had plastered a hairpiece over his bald spot and dyed his hair a dark brown.

After we finished, Harv asked me, "Sandy! Have you heard anything more about Elsie Bloom?"

"You mean her death?" Why was he interested in Elsie all of a sudden?

"Yes. Do the police have any suspects?"

"If they do, they haven't told me."

"You'll keep me posted, won't you?"

"Sure, Harv, although the police haven't been talking to me about the case."

Carl said to the cast, "Has everyone heard the news?"

"The show's cancelled, right?" Joseph was such a

pessimist.

"No, no. The news from head office."

My stomach tightened. Was Ivan announcing his plan to sell the lot? "No, tell us."

The AD said, "Ivan Constantine plans to remodel the buildings on the lot."

"Remodel?"

"He's bringing in a crew to clean the brickwork, fix up the dressing rooms, redo the offices, repair the sidewalks, the works."

"It's about time," Dottie scoffed. "My dressing room hasn't been repainted since Grace Kelly won the Oscar for *The Country Girl*."

I pulled Joseph aside. "Why would Ivan remodel the buildings if he plans to tear them down?"

"You knucklehead, it's a distraction. That's what the kid wants us to think. That way, when he bring in the construction guys to scout out land for the condos, nobody'll suspect a thing."

"That makes sense. Do you know you have a devious mind?"

He chuckled. "Being around average people all the time, I gotta be shrewd."

Royce called me over to the nightclub set to discuss one of my scenes, a piece of business involving some oranges I was supposed to juggle (I'd learned juggling during a *Buddy Brave* episode). He wanted me to use a wine bottle instead and I explained I wasn't *that* good of a juggler. I could only handle small items, preferably ones that didn't break if I dropped them. Royce wanted me to try anyway and he told me to stay put as he went off to find the props manager. As I waited, I practiced juggling the oranges. Then I felt a hand on my shoulder. I put down the oranges and turned round.

Nobody there.

Someone—or something—touched me again.

Puzzled, I looked to either side and then up. One of the large lights suspended from a beam directly overhead swung precariously. The cable broke and the spotlight plummeted to the ground. I jumped out of the way just as the heavy lamp crashed on my tape mark.

The AD ran up. "What happened?"

"I didn't break it!" I was too shocked to say anything intelligent.

Royce ran over. "What's going on? Fairfax, what did you do now?"

I pointed to the pile of bent metal and shattered glass. "That thing almost fell on me!"

Royce stared down at the debris, looked up at the frayed cable swaying to and fro, uttered some four-letter words, and yelled for Ben, the lead rigger. Ben insisted he'd personally inspected each one of the lights and that his crew would never use a faulty cable. While the two argued, Carl picked up the phone to call for a cleanup. I tiptoed my way off the set, careful not to step on the broken glass. Good thing I was wearing the sturdy shoes from wardrobe and not flip-flops. I found a chair off stage and sank into it, nervous from my close call; I had nearly joined Elsie Bloom in the great Green Room in the Sky.

Dottie brought me a bottle of water from craft services. "Sandy, you're white as a ghost."

My hand shook as I took the bottle from her. "Am I?" My voice squeaked. I cleared my throat. "That light almost made a ghost out of me." I unscrewed the bottle cap and took a big gulp of water.

Harv ran up. "Sandy! I heard a light almost fell on you!"

I held up a forefinger and thumb an inch apart. "Missed me by that much."

"That's lucky. Sure would hate to lose you right before the taping."

I glared at him. "Yes, that would be tragic, wouldn't it?"

He looked confused. "What's that supposed to mean?"

"In the four years I worked on *Buddy Brave,* we never had a technical mishap. Five days on this show I'm almost drowned on the back lot. I nearly ate a hash brownie. I came close to being flattened by a falling light." Not to mention my tie-up from yesterday. "Don't you think that's a little odd?"

Harv shrugged. "Accidents happen."

That fallen light was no accident. The crewmembers were experts in rigging the lights. Ben was a stickler for safety measures. Someone had deliberately tampered with the lamp. Why did Royce want me to stand in that exact spot at that time? And who touched my shoulder?

Ben went to fetch a replacement for the broken light. Royce demanded that we push ahead with rehearsal. When Joseph and I finished our scenes, he said he wanted to talk. I stopped by craft services to pick up a chilled Mountain Dew, and we went outside to talk. Sitting at the plastic table, Joseph lit a cigar. I popped open the soda can.

"I hear the sky is falling," he said.

"You're right about that. Did you see anyone tampering with the lights?"

"How am I suppose to see what's going on in the ceiling? I can barely see over a tabletop."

"Did you see anyone go up the ladders this morning?"

"I wasn't paying attention to the crew."

"You were probably too busy trying to look up Dottie's dress."

He chuckled.

"I have to admit, Joseph, I'm spooked. For the rest of the day I'll be waiting for the next shoe—or light—

to drop. Or maybe one of the sets will fall on me. Or a trap door will open and—"

"Sandy! Get a grip!"

He was right. I couldn't do the work if I was constantly watching over my shoulder. "But this must mean I'm close to finding the killer."

"If that's true, why doesn't he just shoot you?"

"That's too obvious. A falling spotlight looks like an accident. Anyway, you had something to tell me?"

"Yeah. You'll love this." From inside his suit jacket he pulled a folded-up newspaper page. He smoothed it across the table. "This is the business section from today's *L.A. Times.* I play the markets so I keep tabs. Stock for Stifert Development is up 10 points from yesterday. What would make a dinky little company like that change so much overnight?"

The stock notations meant nothing to me, but I'd never had a head for numbers. That's why I couldn't hang onto the millions from my records and concerts. "Do you think Leo's deal last night had something to do with this?"

"It has *everything* to do with it."

I scanned the other articles on the page. "Any word in the paper about the developers buying Mammoth?"

"Not a peep."

"So we have no proof of Ivan's plan. Just your word."

"Ain't that good enough?"

The AD called us inside for the dress rehearsal. I headed for the set with the uneasy feeling that this show might be the last program recorded inside this grand old soundstage—a sad epitaph. A technician was sweeping up the broken light. The lighting crew was up in the catwalk, installing a new lamp. I made a beeline for the director.

"Royce, we need extra security on the set."

He gave me one of his usual long-suffering looks. "Why? I don't see hordes of rabid fans chasing you."

"I'm talking about that falling lamp and all the other weird stuff that's been going on this week. Somebody's out to get me."

He smiled and placed a hand on my shoulder. "Relax, Sandy. You're being paranoid."

I brushed his hand away. "Would it hurt to have a few more guards around to make sure nothing else happens? And don't tell me the budget won't cover it."

"You're overreacting to one little incident."

"Royce, that 'one little incident' almost killed me."

He sighed. "All right, Sandy. I'll beef up security just for you."

The director got on the phone and asked the studio security office for one more guard. *One* more? That's hardly what I'd call "beefing up" security.

We started the show from the top. After each scene we had a short break while the cameras moved into place in front of the next set. When my first scene came up, I got in place and glanced at the rafters, ever vigilant for falling objects. I wouldn't want this show as the swan song on my obituary. When the time came for the dog trick, Scruffy barked, leaped upon the desk and started licking my shirt cuffs.

"Easy, boy." I pulled my arms back but Scruffy persisted in nibbling on my sleeves. I pushed him away. "Stop that! Get down!"

"Scruffy, come." On hearing his master's voice, the mutt ran to Frances. She picked him up. "I'm sorry, Sandy. I've never seen him behave this way. I wonder why he did that?"

I couldn't tell her why the dog found my wrists so tasty. I inspected my shirt cuffs, hoping the pooch hadn't caused any damage.

The next few hours flew by as we ran through the

show. Despite the goofy storyline, I enjoyed playing off the other actors. Harv had a great sense of comic timing. Dottie was surprisingly sexy and funny today, although at times one could tell she was reading her lines from her hidden slips of paper. Joseph brought a sarcastic edge to his dialogue that I hadn't heard before, no doubt due to our recent adventure. I hoped none of them were involved in Elsie's murder; I'd hate to see such great talent locked away.

I couldn't say the same about the twins. Their performances had been bland all week, but today they seemed especially out of sorts. They kept blowing lines and missing cues. Royce repeatedly stopped to give them direction. The girls acted hurt by Royce's comments—they looked away, Molly picked at her nail polish and Missy played with a prop. Mrs. Jones was especially testy. At one point Royce threatened to ban her from the set. What would make her so on edge?

We stopped at four o'clock for the dinner break, our last chance for hearty fare before the taping at seven o'clock. The *Off-Kelter* crew and cast, along with those working the other sitcoms shooting tonight on the lot, retired to the commissary for a buffet meal. Harv, Joseph and myself stayed away from the massive feed fest. Joseph wasn't comfortable dining in crowds. Stars like Harv and me preferred privacy. Besides, tonight I had too much on my mind to deal with autograph seekers and glad handlers. A PA brought in the food and set up a folding table and chairs. We couldn't eat at the Kelter dining table because the sets were "hot," meaning everything was in place for taping and couldn't be disturbed. Harv said he had to run an errand, so he picked up his Styrofoam container of food and left. As Joseph and I dined, the dwarf regaled me with raunchy stories about his old acting jobs. That was his way of coping with stage nerves before the big show. After eating, we both retired to our respective dressing rooms to change into a fresh costume.

When I reached my trailer, I found a small, square cream-colored envelope taped to the door. My name was typed in all caps with the word "Urgent!" beneath. Maybe one of my fans had written a "good luck" note or Carl was leaving some last-minute instructions about the show. The envelope had no name or return address. I glanced at my watch; I'd have to hurry to get dressed in time. I placed the envelope on the makeup table and changed into the pinstriped pants.

I was buttoning up a clean shirt when someone knocked on the door. I opened the door and was surprised to see Marshall standing on the top step.

"I'm here to give you moral support," he said.

"I wished you'd brought along a bodyguard. Someone tried to drop a stage light on me."

"Looks like you survived."

"Believe me, if I'd died, you'd be the first to know."

"Outside of that, how are you doing? You feeling okay?"

I took a deep breath and tied the ascot around my neck. "I'm nervous as the devil."

"That's a good sign. That means you're pumped up and ready to go."

"As long as nobody kills me before show time."

"You'll be fine. I have a surprise for you."

Marshall stepped aside so I could see the person standing on the ground behind him. A tall, lanky teenager with shoulder-length blonde hair pushed a lock of hair out of his eyes. The kid wore a T-shirt and jeans; colored briefs peeked out above the waistband. He held a large backpack by one strap.

He said, "Hi, dad."

Chapter 21: Spooky Weirdness

The sight of my thirteen-year-old son made me so happy I almost busted my shirt buttons. "Hello, Chip. Nobody told me that you were coming."

"Becka called and asked if I could pick him up," Marshall said.

Chip shifted from foot to foot, one of his habits when he's nervous. "It was sort of a last minute thing. Me and my buddies were supposed to—"

I interrupted. "My buddies and I."

"What?"

"The correct way to say it is 'my buddies and I.'"

He gave an exasperated sigh. "You're as bad as mom."

"No, I'm not. I just don't want you sounding like a dumb hick, that's all. Now what were you saying?"

"I was going to go to a movie tonight, but Jason got sick and Harold's parents took him out of town to see his relatives and, besides, the only new film out this weekend is some dumb chick flick, and I didn't want to stay home and do nothing on a Friday night."

How nice to know that my boy considered spending time with his dad rated just a little above a sappy romantic film, but I wasn't complaining. "I'm glad you came." I nodded towards the backpack. "What's that? Are you running away from home?"

"Mom said I could spend the night at your house if you didn't mind."

Did I mind? I'd pick up Stage 14 and carry it on my shoulders for the chance to spend time with my boy.

"Sure, that's no trouble at all. I'm always happy to have you. Now pull up your pants, your underwear's showing."

"Dad, that's the style."

"I don't care. People don't need to see if you're wearing boxers or briefs. You look stupid like that."

"You used to wear stupid clothes."

Oh, the backlash of those photo spreads in the old teenybopper magazines. "That was the seventies. Everyone wore stupid clothes back then."

Marshall said, "We'd better let you get ready. I'll make sure Chip gets a good seat in the bleachers. Don't worry, Ernest. You'll be great tonight. If you need me I'll be in the agents' room."

During taping, the various agents were safely stowed out of the way in a separate room where they can watch the proceedings on closed circuit TV and not complain about how their client was treated. I handed my car keys to Marshall and told him to stash Chip's backpack in the trunk. After they left, I closed the trailer door and made use of the bathroom facilities. I sang as I finished dressing, partly to warm up my vocal chords but also because Chip's presence lifted my spirits immensely, as well as increased my anxiety. I had to put on a good performance for his sake. I didn't want my boy to feel that he was wasting time tonight. As I picked up the fedora, I noticed the mystery envelope. Right before I left the trailer, I stuck the note into my jacket pocket to read later when I had time.

On the other side of the street stood a row of people—the folks off the street waiting to fill the bleacher seats. "Hi, Sandy!" Bunny shouted from the line. "Have a good show!"

She and her girlfriends waved at me. I smiled and waved back. Tonight I needed all the friends I could get. The sky was starting to darken—the sun would set soon. Inside the soundstage I sat at the makeup table so the artists could work their magic. Frances dabbed on that blasted liver pate,' although by now Scruffy hardly needed an incentive to lick me. After they finished, I copped a can of Mountain Dew from craft services— what I really needed was a tranquilizer. Between my usual pre-show jitters and the fear of another attack on my life, the last thing I needed was a caffeine-loaded soda.

I had a small bottle of breath spray in my pocket. I offered a squirt to Dottie and helped myself as well in preparation of our upcoming kissing scene. I started carrying breath spray after one of my *Buddy Brave* guest stars ate an onion-and-garlic pizza for lunch right before our smooching scene. Afterwards I needed a half a bottle of mouthwash to feel normal again.

Through the speakers mounted in the back hallway I could hear the activity in the bleachers. The talented warm-up guy was entertaining the audience. Sitcoms use warm-up guys (and a few gals) to hype up the audience for maximum laughter. During the long down times during shooting, the warm-up's job is to relieve the guests' boredom with jokes, interviews, games and merchandise giveaways (although nobody in their right mind would cherish an *Off-Kelter* plastic water bottle). I peeked from behind the living room set. The four videotape cameras were in place to record various angles simultaneously; one camera was set low for Joseph's close-ups. The warm-up was introducing the cast members, who ran out from the set and took bows to tepid audience applause. A security guard was posted at each end of the front bleacher seats and another one was on the floor beside the outside door. This was Royce's idea of "beefed up" security? The meager presence of the guards didn't comfort me. Besides, studio security seldom handled any crime worse than a guest taking unauthorized photos of the actors; the guards never dealt with deadly killers. I was on my own tonight.

After the cast introductions, Royce called for places. The actors in the first scene stepped onto the set. Royce sat in his canvas chair with the script supervisor, the AD and the head writer by his side. The director ordered the sound guy to start the audiotape rolling. A PA stepped in front of the cameras to mark the scene with a digital clapperboard.

Royce called, "Ready, action!" Another fun-filled episode of *Off-Kelter* was off and running.

The opening scenes seemed to drag, mainly because I was anxious to get on stage. Until I can say that first line or sing that opening verse, I'm a basket case. I leaned against the wall, drained the last of the soda from the can and let my mind drift. Thoughts about Elsie Bloom from the past five days floated through my brain. But before the pieces formed a picture, Royce called, "Cut. Moving on," the signal that he was satisfied with the take. The crew pushed the cameras into place for my first scene. The make-up lady and the costumer both gave me a last minute fussing over. I put on my hat, took a deep breath, and waited for Harv's cue. I opened the set door and stepped from the dark backstage into the bright stage lights. I fought the temptation to take a peek at the audience because the cameras would pick up the glance (In the early days of my show, I kept glancing offstage until one of my co-actors sat me down and taught me how to stay focused). I kept one ear tuned to the actors and the other one on the guests. I heard gasps and then hearty applause when the audience recognized me. Bunny and her cohorts offered up screams of delight. The corner of my mouth twitched in a small smile but otherwise I stayed in character. The scene moved along nicely until Dottie mangled a line. As we stopped, I searched for Chip in the bleachers, but with the lights in my eyes I couldn't see. We restarted the scene and my entrance garnered less applause from the already jaded viewers.

My kiss with Dottie elicited considerable audience reaction, including "ooooo!" (from Bunny) and a couple of catcalls (that better not be from Chip). The goofy dog ruined the take by lunging for my wrists again. Frances responded by slapping more goo on my face. With all that liver, I smelled like a butcher's shop. This time I made sure that Scruffy hit his mark by shoving my face up against his nose. When Royce called, "cut, let's move on," the audience responded with heavy clapping. Either they really liked me or else they were relieved at not having to sit through the same scene yet again. The few jokes we had on the show got stale quickly after a couple of takes.

After a couple of hours, the show stopped as Harv and Dottie retired to their dressing rooms for a costume change. During the break, Frances and Scruffy amused the audience with dog tricks (the mutt should have demonstrated his skill in untying knots). I had a long stretch of free time—after the break my pre-recorded dance number would play over the monitors and more scenes would pass before I was due back onstage. I went outside for some fresh air and instead encountered Joseph's cigar.

"The show's going pretty well," I remarked.

He breathed out a well-formed smoke ring. "Just wait until the twins are on again. By the time they get their lines right, they'll be legal age. Say, we got some noisy ones in the audience tonight."

"That'd be my fan club."

"It's nice. We finally got an audience that's laughing instead of snoring during the show. Can we borrow them again for next week?"

I laughed. Darkness had fallen and the outside lights had automatically switched on. Don't know why I thought of it, but I remembered the unread note in my pocket. I took out the envelope and stared at it.

"What's that?" Joseph asked.

"I don't know. I found it taped to my trailer door." I poked a finger beneath the envelope's flap to pry it open.

"Careful, might be a bomb inside that thing."

"Shut up."

"Maybe it's a deadly poison that'll eat right through your fingers."

"Shut up!"

I removed a piece of folded paper with a message typed in all caps: IF YOU WANT TO KNOW WHO KILLED ELSIE BLOOM, GO TO THE BACKLIT DURING THE SHOW OR YOU'LL NEVER FIND OUT. Of course the page had no signature.

I showed the paper to the dwarf. "What do you think about this?" He responded with a most unhelpful "huh."

"Whoever sent this knows where I am tonight."

"That narrows it down to everyone who works at Mammoth. The production schedule ain't exactly a secret."

"Why go to the back lot? Why can't this person talk to me directly? Is the killer watching them?"

"It's a trap, you know, like you see on all the TV shows."

"You manage to see the worst in every situation, don't you?"

"I'm just sayin'."

I folded up the letter and stuck both it and the envelope inside my suit pocket. "I'm going to check it out."

"Now?"

"Royce won't need me for at least forty-five

minutes. The back lot's only two minutes away." I unplugged one of the *Off-Kelter* golf carts from the battery charger and hopped into the driver's seat.

"Wait up."

"You don't need to come along."

"If it's a trap, someone's got to bail you out."

"What are *you* going to do? Bite their ankles?"

Joseph climbed into the front passenger seat. "Let's go, Sherlock."

I felt a little more secure not having to confront the killer alone, although I had my doubts about Joseph's effectiveness in a tight spot. I turned on the cart's headlights, released the parking brake, floored the accelerator, and narrowly missed a page standing by the stage door. I zipped along, with Joseph clinging to the edge of the front seat for dear life. On reaching the back lot I slowed down so I could look around. The streetlights were turned down low to save power. A chill ran down my back.

"I don't see anyone," Joseph said.

"Maybe they're on a different street."

I rounded the corner and drove down the street where I had filmed my dance number. Bare and empty, the street looked different—and scarier. My muscles tightened with fear. Then we both saw it. I stomped on the brake and reached out to keep Joseph from flying out of the cart. When we stopped he stood up on the seat for a better look.

"Son of a buck!" he shouted. "It's Elsie's ghost!"

At the far end of the street stood a woman dressed in a long white dress. In the darkness she gave off a supernatural glow. No mistaking Elsie's distinct features.

Joseph sat and clapped both hands over his eyes. "Go back! Go back! I ain't messin' with no ghost!"

"Don't be ridiculous. Elsie's a friendly ghost. She

knows I tried to help her when she died. She won't hurt me."

"What about me? What about all the times I harassed her? She's out for revenge!"

"I'm going in for a closer look."

I tapped the pedal and eased the cart halfway down the block. I stopped, set the hand brake, and stepped out. Joseph clamored into the back seat and huddled down, out of sight.

"I thought you were here to help me," I said.

"When it comes to ghosts, you're on your own."

"There must be a logical explanation for this."

"Like what?"

I approached the life-size apparition. Even with no breeze her dress fluttered. Her lips moved as if she was talking but she made no sound. Elsie moved her hands and stared off to the side, as if looking at someone standing beside me. She was transparent; I could see right through her. I fought the urge to run away.

"Elsie? Is that you? It's me, Sandy. Remember me? I'm here to help you." She kept moving but didn't reply or look at me. "Elsie? Can you hear me?"

"Sandy, watch out!" At the sound of Joseph's voice, I turned around. His eyes peered out from over the cart's back seat. "Get back here before she sucks out your blood!"

"She's a ghost, not a vampire." I looked at the sprite again. "Elsie? Can you tell me who killed you?"

I reached out my hand to touch Elsie and my fingers passed right through the figure. I pulled back my hand and almost jumped out of my pants with fright. The apparition didn't react.

"Sandy! Don't touch her or you'll die!"

I spun around to face Joseph. "You're not helping!"

I returned to the cart, got in and started to leave when a thought came to me. I looked at Elsie again.

Joseph climbed back into the front seat. "Sandy, let's get out of here!"

"Quiet down, I'm thinking. There's something odd about Elsie."

"There sure is! She's an evil spirit!"

I watched her for a few more moments. That dress looked familiar. She hadn't worn it to the read-through on Monday, but somewhere I'd seen those clothes before. And she kept making the same gestures and mouth movements over and over, as if repeating a set pattern—like a movie stuck on a film loop. I jumped out of the cart and scanned the buildings.

"Up there!" I pointed to the top floor of one of the facades. "Joseph, do you see it?"

"What is it, the Wicked Witch of the West on her broomstick?"

A light shone from a fourth-floor window of one of the brownstones.

I removed my jacket and fedora, laid both items in the cart, and ran down the street. When I reached the front steps of the brownstone, Joseph shouted for me to stop. I waited as he caught up with me, his little legs moving as fast as they could.

He panted. "Don't leave me out here alone with the ghost."

"You know, Joseph, you've played comic sidekicks before. Can't you be a bit more gung ho in real life?"

"If I die from this, you'll hear from my lawyer."

"My lawyer is more expensive than your lawyer."

I climbed the steps into the fake brownstone. The interior was as black as the profit ledger of the *Star Wars* franchise. I felt around for a light switch but found nothing—these facades were only used for exterior shots. Nobody came inside these structures except to rig lights or effects.

"Great. I can't see a thing."

"Sandy, down here." I heard a click, and a flicker of light appeared in the dwarf's hand. He held up his cigar lighter. "Take this."

"Thanks."

I held the chrome lighter ahead of me and climbed the rickety stairs, which hadn't been trod upon since Laurel and Hardy threw their last pie fight. Joseph followed. Our footsteps kicked up small puffs of dust. The tall building had little depth. The ledge behind the front wall was just large enough for an actor or two to stand on and look out the window. The interior had no back wall, just a network of metal pipes to hold up the structure. I walked slowly so my sidekick could keep up. I kept the lighter away from the dry, wooden walls. It'd only take a spark to set these old structures ablaze. We reached the fourth story.

"Look at that, Joseph. There's our 'ghost.'"

On a small cart sat a 35 mm film projector with its lens pointed out the window. A loop of film ran continuously between the two reels. A battery generator powered the contraption. I flipped off the machine's power switch and "Elsie" disappeared from the street below.

Joseph examined the projector. "Son of a gun! The ghost was just smoke and shadows. How did you know?"

"Couple of nights ago I caught one of Elsie's movies on TV. What we saw down there was a clip of her lifted out of that film."

"The guy who set this up is one smarty pants filmmaker. But why the shenanigans? It's a lot of trouble for a practical joke."

"Unless someone wanted to lure us up here."

"Why?"

The answer came all too quickly. An explosion on the ground floor shook the structure and Joseph fell flat on his keister. I grabbed the wall to keep my balance. Huge flames shot up the stairwell, cutting off our only means of escape.

Chapter 22: Burning Down The House

I pulled Joseph to his feet.

"Was that an earthquake?" he asked.

"Worse than that. Arson."

We looked down the stairwell, or rather, what was left of it. The fire was gobbling up the wooden structure. The stairs on the lower levels were already consumed.

"We gotta get out of here!" my sidekick shouted.

"No kidding. But we can't use stairs."

The heat started warping the floorboards and the floor shifted beneath my feet. In minutes we'd both be a couple of barbecued hams.

Joseph screamed, "We're going to die! We're going to die!"

I grabbed him by the shoulders and yelled so he could hear me over the roar of the inferno. "I'll get you out of here, I promise!"

I had enough sweat pouring down my body to fill my swimming pool. The makeup slid down my face and stained my shirt collar. Ashes landed on my clothes, but keeping my costume clean was the least of my worries. I might not make it out of here alive to tape my final scenes. I unbuttoned the cuffs and rolled up my sleeves. We both coughed from the stench of charred wood and scorched metal. I unbuttoned my collar so I could breath. I tied the ascot over my nose and mouth to keep the toxic air out of my lungs. The old paint peeling off the red-hot walls was probably spewing out buckets of lead.

The old fire drills in grade school flashed in my mind. I dropped to my hands and knees. "Get down! There's more oxygen near the floor." Joseph, still standing, looked me in the eye. "I guess you're already down."

The thick smoke reduced visibility to near zero. The heat was worse than an August high noon in Arizona. The fire singed the ends of my hair. I wiped the sweat out of my eyes and crawled around on my hands and knees, searching for an exit. I felt dizzy. I put one hand against the hot wall and waited for my head to clear. If I passed out, our gooses would be literally cooked. My hand touched the projection stand and I got an idea.

"Joseph, were are you?" I heard a faint reply. "Come toward the sound of my voice. I found a way out." I reached into the merciless smoke to find the dwarf.

"Ow! You poked my eye out!"

I grabbed his wrist and pulled him close. With my other hand I tipped over the projector so I'd have a clear shot at our escape hatch.

"Get on my back!" I ordered.

"What?"

"We're leaving through the window."

"Are you nuts? It's four stories to the ground!"

"Hurry up. I can't wait for someone to build an elevator."

A breeze waffled through the window and whipped up the flames. The stairwell crumbled with a crash. The floor swayed beneath me.

"On my back, *now*."

He got on my back, piggyback style, and I stood.

"Hold on tight!" I yelled.

He wrapped both arms around my neck and squeezed.

I gasped for air. "Not that tight!"

With one hand I loosened his death grip against my

windpipe. I grabbed the sides of the window and stepped up onto the sill just as the floorboards where I'd been standing collapsed in a blaze. I sat, crouched on the ledge, and looked down. The ground suddenly moved ten miles away from me. Now I know how Jimmy Stewart felt in the movie *Vertigo*.

"Whatcha gonna do?" Joseph shouted. "Sprout wings and fly?"

"Don't worry. I've done this before."

What I didn't say was that Buddy Brave had done this in broad daylight early in the day when he was well rested, years younger and more spry; when he was rigged up with a safety harness and a net underneath as well as a fire crew standing by to control the flames; and after he'd taken a few tokes of mary jane to calm his nerves. What was I thinking? What kind of fool was I? I was out-of-shape and couldn't climb down a four-story wall in the dark, especially not with a dwarf on my back. This stunt was going to kill both Joseph and myself. But I couldn't have Chip find his dad's charred body on the pavement. I wasn't about to ruin my boy's Friday night fun. Somehow, I had to get out of this mess alive.

I pulled the ascot off my face and stuffed it into my pants pocket. I raised myself into a low crouch. I took a deep breath, held onto the sides of the window, and swung myself around. I couldn't maneuver in those hard-soled shoes, so with my toes I kicked off the studio's footwear. The shoes dropped to the ground. With my stocking foot I gingerly felt around on the outside of the structure for a foothold.

The back lot façades are not made of real brick or stone, but of a plastic-like material created in the studio mill. This synthetic resin is molded into sheets and painted to resemble any type of building material. The sheets are then nailed onto a wooden framework.

Fortunately, whoever constructed this façade had left deep indentations between the fake bricks. A few inches down I found a small ledge just large enough for the toes of my left foot. I followed with my right foot. With my feet planted, I lowered my body and found new handholds. I was too scared to look down, so I had to go by touch alone. I told Joseph to stop fidgeting. His shifting nearly upset my already precarious balance. Flames shot out from the window just feet above me. The wall was hot to the touch and I could only briefly hold onto one spot. I inched my way down the wall. Then I made a horrific discovery.

Plastic melts.

The stone-like resin material beneath my hands and feet began to soften in the heat. Soon I'd have nothing to hang onto. I tried to speed my descent. In my haste my left foot slipped and I dangled precariously. Joseph almost slid off my back. I wiggled my foot around and found a new foothold. I blinked to keep the sweat out of my eyes. The heat made my palms so sweaty I couldn't keep a tight grip. As the foothold dissolved, my wet palms slid off the wall.

Joseph and I both screamed as we fell to the ground.

I landed with a thud, not hard enough to kill me but enough to scare the bejeebers out of me. I lay on the ground long enough to assess the damage. A few aches and scrapes, but nothing broken. Fortunately, we'd only fallen one story up. I got on my hands and knees.

"Joseph? Where are you?"

He moaned. He'd landed on the grassy area to the side of the brownstone's front steps, just inches from the concrete pavement. I crawled over to him. He was face down and not moving. I'd killed him! No, wait, if he was dead he wouldn't be moaning.

"Joseph! Say something! Are you all right?"

"No, I am not all right!"

I sighed in relief. As long as the grouch was his usually cantankerous self, he'd be okay. "Where are you hurt?"

"Everywhere!"

The flames spread to the adjoining structures. In minutes the entire back lot would shoot up in a massive bonfire. With enough marshmallows, chocolate bars and graham crackers, I could make s'mores for everyone on the lot.

"We can't wait here for an ambulance," I said. "I'll have to carry you."

I gently rolled him over. His face was cut and bruised from where he'd landed, but I didn't see any major injuries. I slid my arms beneath him and stood. Lifting a fifty-pound sack of puppies would have been easier. The fire lit up the street like a searchlight at a movie premiere. I ran to the curb just as the wall that I'd been climbing crashed to the ground.

Joseph whined the entire way to the cart. "Ow! Ouch! Take it easy! That hurts!"

"Shut up or I'll really make you hurt!"

I dropped Joseph on the back seat, jumped into the driver's seat, released the brake and hit maximum speed all the way to the studio hospital. I pulled up to the curb.

"Why are we stopping here?" Joseph asked.

"So you can get medical attention."

I turned around. He was sitting up and unwrapping a cigar.

"What are you doing? The way you were carrying on, I thought you'd broken every bone in your body."

"The way you lugged me around wasn't no pleasure cruise."

I deliberately floored the cart, hard enough to knock him back onto the seat. I drove at top speed to the door of Stage 14. I slammed on the brakes and got out. The red light mounted beside the stage door was on, indicating taping in progress. The most grievous sin on the lot was to walk in during shooting. Normally I'd have waited until the light went off, but tonight nothing was normal. I was furious. I grabbed the door latch.

One of the pages attending to the door stepped up to me. "They're taping inside. sir. You can't go in there."

"Watch me!" I yanked opened the door and marched across the floor.

The cameras were aimed at the living room set. Carl was in his chair, intently watching the actors. Royce's chair was empty. The twins and Dottie were onstage. Mrs. Jones was gone from her usual off camera spot. On my entrance, the actors stopped their work and glared at me in shock, that I'd dare violate the sanctity of shooting.

"Cut! Cut!" Carl jumped from his chair. "Sandy, what are you doing? Didn't you see the red light?"

"Call the fire department!" I said. "The back lot's on fire!" Carl stared at me in disbelief. "I'm not joking. The back lot's burning down! Get the firemen out there now!"

Carl told one of the PAs to call, which she did on the floor phone. Carl said, "Sandy, what's this all about?"

"You're shooting without Royce?"

"He had a headache and went to get some aspirin. What happened to your costume?" He glanced at my feet. "Where are your shoes?"

In the heat of the moment (pun intended) I was so preoccupied with escaping the deathtrap that I'd forgotten to retrieve my shoes. There I stood in front of the audience, cast, crew and God Almighty in my stocking feet with half of my costume still in the car, my sleeves rolled up, my ascot off, my shirt stained with makeup, my pants torn and every inch of skin and clothing covered with soot and ashes. This was not one of my better days.

But I had more important things on my mind besides clothes. Across the room, I spied a figure standing at the base of the bleachers. The person stared at me in shock, no doubt surprised that I had survived their trap. The person slid along the front of the bleachers toward the door.

I pointed. "Stop that person! That's Elsie Bloom's killer!"

The person broke into a run, knocking over the crewmembers in the way. The security guards were nowhere in sight. The pages grabbed at the person but the suspect shoved them aside. I was too far away to catch the person before they could dash out the door and escape in the cart I'd conveniently left by the door.

Frances stood nearby, holding Scruffy on a leash. I grabbed the leash from her hand, dropped it, caught the dog's attention and pointed to the suspect.

"Go on, Scruffy, sic 'em!"

The clueless canine sat on his haunches, panted, and gazed at me with his big brown eyes.

"Attack, Scruffy! Kill!"

The moronic mutt barked.

Frances frowned. "Scruffy is an actor! I did not train him as an attack dog!"

The culprit was nearly out the door when my boy came to the rescue. Chip sprang from his seat in the front row of the bleachers, climbed over the railing and dropped on top of the suspect, knocking the person to the floor. They scuffled until Chip rolled the person face down, straddled their back and reached up under the armpits. He laced his fingers behind the person's head and held it down in a full Nelson until the prisoner begged for mercy.

The cast, crew, Joseph, myself, the pages and, last of all, two security guards, surrounded the pair on the floor. Chip relinquished the captive to the guards. My boy stood beside me as the guards squatted on either side of the person.

Leo pushed his way through the huddle and glared at the captive. "What's this all about?"

Troy, sprawled on the floor and looking forlorn, gazed at the studio chief with moist eyes. "I did it for you, dad."

Chapter 23: A Hard Day's Night

The people around me murmured in astonishment, including Mrs. Jones, who had just returned from the backstage restroom.

"Did Troy call Leo his *dad*?" Joseph asked

"It's true," I said. "Troy is Leo's love child. So Elsie wasn't lying. Had she married Troy, the big guy would have been her father-in-law."

Leo crossed his arms and said to Troy, "Do what? What did you do for me?"

Tears ran down Troy's cheeks. "When Elsie was in Spain shooting a movie. She found out what you did. She talked to the man you hired. Elsie was going to tell. I couldn't let that happen. I tried to protect you. I thought you'd love me if I kept you safe, dad."

Leo's face turned as red as the flames in the back lot. "Stop calling me that! I am not your father!"

From the way he blushed, we all knew he was lying.

Ivan came down from the front row of the bleachers. "What? Is this true? Is that hack actor my brother?" He sounded more angry than joyful at the unexpected family reunion.

The elder Constantine ordered, "Go back to your seat, Ivan."

"What's he talking about? Who is this man you hired in Spain?"

"He's crazy! That man on the floor is delusional!"

I prompted, "It has something to do with your mother, Ivan."

"My mother? What about my mother?" The pitch of

his voice rose with anxiety. "Leo, what did you do to my mother?"

"We'll talk about this later, son."

Leo rushed out the stage door with his legitimate child following, pleading and yelling. I had a feeling that next year Ivan wouldn't be sending any Father's Day cards. I asked the security guards if they could hold Troy until the police arrived. I told the AD to call for the real cops. Carl got on the phone as the guards helped Troy to his feet. When the guards opened the stage door to leave, the studio fire engine roared down the street with its siren blaring.

Royce, holding a large bottle of aspirin, walked up. "Why is everyone standing around? Why aren't we shooting?" He noticed my disheveled appearance. "Fairfax. I should have known. I let you out of my sight for one minute and you get into trouble."

"I just caught Elsie Bloom's murderer," I said.

"That's nice, but we got a show to get in the can before the crew goes into golden time. Everyone, back in position!" Royce shot me a glance, then uncapped the aspirin bottle, poured out a handful of pills, and swallowed them. The he hollered to the warm-up guy to calm down the audience. The two hundred people in the bleachers were riled up about Troy's capture. Those in the back seats were standing for a better look and the rest were talking. The warm-up tried one of his tried-and-true monologues but nobody was listening. We couldn't shoot with the guests rioting. I glanced at my watch: eleven o'clock, and we still had three scenes left. I asked the warm-up to hand me his microphone. He dropped the mike over the railing.

I spoke into the mike. "Hi, there. Sandy Fairfax here. If all of you will simmer down, I'll sing for you. Would you like that?" Of course my fan club screamed in glee. "But everyone has to sit down and be quiet. We have to finish the show and we need everyone's cooperation to make that happen. Okay?"

The people reluctantly sat. I sang one of my old hits a capella. I have perfect pitch, so staying on key without a backing band wasn't a problem. Can't say this was one of my best performances, but considering the circumstances, I did okay. A few bars into the song the audience looked relaxed (maybe I should record an album of lullabies for insomniacs). I finished to applause more generous than my effort warranted and I returned the mike to the warm-up guy.

Chip was still standing on the stage floor. "Thanks for helping me catch that creep," I said. "Where did you learn to fight like that?"

"I used to beat up the kids at school when they called you a drunken bum."

"Why didn't I ever hear about that?"

"I guess mom didn't tell you."

"I don't want you picking fights. Beating up people doesn't solve any problems."

"Yeah, dad."

I put my hand on his shoulder and smiled. "But I appreciate the fact that you stood up for your old man."

He pushed the hair out of his eyes and grinned. "Yeah. I really licked some of them too."

"I bet you did."

Royce said, "Can we have quiet on the set? And Sandy, get some decent clothes."

I told Chip to get back in his seat. While he dashed up the steps I silently padded (I'm still shoeless) backstage. Joseph's costume was also a mess, but he hadn't changed after dress rehearsal so he put on the second outfit in his dressing room. When Edith saw my distressed costume, her head nearly exploded. She grabbed my wrist and dragged me into a backstage room. I didn't have a stand-by costume since nobody had expected me to do stunt work. The wardrobe building had closed for the day, so Penny had to make do with the clothes on hand. Edith sent a PA to retrieve my jacket and hat from the cart and then ordered me to take off my clothes. Yes, that's right. She wanted to give my shirt and pants a quick sponging and ironing. I balked at the idea of standing around in only my Jockies but she insisted. Edith searched a closet for something I could wear while she worked on the costume but all she found that fit me was a large, frilly pink ladies' robe with a hemline that ended above my knees. But it had to suffice. I put on the robe just as Harv and Joseph walked by the open doorway. The dwarf gave me a hearty wolf whistle and Harv looked me over appreciatively. I crossed my arms and pretended to ignore them.

Edith cleaned and pressed the jacket, pants and the ascot, but the shirt was ruined beyond repair. She found a clean white shirt that was a size too big. No matter. I put it on and buttoned the jacket over it to hide the shirt. Edith didn't have any men's shoes in my size so a PA fetched my sneakers from the trailer. The makeup gal did a fast repair of my face and trimmed the burnt ends of my ponytail. Hopefully the audience wouldn't notice the discrepancy in my hair and clothes. Royce changed the blocking so the cameras only shot me from the waist up to hide my footwear and the burn marks on the trousers.

Because of the late hour, people in the bleachers started leaving until only a handful of family members and my fan club remained. Exhausted, I played my last scene on adrenaline fumes and to a half-empty house. When Royce called "that's a wrap" shortly after midnight, everyone cheered out of gratitude that we could finally go home. The warm-up guy called the actors out for a quick curtain call to a tiny but appreciative audience. My fan club gave me a standing ovation. As the crew packed up, the audience came onto the floor to congratulate us for surviving the show.

The agents were released from their holding area and Marshall approached me with fire steaming from nostrils. "Ernest! What were you doing, giving a concert without a contract!"

"Hello to you too, Marshall. I didn't give a concert, I sang one little song."

"A song for which the producers did not pay you to perform! Why do you keep giving away your talent for free? Are you trying to give me a heart attack?"

"Yes, then you won't scold me as much."

"What is it with you getting mixed up with murderers?"

"I don't know, Marshall. These things happen."

He glanced over my clothes. "You look like you've been smacked by a steamroller."

"Feel like it, too. So how was the show, or were you too busy schmoozing with the other agents to watch?"

Marshall and I discussed a couple of quick business matters, then he returned my car keys and went on his way. I turned my attention to my son.

"So, Chip, how did you like the show?"

"It was all right. Kinda dumb story. The best part was catching that killer." Not a word about my performance. "Can you introduce me to the twins? They're pretty hot."

So Chip had an eye for the pretty girls. Like father, like son. I proudly presented him to the rest of the cast and left him on his own to finagle a date from the twins while I met with my fan club. Bunny had gathered up some stray scripts left by the crew and I autographed the pages for the fans.

"That was a super duper show, Sandy! I loved it!" I could always count on Bunny for a compliment. "I never knew making a sitcom was anything like this!"

"Most sitcoms don't have a killer running loose or the back lot burning down but, yes, otherwise, this was a pretty typical shoot."

"You'll have to tell me all about it so I can write it up for the fanzine!"

"Maybe later. Remember the ghost I told you about, Bunny? This morning she saved my life. Freda tapped my shoulder and warned me that a spotlight was going to fall on me."

Bunny whispered. "Really? Is the ghost in here right now?"

"Possibly. She may be watching and laughing at how silly we are."

"But you solved another mystery, Sandy! You're a real detective!"

"No, I'm just an entertainer."

"So are you going to do any concerts real soon?"

Concerts? I hadn't thought that far ahead. Only an hour ago I wasn't sure that I'd live long enough to finish the show. I thanked the gals for sticking around to the bitter end, wished them a safe trip back home, and bid them good night. after they left, I had another visitor.

"Do I get an autograph too?" I spun around to see Cinnamon. "Surprised?"

"Yes, I am. Were you here for the show?"

"Certainly. I had to see how your dance looked in the final cut."

"Are you pleased with it?"

"Very much so."

"You ran off after the shoot on Wednesday. I thought you were unhappy with me."

"I'm sorry. I had an appointment across town."

"I'm glad you came tonight."

"I am too. You were the best part of the show."

"Um, thanks." Why couldn't I think of something intelligent to say? Around my fans I was bold and confident, but beside Cinnamon I felt like a teenager with his first crush.

After an uncomfortable pause, she said, "Well, I have to go now."

"Wait!"

"What is it?"

"Can I have your phone number?"

"My what?"

"Well, Cinnamon, I might be doing some concerts soon and when I do I'll need a choreographer to do the choreography. You know, for the dancing and, well, I was wondering—" She smiled in amusement as I rambled. "Since you're a choreographer, if I had your number I could call you to come and, um, do the choreography for the dance numbers. If that's something you'd like to do."

Cinnamon flashed two rows of the whitest teeth I'd ever seen. "Sandy, I'd like that very much." She took a business card from her purse. She placed the card in my palm, closed my fingers and laid her hand atop of mine. "Here's my number. Call me soon, okay?"

Our eyes met and my head nearly spun out of control. She released her hand and gave me a small wave. I watched her every step of the way as she left the building. Then I noticed Chip starring at me. How long had he been watching and how much had he heard?

Joseph yanked on my trouser leg. "Okay, Mister Sammy Shovel, ace detective. Tell us how you fingered Troy as the murderer."

The other cast members also demanded an explanation. I handed off my jacket and hat to Penny and the craft services guy brought me an ice-cold Mountain Dew. The soda helped to wash the taste of the ashes out of my mouth. The actors sat around the living room set to listen to my tale. I perched on the top rung of the stairwell so everyone could see me. Royce and Carl stood outside the set to listen.

Some of what follows I learned later as Troy confessed to the cops and the local investigative reporters dug into the story. When Elsie had shot that spaghetti western in Spain (the one that I saw on TV), she ran into the low-life that Leo had paid to poison poor Yolanda. She didn't think much about it until later when she started dating Snooky Doodle, her pet name for Troy, and learned that Leo was his dad. Leo kept Troy's identity a secret to retain his respectability. Mr. Constantine tried to placate his misbegotten child by throwing a few bones his way, like the *Space Posse* gig. Despite the low ratings, Leo kept the show on the air to give Troy a job. The "TY" dates in Leo's calendar were the times he visited Troy, usually at a cheap restaurant away from the well-to-do Westside crowd.

But over time, the son felt he deserved more from his dad than a small role in a bad show and lunch dates on the sly. Troy, who was never a good actor, took filmmaking classes in hopes that he could move into directing or producing, but Elsie threatened to jeopardize the plan if she went to the police. If Leo went to jail for murder, Troy's career was over. Besides, Troy still felt some loyalty to his dad. In his own twisted way the actor thought if he kept Leo out of prison, his father might love him more.

I sensed something was going on between father and son when I overheard the actor asking for an *Off-Kelter* directing job. Newbies in the industry don't run to the studio boss to ask for work. Since Troy was already on the *Space Posse* payroll, logically he'd first direct for that show, not a sitcom for which he'd had no prior experience.

At the studio, Troy had access to the resources to not only make the poison that killed Elsie but to set up the ghost film on the back lot. He knew the *Off-Kelter* schedule and room layout so he could slip in and out of the stage unseen. He planted the hash brownies and, having taken a lighting class at USC, also rigged the light to fall (he learned how to tie knots in class as well). On Thursday when I was on my way to the administration building, Troy was outside with the *Space Posse* cast. He assumed I was on my way to tell Leo what I knew about Elsie's death. He followed at a distance. When Troy saw me inside the executive suite, he panicked and knocked me out. He carried me on his shoulders out of the building to the empty soundstage next door. Troy had left the poison at home so he, thankfully, couldn't kill me right away. By the time he returned, I'd split, thanks to the efforts of man's best friend.

The suspect hadn't planned to burn me alive in the back lot. Troy had left the note on my trailer door and hid in a brownstone to see if I'd show up for his spooky movie. Actors are highly superstitious and he assumed that Elsie's "ghost" would scare me off. But when Joseph and I discovered the camera, Troy tried to stop us permanently.

As for the clandestine meeting between Elsie and Leo in the studio park, that's when the actress announced her very real pregnancy.

Dottie raised her hand. "But how did Troy put the poison in Elsie's eye drops? She used her drops Monday morning during the table read and was just fine."

"Troy switched the bottles during the lunch break. He knew Elsie always left her bag in her dressing room when she went out for lunch."

Carl said, "But Troy was working on his show that

morning. We saw him on our way to the commissary."

"That puzzled me too until I remembered something that one of my fans said: 'It could be anyone under all that makeup.' When we met the Gorgandian on Monday, he grunted and walked away. But the other times when I saw Troy in makeup and costume, he talked. On Monday, Troy had paid another actor to take over his role. Since his character spoke gibberish, nobody noticed the swap."

"What about the hamburger wrapper in Elsie's waste basket?" Joseph asked.

"Again, that was Troy. Since he was playing hooky, he couldn't go to the commissary and let anyone see him out of makeup. He grabbed a bite to eat off the lot."

After Troy's arrest, the LAPD finally tested the bottle of eye drops I turned in and, yes, traces of cyanide were found. Troy's lawyer later tried to discredit the find, claiming I had "contaminated" the evidence, as if an out-of-work former teen idol would keep cyanide around his house. Over the following weeks, the tabloids had a blast dishing out dirt about Leo's love child, but the elder Constantine was occupied with other problems. Ivan slapped a civil suit onto his dad for his mother's death. The current Mrs. Leo Constantine filed for divorce. Leo and Ivan both resigned from the studio, and daddy fled to Switzerland before the cops caught up with him.

On a happier note, the resulting publicity gave *Off-Kelter* a helpful boost in the ratings and a season renewal. The role of Miss Tucker was recast and a talented young comedienne breathed new life into the character. The sitcom's new producer fired all the writers and hired better ones who revamped and improved the show. The twins stayed on, but only to use the show as a springboard to promote their line of teen fashions. Once the clothes started selling, Mrs.

Jones was happy to let the girls ease out of acting and devote their energies to more profitable retail sales.

But for now in the studio, I said my goodbyes to the cast amidst hugs and the standard promises of "let's do lunch" that seldom materialize. Dottie introduced her neighbor, Mrs. Fitch, and told me that she planned to hire a full-time chauffeur "so I can focus on my acting and not worry my head about driving." Sounded like a good plan to me.

I tried to avoid Royce, but he cornered me. "Did you honestly think I was involved with Elsie's death?"

"I have to admit, Royce, I thought you were trying to drown me Wednesday in the back lot."

"Mechanical malfunction with the pipe. One of the crew guys told me that a switch got stuck."

"And I was suspicious when I saw Leo's memo about Elsie's pregnancy."

"If you must know, I told Elsie that if she proved the child was mine, my wife and I would adopt the little tyke."

"You would?"

To my surprise, Royce looked happy. "Years ago a team of doctors said I could never father a child. I was hoping Elsie would prove them wrong."

By now, the room was nearly empty except for a crewman shutting down the last of the work lights. A tug on my pant leg meant that Joseph wanted to speak to me. I squatted to look him in the eye. A charming female dwarf stood with him.

"Hey, big guy. Looks like you survived your week on *Off-Kelter*."

"I guess you could say we set this show on fire."

"Very punny. Say, I wanna introduce my better half, Linda."

"Hello, Linda." Feeling gallant, I kissed her chubby little hand. "Very nice to meet you. Joseph's been telling me how much he loves that health food you cook for him."

"Don't listen to him, he's crazy. Say, the little woman and I are going out for a late supper. Wanna join us?"

"Can I take a rain check on that? My son's with me and I need to get him home."

"Is that him over there? Looks just like you, the poor kid."

"That's why we call him Chip, for 'chip off the old block.' Well, Joseph, we caught Elsie's killer but we didn't stop Ivan from selling the studio."

The dwarf grinned. "Don't worry about that. Monday morning I'll be calling the 'Entertainment Tonight' people with a hot tip. Once their reporters break the story, Ivan's gonna look pretty stupid for selling the studio while his pop and stepbrother are murder suspects. That family's gonna keep a fleet of lawyers in gravy for years."

"I was right, you do have a devious mind. Joseph, thanks for all your help with my investigation. I couldn't have done it without you."

"Nothing personal, Sandy, but next time you're on a show, don't call me. Working with you is too dangerous. "

SATURDAY: AT LIBERTY
Chapter 24: Beautiful Boy

The Graves left and Chip said, "Dad, can we go now?" He sounded bored and tired.

He and I were the only ones still in the building. Before we left, I gave Stage 14 one last, nostalgic look. I stopped at my trailer long enough to get out of my filthy costume and take a quick shower to remove the makeup and soot; Chip waited outside and chatted with one of the female pages. After I finished dressing, the two of us bundled into the Mustang and I waved at the gate guard as I drove out. Famished, I swung by the In-and-Out drive-through on West Sunset to pick up two orders of double cheeseburgers, fries and chocolate shakes. When we go to my house, Chip said he had to call his mother.

"You mean now? It's past midnight. She's probably asleep."

"She said I had to call when I got to your house."

"She's afraid I'll take you to the airport and fly off to South America. Sure, go ahead. Use the kitchen phone."

As he dialed, I set out the fast food on the kitchen island. I listened to Chip's end of the conversation.

"Hi mom...yeah, I know, but the show ran late and we just now got in...yeah, I had a good time...I helped dad catch a murderer."

At that point Chip held the receiver away from his ear because Becka was yelling louder than the fan screams at one of my concerts. I better do some damage control. I turned on the living room light and picked up the extension phone on the sofa end table.

"Becka, it's me...calm down, everything's all right. Chip is fine...he was never in any danger...yes, you heard him, we caught the man who killed Elsie Bloom. Actually, Chip caught him. I just pointed the guy out."

"Stanford Ernest Farmington!" Becka never used my full name unless she was annoyed at me. "I did not let you have my boy tonight so he could get mixed up with criminals!"

"He's my son too, and I'm proud of what he did. Takes a hero to wrestle down a killer."

"Wrestled? Chip was fighting? Did he get hurt?"

"No, mom, I'm okay." My boy was still on the other line.

"Ernest, what's going on? I let you have Chip for one night and look what happens!"

"How was I supposed to know Elsie's murderer was going to show up tonight? Besides, it'll give him something to brag about to his friends."

"I don't want Chip playing cops and robber with you, Ernest."

"I'll have you know Chip almost lost his dad tonight. The murderer tried to burn me up in the back lot. And don't tell me that you wished he'd succeeded."

"I'm not surprised, Ernest. Seems like everything that happens to you is overly dramatic."

"As I recall, you married me because you found me exciting."

Chip blurted in again. "Dad, our food's getting cold."

"Chip, did you tell your father that I'm picking you up tomorrow evening?"

"Not yet, mom."

"Why can't I have Chip for the whole weekend?" I said. "I can bring him back Sunday night."

"Because he has homework to do, and he won't get any done at your place. Besides, he needs at least one healthy meal this weekend. You'll just fill him up with cheeseburgers and pizza."

"Will not!" I said.

"I want him home in one piece, so no tearing around town on your motorcycle."

"I don't 'tear around town.'"

"I've seen you drive."

"Don't be such a worry wart. I won't let anything happen to my kid."

She yawned. "I need to get back to sleep. Get off the line, Ernest, so I can say good night to Chip."

"All right, Becka. 'Bye now. Thanks for letting Chip spend at least one night with me."

The words came out more sarcastic than I intended. Of course, I was grateful for whatever time I had with my kids, but Becka wasn't about to grant me one more second than necessary. I hung up and let Chip finish his call. When he sat at the island to eat, he looked flustered. Over the years he'd heard Becka and me fight far too many times. Tonight's bout was one of our tamer sessions, but I'm sure Chip hated getting stuck in the middle. We unwrapped our juicy burgers and dug in.

"I hope your mom isn't mad at you, Chip."

"Naw, she's cool with me. I think she's mad at you."

"What else is new? It's not my fault the show ran late."

"Mom's upset about that crook."

"Don't talk with your mouth full. Anyway, it's good for you to get out of the house and have some adventures and do something besides watch *National Geographic* specials on TV with your stepdad." I stuffed some fries in my mouth. "What's that on your arm?"

Chip held out his left arm, which had seven numbers inked on it. "One of the twins gave me her phone number."

"Don't get your hopes up. Girls like her like to string guys along."

Chip sucked on his straw and loudly drained his milkshake to the bottom of the cup. "Who was that girl you were talking to, the one with the long black hair?"

"You mean Cinnamon? She's a woman, not a girl. You date girls. I date women. She was my choreographer. She taught me that dance number you saw on the monitor."

"She's got the hots for you."

I nearly choked on a fry. "She does not!"

"Do you like her?"

I changed the topic and asked Chip about school. He said his classes bored him. We finished our late night dinner. Ordinarily we'd have watched a movie on video, but he was nodding off and I was fading too. We'd never stay awake past the opening credits. I turned out the light (I'll clean up tomorrow) and we headed to the second floor. I rummaged around in the linen closet until I found some clean sheets and made up the bed in the guest room. We said goodnight and retired to our respective bedrooms. I put on my pajamas and fell asleep almost before I hit the pillow.

We both slept in late. When I got up I did a quick cleanup and shave, threw on some old clothes, and headed downstairs to find that Chip was already up and watching *Teenage Ninja Mutant Turtles* on the living room TV. He had on a clean shirt and blue jeans.

"Good morning," I said. "Aren't you a bit old for cartoons?"

"The turtles are cool and, besides, there's nothing else on except kid stuff."

"Have you had breakfast?"

"I found an open bag of chips in the kitchen."

My kid is so resourceful. "I'll make us some brunch."

I watched the morning news on the kitchen TV as I whipped up steaming waffles, sizzling bacon and glasses of ice-cold orange juice. In the story about the Elsie Bloom murder, Detective Hernandez took full credit for cracking the case. I stopped pouring batter into the hot waffle iron long enough to yell at the TV.

"Hey! What about me! I'm the one who figured out who dunnit!"

Chip wandered in from the living room, tossed the empty chips bag into the trashcan, and glanced at the TV.

"Hey, dad, isn't that the cop who arrested you for beating up that guy in the bar?"

I closed the lid on the waffle iron. "How did you know that?"

"I saw him on the TV when it happened."

How nice to know that my boy kept up with his father's activities. "Getting in a bar fight was a very stupid thing for me to do, and I hope you never do anything like that. Did your mother tell you that I stopped drinking?"

"Yeah, but she doesn't think that you can do it."

"Is that so? Just watch me. I won't take a sip of booze this entire weekend."

He looked disappointed. "You're kinda funny when you're drunk. You act all goofy and nutty."

Out of the mouths of babes....

I told him to turn off the living room TV and sit down so we could eat. I turned down the sound on the kitchen TV and then set out the food on the kitchen island. After shutting off the TV, Chip plopped onto one of the island stools.

"Do you want whipped cream or chocolate sauce on

your waffle?" I asked.

"Mom only lets me have low-calorie syrup."

"Your mother is starving you. So which is it, whipped cream or chocolate sauce?"

He grinned. "Both."

Yep, this kid's got my genes.

After we polished off our sinfully sweet and fattening brunch, I asked Chip what he'd like to do for the day. I suggested going to Griffith Park or the newly opened Universal CityWalk but he wanted to doodle around in my home recording studio. To my regret, I didn't encourage my kids to study music—I resented my father forcing lessons on me—so Chip's request came as a pleasant surprise. I showed him how to operate the control board. I handed him one of the right-handed acoustic guitars that I keep on hand for when my rock and roll friends drop by. I showed him some chords but he one-upped me with some fancy riffs.

"Where did you learn to play guitar?"

"Some of my friends play guitar. And Uncle Warren showed me some stuff."

So that know-it-all brother of mine was teaching my kid the things that he should be learning from me. I was going to have to move fast to catch up with this parenting game. I took my left-handed acoustic and taught Chip a simple duet. He had a good singing voice, untrained but bursting with potential. We recorded the song and I gave him the tape reel as a memento. By then, we were both hungry again so I ordered out for pizza. We had finished gobbling up a large pizza loaded with everything when Becka phoned to say she was on her way over. I sent the boy upstairs to pack his stuff while I cleaned up the kitchen. He came downstairs with his backpack just as Becka called from the security gate. I buzzed her in. Chip and I met her on the front porch. She parked her SUV and walked over to us.

Becka had a brown paper sack in her hand. "Did you have a good time, Chip?"

"Yeah, it's cool. Dad's got a girlfriend."

I protested. "I do not!"

Becka eyed me. "Another girlfriend? Who is it this time?"

"She isn't a girlfriend. She...we worked together on the show. That's all. Chip, why don't you wait in the van while I talk to your mother?"

He pushed the hair out of his eyes. "Thanks for letting me stay over, dad."

"I'm glad you came. See you again soon, okay?"

I put my arm around the boy and gave him a hug that embarrassed him to death. After Chip was out of earshot, I spoke to Becka.

"See? I didn't ruin him. The boy is still alive."

"Yes, I can see that."

"Is Chip in any music programs at school? Band, choir, that sort of thing?"

"No. Why?"

"We were playing around in my studio. Chip's a natural talent. With some coaching he could be a good musician. I want him to start taking lessons."

"I don't think that's a good idea."

"Why not? He said he was bored with school. This might be the thing to perk him up."

"He doesn't need to be prancing around like a rock star and hanging out with groupies. I want Chip to go to college and make something of him."

"What you're really saying is you don't want him to end up like me." She opened her mouth for a rebuttal but I kept going. "I'll find the teachers and pay for them. If he doesn't have a guitar, I'll get him one. If you don't want to drive him to classes, I'll hire a taxi. But I'm the boy's father, and I say he's getting the lessons."

I braced myself for the volcanic eruption that I was certain would follow—but it never came.

After a moment, she said, "If Chip gets his grades up and as long as I don't have to push him to practice, then okay."

I almost turned a somersault with joy. "I'm sure he'll do fine."

She handed me the brown paper bag. "This is for you."

"What is it?"

"I knew you wanted to see Robin's dance recital, so we taped it for you."

"Why, thanks." Totally unexpected but appreciated.

"I have to go now. So long, Ernest."

"Bye, Becka. I'm sure we'll be speaking together again real soon." She shot me a look before heading off. As she got in the vehicle, I called out, "And I don't have a girlfriend!"

As the car pulled away, Chip and I waved at each other. The security gate automatically opened as the SUV approached. I went inside and found a videocassette inside the bag along with a handwritten note:

Daddy,

Thank you for the lovely flowers. They're beautiful. I wish you were here tonight. I miss you. Lots of love,
                                                Robin.

I wiped a tear from my eye, went into the den and popped the tape into the VCR machine. Despite the homemade quality of the tape, I had a wonderful time watching my little girl dance her heart out. After a couple of viewings, I ejected the tape, put it back in the cardboard cover, and placed it in the video cabinet. With Chip gone, the house felt too quiet. As I headed to the kitchen for a bottle of O'Doul's, I passed by the living room and saw the light blinking on the answering machine. Someone must have called while Chip and I were in the studio. I pressed the play button; Marshall had left a message that he had a new gig for me. What good timing. A job would keep my mind off my loneliness and Becka might see me as a responsible dad.

I called my agent at home. "Marshall, I'm returning your call. I thought you and your wife would be out and about on a Saturday night."

"We have friends coming over later for drinks and cards."

"So what's this new job? If it's another sitcom, forget it."

"Far from it. How does working on board a cruise ship sound? Two shows a night for five days. Interested?"

I sat on the sofa. "Keep talking."

"The only catch is that the agency wants two singers. I think you and your sister would make a great team."

"My sister?" My good spirits instantly sagged. "I don't think that's possible."

"Why not?"

"She still hasn't forgiven me."

THE END

Sandy Fairfax Discography

(All records except *Sessions* and *Black Wave* originally released on the SuperTonic label)

Sincerely Yours, Sandy. "Girl of My Dreams"/"Spark of Love " 1975

Soda Shoppe. "Cuddle Close"/"Sweet As Can Be" 1976

Walk In The Park. "Weeping Willow"/"Every Jack Has His Jill" 1976

Stars In My Eyes. "Little Bunny Bright Eyes"/"Didn't I See You Looking (at Another Boy)" 1977

Dancin' Sandy. "Meet Me At The Disco"/"Swing To The Beat" 1977

Sandy Sings Live For You (concert album) 1977

Knight In Shining Armor. "Tell Me True (I Love You)"/ "Tomboy In Pink Ribbons" 1978

Sandy Rings In The Holidays. "Mistletoe Kiss"/"Sugar Plums and You" 1978

Castles In The Air. "Moonbeam Melinda"/"The Picture In The Locket" 1979

Sandy's Tastiest Treats (greatest hits) 1980

Peanut Butter And Jam Sessions (independent label) 1985

Black Wave (with the band Shipwreck)1988

Movies And Television

Buddy Brave, Boy Sleuth (live action TV series) 1975-1979

Buddy Brave And The Suspicious Spy (movie) 1975

Buddy Brave And The Dangerous Demon (movie) 1976

The Secret Files Of Buddy Brave (animated TV series) 1979-1980

Charlie's Angels (guest appearance) 1980

Fantasy Island (guest appearance) 1983

The Love Boat (guest appearance) 1985

Off-Kelter (guest appearance) 1993

TEEN IDOL QUIZ

A true fan knows everything about her idol! See how much you love Sandy Fairfax, star of the smash 70s TV show, *Buddy Brave, Boy Sleuth*. All the answers can be found in *The Sinister Sitcom Caper*.

1. What kind of car does Sandy drive?

2. What are the names of his siblings?

3. What's the name of the orchestra his father conducts?

4. Name the *Buddy Brave* episode where our hero is tied up with strands of cooked spaghetti.

5. What actor starred in the dance movies that Sandy loved to watch?

6. What's Sandy's favorite snack when working on the set?

7. Name the studio where *Buddy Brave, Boy Sleuth* was filmed.

8. How old was Sandy when he shot the pilot episode of *Buddy Brave*?

9. What model of motorcyle does Sandy ride?

10. What is the name of Sandy's biggest fan club?

Count up your correct answers. How well did you score?

0 to 2—Struggling actor
3 to 5—Bit player
6 to 8—Supporting role
9 to 10—Movie star

Quiz Answers

1. 1964 poppy red Mustang convertible
2. Warren and Celeste
3. Golden Wing Philharmonic
4. "The Perilous Pasta Caper"
5. Gene Kelly
6. Brownies (soft and gooey)
7. Mammoth Picture Studio
8. Eighteen
9. '68 Shovelhead Harley-Davidson
10. Sandy's Buddies

ABOUT THE AUTHOR

 Sally Carpenter is native Hoosier now living in Moorpark, Calif. She has a master's degree in theater from Indiana State University. While in school her plays "Star Collector" and "Common Ground" were finalists in the American College Theater Festival One-Act Playwriting Competition. "Common Ground" also earned a college creative writing award. "Star Collector" was produced in New York City and also the inspiration for her book series. Carpenter also has a master's degree in theology and a black belt in tae kwon do. She's worked as an actress, freelance writer, college writing instructor, theater critic, jail chaplain and tour guide/page for a major movie studio. She's now employed at a community newspaper.

Her first book in the Sandy Fairfax Teen Idol mystery series, "The Baffled Beatlemaniac Caper," was a 2012 Eureka! Award finalist for best first mystery novel. Her short story, "Dark Nights at the Deluxe Drive-in," is published in the anthology, "Last Exit to Murder." "Faster Than a Speeding Bullet" is in the "Plan B: Vol. 2" e-book anthology.

She's a member of Sisters in Crime/Los Angeles. She's "mom" to two black cats. Contact her at Facebook or scwriter@earthlink.net. She blogs at http://sandyfairfaxauthor.com.